U0127331

IELTS雅思聽力

最後 9 堂課

劍橋台北語文中心資深講師
Robyn Blocker —— 著

眾文圖書股份有限公司

Dedication

Many thanks to the following people for their help, support, patience, and encouragement during the writing of this book: Jocelyn Lu, Jill Lee, the staff of Cambridge Taipei, and Michael Piraino. Also worthy of thanks are my family, who listened patiently for months while I talked about nothing but this project and were a constant source of reassurance.

Author's Words

To the students of this textbook:

I very much respect anyone who sets out on the journey of tackling the IELTS, and I have even *more* respect for the people who see this journey to completion. Doing so requires a great sacrifice of your time and effort. As a result, most people prepare for this exam for at least weeks, but more often months. That means *hours* per week.

Some days, you may feel that the path to your particular IELTS score is too long, or that there are too many obstacles in your way. You may feel quite frustrated with yourself. 'In the beginning of my studies,' many IELTS candidates say, 'I saw such fast progress. Now I've slowed down. Am I still progressing at all?' To this, I ask you to remember that all learners of all skills (even physical training) hit a plateau when they have reached a high enough level in their skill acquisition. It may be frustrating, or even dull, but you must continue to persevere.

誌謝

非常感謝陸文玲女士、Jill Lee、劍橋台北語文中心同仁,以及 Michael Piraino 在我撰寫這本書時的協助、支持、耐心和鼓勵。也謝謝我的家人,他們有好幾個月都只能聽我大談特談這本書的構想,並給我無限的信心和支持。

作者的話

給這本書的讀者:

我非常敬佩所有決定報考 IELTS 的考生,更敬佩能夠完成這趟旅程的人。應考 IELTS 必須耗費許多時間和心力,很多人至少會花上好幾週,更多人則是花好幾個月準備,意思是每週都必須投入好幾個小時學習。

有時候,你可能會覺得要考到理想的 IELTS 分數過程很漫長,又充滿阻礙,你也可能會感到很挫折。很多 IELTS 考生會問:「我剛開始進步很快。但現在慢下來了,這樣我還有在進步嗎?」關於這點,一定要記得:學習任何東西(健身也一樣!)在能力達到一定程度的時候,就會碰到進步的停滯期。這可能會讓人非常沮喪或失去興趣,但你一定要堅

Though it may feel like you are not moving, in truth you are not 'stuck.' It only *feels* that way because the developments and connections your brain is making at this crucial point are happening on such a deep level that you cannot see them.

The reward you will gain when you break through that plateau will be worth the hours of practice and review. Imagine the moment you get the score you need on that exam. What does that score mean? Does it mean going abroad to study or live? Does it mean getting a job you have coveted for months? Does it mean getting into a school or programme where you will learn so much and meet so many great new people? In the end, always remember that the IELTS is merely a stepping stone to this longer-term goal. One day in the future, you will be so immersed in the life that your IELTS score brought you that you will not even remember the hours of hard work at all.

持下去。雖然你會覺得自己沒有在前進，但實際上，你並不是真的「卡住」。這是因為在這個關鍵階段，你的大腦所發展和建立的連結都很深層，所以你才無法輕易察覺。

在你突破停滯期之後所得到的成果，會值得你花費無數小時練習、複習。想像一下你取得理想成績的那一刻。那個成績代表了什麼？是出國讀書或生活？是得到你渴望好幾個月的工作？還是進入學校或學程，讓你可以學到很多、認識很多很棒的人？無論如何，永遠記得 IELTS 只是你長遠目標的一個踏腳石。將來有一天，你會享受 IELTS 成績為你帶來的生活，到時候你根本就不會記得現在有多辛苦了。

About the Author

關於作者

Originally from the Dallas, Texas area, Robyn Blocker graduated with a Bachelor's degree in English: Creative Writing from the University of North Texas. Soon afterward, she received TESOL Certification in Zhuhai, China and moved to the famous city of Hangzhou, where she spent nearly four years as an EFL instructor, curriculum developer, teacher trainer, and occasional resource manager.

Robyn Blocker 來自德州達拉斯，於北德州大學取得英語創意寫作學士學位。接著她在中國取得了 TESOL 英語教學教師證照，並在當地擔任英語教師、課程開發專員及師資培訓顧問將近四年。

With the aim of enhancing her knowledge and effectiveness as a teacher, Robyn moved back to the United States and subsequently graduated with a Master's in TESOL from Western Carolina University, located in the beautiful state of North Carolina. Part of her degree work included a teaching practicum in the field, and thus her final year of graduate school took her to Guilin, China, where she taught Listening to second-year university students at Guangxi Normal University.

After finishing her contract in Guilin, Robyn moved to the vibrant city of Taipei. There, she taught young learners for one year before finding her way to the wonderful field of IELTS. She taught students how to tackle all four parts of the IELTS exam (Listening, Reading, Speaking, Writing) for nearly ten years.

為了提升作為教師所具備的知識和實力，Robyn 回到美國，在北卡羅來納州的西卡羅來納大學取得了 TESOL 碩士學位。她的學位要求包含教學實習，因此她畢業前一年前往中國，在廣西師範大學指導大二學生英語聽力。

結束在中國的工作後，Robyn 搬到充滿活力的臺北。她先教授兒童英語一年後，轉而專精於 IELTS 的教學。她至今已經有教授 IELTS 四個部分應考技巧（聽力、閱讀、口說、寫作）長達十年的經驗。

How to Use this Book | 如何使用本書

This book has nine lessons, focusing on different question types in the IELTS listening section. Each lesson consists of four parts:

1 Lesson Vocabulary Bank
2 Pre-Lesson Skills Practice
3 Listening Strategies
4 Task Practice

本書的 9 堂課分別針對 IELTS 聽力測驗的不同題型提供答題策略。每堂課都包含四個部分：

① 課程字彙庫
② 高分技巧訓練
③ 聽力答題策略
④ 題型練習

1 Lesson Vocabulary Bank

課程字彙庫

This section presents a varying number of words (and occasionally phrases) that you might hear in that lesson's Pre-Lesson Skills Practice, Listening Strategies and Task Practice sections. Four forms of the word are given: the infinitive (base verb), the adjective, the noun, and a final category: the 'agent noun,' or the person or entity that performs the verb. Not included are forms like past tenses, past participles, adverbs, etc.

課程字彙庫收錄了在「高分技巧訓練」、「聽力答題策略」和「題型練習」可能會聽到的相關單字或片語，一共列出四種形態：原形動詞、形容詞、名詞，以及動詞的「動作者」。不收錄過去式、過去分詞、副詞等。

The Lesson Vocabulary Bank is NOT an 'answer list' for your IELTS listening practices. It is a collection of words relevant to the lesson's general topic and which you may hear on the IELTS. For instance, in Lesson 3, we have:

字彙庫並不是聽力練習的答案表，而是收錄和每一堂課主題相關的單字，這些單字都可能會在 IELTS 中出現。舉例來說，第 3 課收錄了：

○ educate [ˋɛdʒʊkeɪt] 動 教育
○ educational [ɛdʒʊˋkeɪʃ(ə)n(ə)l] 形 教育的（↔ noneducational 非教育的）

○ education [ˌedʒuˈkeɪʃ(ə)n] 名 教育

○ educator [ˈedʒukeɪtə(r)] 動作者 教育者

You should:

- Make sure you know the meaning of the words at the very least.
- Practise saying the words so that you hear them if time allows you to prepare more thoroughly. (Standard British pronunciation is given.)

你應該：

- 確保自己至少知道每個字的意思。
- 時間充裕的話，練習把單字唸出來，熟悉發音。（本書附有單字的英式發音）

For further practice, you might look for example sentences of the word in books or on the Internet. When you have already completed the lesson, you can see how the words are used in the scripts. Do NOT look at the scripts before you do the lessons.

如果想更進一步練習，你可以從書籍或網路上搜尋包含這個單字的句子。練習完一課之後，也可以從音檔逐字稿中看看這些單字怎麼用。但還沒練習完一課之前，請先不要看逐字稿。

You may occasionally see a word in a vocabulary list that is used in a different way than you are used to. Furthermore, the other uses of the word seem to be ignored. This means we are focusing on a different usage of the word. For instance, look at this entry for 'academic' in Lesson 5.

你可能會發現字彙庫中收錄的單字和你過去習慣的用法不同，或似乎省略了一些用法，這表示我們想把重點放在這個字的另一個用法上。舉例來說，第 5 課收錄了「academic」：

○ academic [ˌækəˈdemɪk] 名〔人〕學者

In this lesson, we are ignoring the obvious adjective form of the word because this lesson features the word 'academic' in its noun (person) form.

這裡省略了 academic 最常見的形容詞用法（學術的），因為這堂課中用到的是它的名詞用法。

Many English words have slightly different meanings dependent on context. In our textbook, we will focus on the words as they are used in the context of that particular listening passage.

許多英文單字會根據前後文而有不同的意思。本書中，我們會以聽力測驗內容出現的用法來學習單字。

On a final note, be aware that words have been chosen for their helpfulness in your IELTS preparation. If a word exists but is highly uncommon in English and never used on the IELTS, it will not be included in a word bank.

○ reduce [rɪˋdjuːs] 動 減少
○ reduced [rɪˋdjuːst] 形 降低的
○ reduction [rɪˋdʌkʃ(ə)n] 名 降低，減少

For instance, the word 'reducer' exists in English, but it is not included in this entry because it is a highly specialised, technical word rarely used in common English and thus probably not mentioned at all in IELTS listening. At this stage in your test preparation, it is crucial not to waste your valuable time with information unhelpful to achieving your required IELTS score.

最後一個小提醒，字彙庫收錄的都是能幫助你準備 IELTS 的單字。如果是非常少見、從來沒有出現在 IELTS 中的單字，就不會列入字彙庫中。

舉例來說，reducer（還原劑；減速器）這個字雖然存在，但沒有列入字彙庫，因為它是個相當專業的術語，很少用在日常英文，也應該不曾出現在 IELTS 的聽力測驗中。在準備考試的這個階段，千萬不要把寶貴的時間耗費在無法幫助你提升成績的資訊上。

2 Pre-Lesson Skills Practice

高分技巧訓練

This section presents you with listening tasks that highlight and target the abilities needed in IELTS listening parts and specific questions. Thus, the practices vary from lesson to lesson.

高分技巧訓練針對 IELTS 聽力測驗的不同部分和題型提供所需要的技巧。因此每堂課的練習都不同。

This section has several aims:
- Engaging your focus so that you are ready to listen with full attention to the upcoming IELTS tasks.
- Showing you exactly the way you will need to 'use your brain' for the upcoming IELTS tasks.
- Highlighting the particular challenges of each IELTS listening question type.

這部分有幾個目標：
- 讓你集中注意力，準備好專心面對接下來的 IELTS 聽力測驗。
- 讓你熟悉在面對各種題型時要怎麼思考、作答。
- 讓你加強訓練不同聽力題型可能遇到的困難之處。

Essentially, every type of listening question on the IELTS is designed to 'trick' or misdirect you in some way. (This does not mean the questions are 'unfair.' They are fair. They are just not always simple or easy.) The Pre-Lesson Skills Practice gives you a taste of what that trick or misdirection will look like. In some cases, it is merely a matter of spelling ability, while in others the 'trick' is more sophisticated and likely to fool someone whose English ability is lower or who has not practised the IELTS skills drilled in these sections of the book.

基本上，IELTS 聽力測驗的題型都有陷阱，或很容易誤導你（題目沒有不合理，只是不太容易）。高分技巧訓練會讓你稍微體會一下陷阱可能是什麼樣子。有時候，題目考的只是拼字能力，但有時也會有很細節的陷阱，英文程度比較基礎或沒有練習過這部分 IELTS 答題技巧的人就可能會上當。

Q When should I do the Pre-Lesson Skills Practices?

A Along with the Lesson Vocabulary Banks, consider the Pre-Lesson Skills Practices your homework. Complete each one before you start the Listening Strategies sections.

我該什麼時候做高分技巧訓練？

和課程字彙庫一起，可以把高分技巧訓練想成預習的作業。盡可能在開始「聽力答題策略」前完成。

Q How many times should I do each Pre-Lesson Skills Practice?

A As many times as you need to feel comfortable with the tested skills.

我應該練習幾次高分技巧訓練的題目？

練習多少次都沒關係，直到你對答題技巧有信心就可以。

Q What if I didn't catch what the speakers said in the Pre-Lesson Skills Practice?

A You may listen to the tracks more than once. However, if your general listening is still not strong, consider reading along with the scripts while listening. Afterwards, listen again without the scripts. In this way, you can still practise your IELTS listening abilities.

要是我聽不懂高分技巧訓練的音檔在說什麼怎麼辦？

你可以再聽一次。如果你整體聽力表現還是不太好，可以試著邊聽邊看逐字稿。之後不看逐字稿再聽一次。這樣你還是可以練習到聽力。

3 Listening Strategies

聽力答題策略

The IELTS listening task(s) that you will learn about in each lesson are presented in the Listening Strategies section. After you view an example of the task, you will be given general tips for how to handle that task type. Next, there will be specific instructions about what to do immediately before you listen. Last, you will listen to the recordings and answer the questions.

聽力答題策略將會在每一課中分別介紹 IELTS 聽力測驗的各種題型。你會先看到各題型的例題，以及基本的答題策略，接著會更詳細指引你在聆聽題目之前應該先做什麼。最後，你可以透過例題驗收成果。

4 Task Practice

題型練習

After all the new tasks in that lesson have been introduced, you will practise the relevant IELTS tasks on your own in the Task Practice. Some lessons' Task Practices will include question types from previous lessons in addition to the new tasks from that lesson. This is not only to help you review, but also to expose you to that question type in different parts of the IELTS listening paper.

每一課介紹完答題策略之後，你將會在題型練習實際演練。有些題型練習會包含前幾課介紹過的內容，這不只是為了幫助你複習，也能讓你熟悉該題型在聽力測驗不同部分出現的形式。

You will both preview and complete the tasks using the strategies we went over in the Listening Strategies. At the end, you will check your answers.

你會用到我們在聽力答題策略中學到的技巧，完成題型練習，最後再對答案。

Listening Test Basics | 聽力測驗簡介

Overview

概述

The IELTS Listening section comprises 4 parts (4 recordings) and contains 40 questions in total. It lasts approximately 30 minutes, with an additional 10 minutes to transfer answers. However, for the computer-based test, this extra time is reduced to just 2 minutes for reviewing answers. All the recordings will be played only once.

There will be a variety of different accents in the recording, so you should practise listening to different accents when preparing for the test. Note that the listening sections are identical for both the Academic and General Training tests.

IELTS 聽力測驗包含四個部分，一共有 40 題。測驗時間大約 30 分鐘，還有額外 10 分鐘讓你填寫答案。但請注意，如果是電腦測驗，你只會有額外 2 分鐘確認答案。所有的音檔都只會播放一次。

聽力測驗的音檔中可能會有多種口音，所以務必要練習聽不同口音的人說話。特別注意，「學術組」和「一般訓練組」的聽力測驗是一樣的。

PART 1
- Questions 1-10
- A conversation between two speakers
- An everyday context, e.g. booking a room at a hotel, asking questions about a venue or an event

第一部分
- 第 1〜10 題
- 兩人對話
- 非學術的對話主題，如：預定飯店住宿、詢問場地或活動等

PART 2
- Questions 11-20
- A monologue (one speaker only)
- An everyday context

第二部分
- 第 11〜20 題
- 單人獨白
- 非學術主題

PART 3
- Questions 21-30
- A conversation between two or more speakers

第三部分
- 第 21〜30 題
- 多人對話

- An academic context, e.g. education or training situations

- 學術的對話主題，如：教育、培訓等

PART 4

- Questions 31-40
- A monologue (one speaker only)
- An academic context

第四部分

- 第 31～40 題
- 單人獨白
- 學術主題

Grading Criteria

- Each correct answer is awarded 1 mark, with a possible total of 40 marks. Based on this total (the raw score), a band score ranging from 1.0 to 9.0 is given.
- Both North American and British spelling conventions are acceptable, but do not switch between them during the test.
- You can write all your answers in capital letters, but it is not a requirement.
- Spelling is crucial in the IELTS. You will not get a mark if you spell a word incorrectly.
- All correct formats of written numbers, times and dates in English are acceptable.

評分標準

- 答對一題會得到 1 分，最高 40 分，最後再以這個分數計算出 1.0～9.0 的級分。
- 使用美式拼字或英式拼字都可以，但在考試中要維持一致，不要任意切換。
- 答案可以用大寫，但並非必要。
- 拼字在 IELTS 中非常重要，拼錯字就不會得到分數。
- 任何數字、時間和日期的寫法，只要在英文中是正確的格式就可接受。

CONTENTS

目 錄

「聽見眾文」APP 操作說明

STEP 1

請掃描本書專屬 QR Code 登入帳號後，
輸入兌換序號（engrossed）

（首次使用，請先註冊成為「聽見眾文」APP 會員）

STEP 2

打開「聽見眾文」APP，
點選本書即可免費聆聽。

LESSON 1

Form and Table Completion

表單和表格填空題

Form and Table Completion
表單和表格填空題

Lesson Overview

In this lesson, you will become familiar with the *form completion* and *table completion* questions on the IELTS. You will learn how to approach the two tasks and will become aware of common problems that IELTS candidates encounter in these questions.

We will be working with IELTS Listening Part 1 for these two task types.

♦ **Listening Part 1**
- Questions 1-10
- A conversation between two speakers
- The topic is non-academic, e.g. job interview, booking accommodations, etc.
- Form completion task is common in Part 1, but any question type is possible

本課內容

在這堂課中,我們將會介紹「表單填空題」和「表格填空題」。你會學到這兩種題型的答題技巧,以及一般考生最常遇到的問題。

我們會透過 IELTS 聽力測驗 Part 1 來練習這兩種題型。

聽力測驗 Part 1
- 第 1~10 題
- 兩人對話
- 非學術的對話主題,如:工作面試、預訂住宿等
- 表單填空題在 Part 1 相當常見,但也可能是其他題型

Lesson Vocabulary Bank:
Volunteering / Venue booking

課程字彙庫：
志工服務 / 預定場地

🔊 MP3 01

- accommodate 動 容納
  [əˋkɒmədeɪt]
- accommodating 形 親切的
  [əˋkɒmədeɪtɪŋ]
  (↔ unaccommodating 不通融的)
- accommodation 名 住宿
  [ə͵kɒməˋdeɪʃ(ə)n]

- atmospheric 形 有氣氛的
  [͵ætməsˋferɪk]
- atmosphere 名 氣氛
  [ˋætməsfɪə]

- attend 動 參加
  [əˋtend]
- attendee 動作者 出席者
  [ə͵tenˋdi:]
- attendant 動作者 服務人員
  [əˋtend(ə)nt]

- cater 動 迎合，滿足需求
  [ˋkeɪtə(r)]
- catering 名 承辦宴席
  [ˋkeɪtərɪŋ]
- caterer 動作者 外燴業者
  [ˋkeɪt(ə)rə(r)]

- ceremonial 形 儀式的
  [͵serɪˋməʊnɪəl]
- ceremony 名 典禮，儀式
  [ˋserɪməni]

- compulsory 形 強制的
  [kəmˋpʌls(ə)ri]

- confer 動 授予（學位）；協商
  [kənˋfɜ:(r)]
- conference 名 會議
  [ˋkɒnf(ə)r(ə)ns]

- consist (of...) 動 由…組成
  [kənˋsɪst]
- consistency 名 一致性，連貫性
  [kənˋsɪst(ə)nsi]

- deposit 動 存（錢）；放置 名 存款；訂金
  [dɪˋpɒzɪt]

- litter 動 亂丟垃圾 名（小型）垃圾
  [ˋlɪtə(r)]
- litterer 動作者 亂丟垃圾者
  [ˋlɪtərə(r)]

- podium 名 演講台
  [ˋpəʊdɪəm]

- spacious 形 寬敞的
  [ˋspeɪʃəs]
- space 名 空間
  [speɪs]

- venue 名 會場，（事件）發生地
  [ˋvenju:]

＊本書音標採用 IPA 音標系統

Pre-Lesson Skills Practice | 高分技巧訓練

Skill 1　Writing letters or numbers | 技巧 1：寫字母或數字

- Two of the same number or letter side by side can be referred to as **'double + [letter or number].'**
  - 35569: 'three-double five-six-nine'
  - Smallie: 'S-M-A-double L-I-E'

連續兩個相同的數字或字母可以唸成「double + 數字／字母」。
- 35569 唸成「three-double five-six-nine」。
- Smallie 唸成「S-M-A-double L-I-E」。

- The word **zero** is often spoken as **'oh'** for convenience.
  - 302: 'three-oh-two.'

為了方便，數字「0」常常會唸成「oh」。
- 302 唸成「three-oh-two」。

- Some letters, especially **vowels**, can sound very different depending on the accent of the English speaker.

有些字母（尤其是母音）會因為不同口音而聽起來非常不一樣。

During one particular listening practice test, 99% of my students across ten years heard the letter 'A' as sounding like 'I' when pronounced by someone with a strong Australian accent! The word 'sailor' sounded to them like 'syler,' which is not a real word.

在我教學 10 年來，有 99% 的學生會把某個聽力考題中澳洲口音很重的「A」聽成「I」！他們會把 sailor（水手）聽成「syler」，但這個字並不存在。

Listen to each short extract. Write the letters or numbers that you hear.
請聆聽音檔，寫下你聽到的拼字或數字。

🔊 MP3 02

Example: <u>Whitehall</u>

1 ....

4 ....

2 ....

5 ....

3 ....

*Answer Key p. 22

Skill 2 Predicting

If you know what kind of word the answer is going to be, you are more likely to catch it when listening. You can nearly always predict this information by paying attention to keywords in the questions.

- **When** did the man finish his project?
  - The answer is likely either a day, year, time, or other adverb of time.
  - Example answers: on Sunday, in 2021, at 3:30, recently

- **How much** is a ticket to Paris?
  - The answer is likely a number.
  - Example answer: £12

- **What country** do kangaroos come from?
  - The answer is likely a proper noun, specifically a country's name.
  - Example answer: Australia (technically the only answer! Sorry—the IELTS will not be that easy.)

技巧 2：預測答案

如果你事先知道要填入什麼類型的答案,聆聽時就更能仔細注意。事實上,你幾乎可以透過題目關鍵字準確預測答案的類型。

那個男子何時 (when) 完成他的報告?
- 答案很可能是某天、某年、某個時間或時間相關的副詞。
- 例如:on Sunday（星期天）、in 2021（2021 年）、at 3:30（3 點 30 分）、recently（最近）

一張去巴黎的票要多少錢 (how much)?
- 答案很可能是個數字。
- 例如:£12（12 英鎊）

袋鼠源自於哪個國家 (What country)?
- 答案很可能是個專有名詞,更明確來說,是個國家名稱。
- 例如:Australia（澳洲,這個例子的答案很明顯是澳洲,不過很可惜,IELTS 實際上不會這麼簡單）

- Some keywords indicating **'number'** answers:
  - **How much**

    How much is it? / How much does it cost?
  - **Fee**

    There is a late fee of $1 for library books.
  - **Fine**

    I had to pay a $200 fine for driving too fast.
  - **How old**

    How old is your brother?
  - **Age**

    Could you tell me your age?
  - **What time**

    What time will the family leave?

Currency symbols such as $ or £ are usually given to you on the IELTS. In this case, you will not need to write them yourself. This makes it easier to see that the answer is going to be a number!

- Some keywords indicating **'number + noun'** answers:
  - **How many**

    How many chairs do they need?
  - **Address**

    What's your address?
  - **How tall / wide / heavy**

    How wide is the doorway?
  - **Height / width / weight**

    What's the doorway's width? / What's the width of the doorway?

These questions would need 'a number + a noun'

有些關鍵字顯示出答案是**數字**：

- How much is it? / How much does it cost?（這個要多少錢？）
- There is a late fee of $1 for library books.（圖書館的逾期費用是 1 美元。）
- I had to pay a $200 fine for driving too fast.（我得付 200 美元的超速罰款。）
- How old is your brother?（你弟弟幾歲？）
- Could you tell me your age?（請問你的年齡是？）
- What time will the family leave?（那家人何時要離開？）

貨幣符號（例如 $ 和 £）在 IELTS 題本上通常會印出來，答案中就不用再寫一次，而且會讓題目更簡單，因為答案一定是個數字！

有些關鍵字顯示出答案是**數字 + 名詞**：

- How many chairs do they need?（他們需要多少張椅子？）
- What's your address?（你的地址是什麼？）
- How wide is the doorway?（門口有多寬？）
- What's the doorway's width? / What's the width of the doorway?（門口的寬度是多少？）

這些問題的答案會是數字加上名

as an answer, e.g. *two chairs*, *36 inches*. For addresses, listen carefully; they could be anything.

詞的組合，例如：two chairs（兩張椅子）、36 inches（36 英寸）。至於地址，因為組合比較複雜，一定要仔細聽。

- Some keywords indicating **'noun'** answers:
  - **Name**
    What's his name? / Do you know the name of the song?
  - **Called**
    It's called 'Titanic.' / We called him 'Tall Peter.' / What's it called?
  - **Country**
    What country are you from?
  - **Nationality**
    What's your nationality?
  - **What + [noun]**
    What school did you go to? / What store is your favourite? / What animals do you like?

有些關鍵字顯示出答案是**名詞**：
- What's his name?（他的名字叫什麼？）/ Do you know the name of the song?（你知道這首歌的歌名嗎？）
- It's called 'Titanic.'（那部電影叫做《鐵達尼號》。）/ We called him 'Tall Peter.'（我們叫他「Tall Peter」。）/ What's it called?（它叫什麼？）
- What country are you from?（你來自哪個國家？）
- What's your nationality?（你的國籍是什麼？）
- What school did you go to?（你從什麼學校畢業？）/ What store is your favourite?（你最喜歡什麼店？）/ What animals do you like?（你喜歡什麼動物？）

These questions, with the exception of 'What animals do you like?', would require proper nouns as answers. Proper nouns are names. They must be capitalised, e.g. *John*, *Singapore*, *Cambridge University*.

以上這些問題，除了「你喜歡什麼動物？」之外，答案都會是專有名詞。專有名詞第一個字母必須大寫，例如：John、Singapore（新加坡）或 Cambridge University（劍橋大學）。

- Some keywords indicating **'verb'** answers:
  - **What ... do**

有些關鍵字顯示出答案是**動詞**：
- What does John think you

What does John think you <u>should do</u>?

- **What ... did**

  <u>What</u> was the last thing you <u>did</u> yesterday?

- **What ... have done**

  <u>What has</u> the teacher <u>done</u> today?

- **What ... will do**

  <u>What will</u> you <u>do</u>?

should do?（John 覺得你應該做什麼？）

- <u>What</u> was the last thing you <u>did</u> yesterday?（你昨天最後做了什麼？）

- <u>What has</u> the teacher <u>done</u> today?（老師今天做了什麼？）

- <u>What will</u> you <u>do</u>?（你會做什麼？）

● Some keywords indicating **'adjective'** answers:

- **... look like**

  What does the building <u>look like</u>? / Would you tell us what she <u>looked like</u>?

- **... [be verb] + like**

  What <u>is</u> your mother <u>like</u>? / What <u>was</u> your grandmother <u>like</u>?

- **Appearance**

  In terms of <u>appearance</u>, I'd say she was tall, quite pretty, and had red hair.

- **Personality**

  He has a great <u>personality</u>. He is friendly, funny, and generous.

- **What colour**

  <u>What colour</u> are your eyes?

有些關鍵字顯示出答案是**形容詞**：

- What does the building <u>look like</u>?（那棟建築看起來像什麼？）/ Would you tell us what she <u>looked like</u>?（請告訴我們她看起來是什麼樣子？）

- What <u>is</u> your mother <u>like</u>?（你媽媽<u>是</u>怎麼樣的人？）/ What <u>was</u> your grandmother <u>like</u>?（你奶奶是怎麼樣的人？）

- In terms of <u>appearance</u>, I'd say she was tall, quite pretty, and had red hair.（以<u>外表</u>來說，我會說她很高、滿漂亮、有一頭紅髮。）

- He has a great <u>personality</u>. He is friendly, funny, and generous.（他<u>個性</u>很好，親切、有趣，還很慷慨。）

- <u>What colour</u> are your eyes?（你的眼睛是什麼<u>顏色</u>？）

*Listen to each question. Write letters **A-G** to say what kind of answer is needed.*
請聆聽音檔中的題目，判斷答案可能是什麼內容，寫下字母 A-G。

🔊 MP3 03

Example: ___D___

Answer choices:

A a proper name (e.g. *Mary, Oxford University*)

B an adjective (e.g. *short, nice-looking, well-dressed*)

C a time phrase (e.g. *in the winter, July*)

D a number or a price after a money symbol (e.g. *30, $16*)

E a number and a noun (e.g. *6 weeks*)

F a past tense verb (e.g. *ate, did not go*)

G a present tense verb (e.g. *take*)

1	**5**	**9** ....
2	**6**	**10** ....
3	**7**	
4	**8**	* Answer Key p. 22

Skill 3 **Identifying parts of speech**　　技巧 3：判斷答案的詞性

There are **eight parts of speech** in English that words are grouped into: nouns, verbs, adjectives, adverbs, prepositions, conjunctions, articles, and interjections. On the IELTS, knowing a word's part of speech in a sentence can help you choose or write more correct answers.

英文中有八種詞性：名詞、動詞、形容詞、副詞、介系詞、連接詞、冠詞、感嘆詞。知道一個字的詞性可以幫助你在 IELTS 測驗中選出或寫出更正確的答案。

- For most English words, **the word form is different** for different parts of speech.

大部分的英文字，只要詞性不同，拼字就會改變。例如：名詞

- Noun: beauty
- Verb: beautify
- Adjective: beautiful
- Adverb: beautifully

beauty、動詞 beautify、形容詞 beautiful、副詞 beautifully。

Writing the wrong form of a word on the IELTS will equal a wrong answer, for example:
✗ He thinks the park is very <u>beauty</u>.

在 IELTS 測驗中，如果寫了錯誤的詞性，答案就會是錯的。
✗ He thinks the park is very <u>beauty</u>.（beauty 是名詞，這裡應該用形容詞 beautiful 才對）

- Not all words have all forms.
  - Noun: deliciousness
  - Verb: ✗
  - Adjective: delicious
  - Adverb: deliciously

並不是所有字都有每一種詞性。例如：名詞 deliciousness、形容詞 delicious、副詞 deliciously，沒有動詞形態。

- For some words, **the forms look the same** for different parts of speech.
  - Verb / Adjective: clear
  - Verb / Noun: bore

有些字可以兼具不同詞性。
- clear：動詞（清理）、形容詞（清楚的）
- bore：動詞（使無聊）、名詞（無聊的人或事）

- Some words have **more than one form** for the same part of speech. The underlined words below are all adjectives:
  - I'm so <u>exhausted</u> / <u>tired</u> / <u>bored</u> / <u>excited</u>.
  - Learning is so <u>exhausting</u> / <u>tiring</u> / <u>boring</u> / <u>exciting</u>.

有些字的同個詞性會有不只一個字，例如以下的形容詞就有 -ed 和 -ing 兩種形式：
- I'm so <u>exhausted</u> / <u>tired</u> / <u>bored</u> / <u>excited</u>.（我好累 / 無聊 / 興奮。）
- Learning is so <u>exhausting</u> / <u>tiring</u> / <u>boring</u> / <u>exciting</u>.（學習讓人很累 / 無聊 / 興奮。）

Now, let's do some warm-up exercises. What part of speech is the missing word in each sentence below? Choose from noun, verb, adjective, adverb, or preposition.

我們現在來練習一下。請看以下句子，空格中應該是什麼詞性？請填入名詞、動詞、形容詞、副詞或介系詞。

The .... are playing outside.

Answer: noun

Some correct possible nouns or noun phrases for the sentence above:

○ big dogs ✕ big dog
○ children ✕ child
○ teams from Australia ✕ team from Australia
○ professional musicians ✕ professional musician

Notice the four phrases marked ✕ are singular. That means they refer to only one dog, child, team, or musician. Remember the original sentence: 'The … are playing outside.' 'Are' indicates that there is more than one dog, child, team, or musician.

答案：名詞

以下是一些可以填入空格的名詞和名詞片語：

四個打 ✕ 的名詞或片語都是單數，指的是一隻狗、一個小孩、一個小組或一位音樂家。題目中的動詞是 are，表示主詞是複數。

Long books .... her.

Answer: verb

Some correct possible verbs or verb phrases for the sentence above:

○ bore / are boring to ✕ boring
○ excite / are exciting to ✕ exciting
○ tire / are tiring to ✕ tiring
○ interest / are interesting to ✕ interesting

答案：動詞

以下是一些可以填入空格的動詞或動詞片語：

Note that the four words marked ✕ are adjectives and not verbs, and thus do not fit the sentence.

四個打 ✕ 的字在此是形容詞，而不是動詞，因此不能填入空格中。

Let's change up how we approach this idea. Which words or phrases could correctly finish the sentence below? Write the letters in the gap.

讓我們換個方式練習。以下哪些選項可以放入這個句子的結尾？請在空格中填入字母。

> They work ....
>
> A well   C next to me   E make money
> B my company   D twice a week   F so exhausting

Answers: A, C, D

答案：A、C、D

A describes how they work. C describes where they work. D describes how often they work.

A 說明工作的「情況」，C 說明工作「地點」，D 說明工作「頻率」。

Why not B?—'My company' is just a noun phrase. It doesn't tell us anything about the verb 'work.' If we had '**at** my company,' this would be okay. It would become a phrase telling us where they work.

為什麼 B 不對？My company 是個名詞片語，不能修飾動詞 work。如果是 at my company 就沒問題，這樣會是個說明地點的片語。

Why not E?—'Make money' is a verb phrase. This sentence already has a verb. If we wrote '**to** make money,' this would be okay. It would become a phrase telling us why they work.

為什麼 E 不對？Make money 是個動詞片語，但句子中已經有動詞了。如果換成 to make money 就沒問題，這樣會是個說明目的的片語。

Why not F?—'Exhausting' is an adjective. Adjectives modify nouns, not verbs.

為什麼 F 不對？Exhausting 是個形容詞，可以修飾名詞，但不能修飾動詞。

*Listen to each word as it is used in the sentence. Is it a noun, verb, adjective, adverb, or prepositional phrase? Write **N** for noun, **V** for verb, **Adj** for adjective, **Adv** for adverb, or **Prep** for prepositional phrase.*

請聆聽音檔，音檔會先唸一個字詞，再唸一個造句，最後重複一次字詞，請判斷字詞是名詞、動詞、形容詞、副詞，還是介系詞？名詞寫 N，動詞寫 V，形容詞寫 Adj，副詞寫 Adv，介系詞寫 Prep。

◀)) MP3 04

Example: ___V___

1 ....   3 ....   5 ....

2 ....   4 ....   * Answer Key p. 22

Skill 4 Spelling common words

技巧 4：拼寫常見字彙

- Spelling counts on the IELTS. If you spell a word incorrectly, you don't get a mark for a correct answer.

拼字在 IELTS 中很重要。如果你拼錯字，就得不到分數。

- Be consistent with your spelling of words like 'color / colour,' 'favorite / favourite,' 'flavor / flavour,' and 'center / centre.' Choose either North American OR British spelling conventions, and don't switch during the test.

要用英式拼字或美式拼字都可以，但在考試中請統一，不要任意切換。例如：color / colour、favorite / favourite、flavor / flavour、center / centre。

- At the very least, you should know how to spell words like:
  - numbers (e.g. *thousand, million, billion*)
  - colours
  - jobs
  - days of the week
  - months
  - basic animals and plants

你至少應該要會拼這些類別的字：
- 數字，例如 thousand（千）、million（百萬）、billion（十億）
- 顏色
- 職業
- 星期幾
- 月分
- 基本的動植物

- famous countries and cities
- famous universities (e.g. *Oxford, Yale*)
- places in towns and cities
- rooms and basic objects in homes
- rooms and basic objects in schools and universities

- 知名的國家、城市
- 知名的大學，例如 Oxford（牛津）、Yale（耶魯）
- 城鎮中的地點
- 家中的房間和基本物品
- 校園中的空間和基本物品

Listen and spell the indicated word.

請聆聽音檔，音檔會先唸一個單字，再唸一個造句，最後重複一次單字。請將單字拼寫出來。

◀)) MP3 05

Example: rose

1 ....   5 ....   9 ....

2 ....   6 ....   10 ....

3 ....   7 ....

4 ....   8 ....   * Answer Key p. 22

Listening Strategies ❶
Form Completion

聽力答題策略 ❶
表單填空題

Look at the example of a form completion task below.

請先看以下「表單填空題」的例題。

Complete the form below.

*Write **NO MORE THAN THREE WORDS AND/OR A NUMBER** for each answer.*

Animal Shelter Volunteer Form

Name:	Tim **1** ....
Phone:	**2** ....
Address:	**3** ....
Age:	19
Experience (1):	local **4** ....
When:	every year
Tasks:	helps prepare Christmas meal, washes dishes
Experience (2):	beach clean-up crew
When:	**5** ....
Tasks:	**6** ....
Animal preferences:	**7** ....

Tips

Grammar, spelling, and punctuation are important on all completion tasks. If one of these features is wrong, your answer is not counted as correct. Read all directions carefully before each new section to avoid writing too many words.

Note if the answer can be **words and/or numbers**, or merely **words or numbers**. Words and/or numbers means an answer like '2 times' is possible. Words or numbers means the answer does not allow words and numbers. '2 times' would not be possible answer because it includes a word and a number.

Finally, be aware that in all Listening parts, the IELTS gives you a short time to look at the next questions. You should preview the information by asking yourself the questions below.

在所有填空題中，文法、拼字和標點都非常重要。如果任何一處出錯，那你的答案就是錯的。一定要仔細閱讀題目說明，以避免寫太多字。

要注意答案是要填「words and/or numbers」還是「words or numbers」。第一種表示答案有可能是「2 times」這種數字加上單字的組合，第二種則表示不能同時出現單字和數字，「2 times」在此就不可能是答案。

最後，別忘了在 IELTS 聽力測驗的每個部分之間，你會有很短的時間可以先瀏覽接下來的題目。你應該在看題目的時候先問問自己以下的問題。

1.1

Study the form completion task above. Answer the following questions.

請觀察上一頁的表單填空題，並回答以下問題。

❶ What is the word limit? Can the answer be a number?

....

❷ Which question(s) require only a word or words as the answer?

....

① 字數限制幾個字？答案可以是數字嗎？

② 哪些問題的答案只能是英文字？

❸ Which question(s) require only a number as the answer?

③ 哪些問題的答案只能是數字？

....

❹ Which question(s) require both a number and a word as the answer?

④ 哪些問題的答案是字和數字？

....

❺ What questions might the speaker ask to elicit the information required for the gaps? For example, *Name*: Could I get your name? / What's your name?

⑤ 說話者可能問哪些問題來得到空格應填入的資訊？例如「姓名」欄：請教你的姓名？你的名字是？

....

∗ Answer Key p. 22

1.2   ◀» MP3 06

Now, listen to the recording of the form completion task on p. 15. As you listen, write the answers in the gaps.

現在請練習第 15 頁的表單填空題，將答案填入空格中。

Do not worry about spelling while you listen and write, but after you finish the listening practice, give yourself a few minutes to consider your spelling.

邊聽邊寫的時候不用在意拼字，但在聽力播放結束後，記得花幾分鐘檢查一下。

∗ Answer Key p. 23

Listening Strategies ❷
Table Completion

聽力答題策略 ❷
表格填空題

Look at the example of a table completion task below.

請先看以下「表格填空題」的例題。

Complete the table below.

*Write **NO MORE THAN ONE WORD AND/OR A NUMBER** for each answer.*

Event	Date	Time
8 .... Orientation (all volunteers)	31 July	10:00 AM-10:30 AM
Cat Class	31 July	12:00 PM-12:30 PM
Dog Class	**9**	**10** .... AM-12:00 PM

Tips

We approach table completion tasks similarly to how we approach form completion tasks. There are some differences, though. If the table occurs in Part 1 or Part 3 (conversations), the speakers will sometimes cue you as to which point you are on by asking questions like they do in form completion tasks. For example, if the speaker asks, 'What time is the Dog Class?' then you know you are on Question 10.

However, the speaker may not ask a question to cue you to which point you are on, so always preview by

表格填空題的答題策略和表單填空題非常像,不過還是有一點不同。如果表格填空題出現在 Part 1 或 Part 3(對話題),說話者有時候會像表單填空題一樣,透過問問題,暗示他正在講哪題的答案。舉例來說,若是說話者說「狗狗課程的時間是什麼時候?」你就會知道現在是在第 10 題。

然而,說話者不一定都會這樣問問題作為提示,所以你還是要在

asking yourself the questions below.

瀏覽題目時，先問問自己以下的問題。

2.1

Study the table completion task above. Answer the following questions.

請觀察上一頁的表格填空題，並回答以下問題。

❶ What is the sequence of the questions? Quickly touch each question in order with your finger or pencil. Because of the format, IELTS candidates sometimes 'lose a question' in tables or get confused.

① 題目的順序是什麼？用手指或鉛筆快速按照順序指出題目。IELTS 考生有時候會因為表格格式不同而找不到下一題在哪裡。

❷ What is the word limit? Can the answer be a number?

② 字數限制幾個字？答案可以是數字嗎？

....

❸ What kind of answer does each gap require? (e.g. noun, adjective, verb, number, etc.)

③ 每個空格應填入什麼樣的答案？（例如：名詞、形容詞、動詞、數字等）

....

＊Answer Key p. 23

2.2   ◀)) MP3 07

Now, listen to the recording of the table completion task on p. 18. As you listen, write the answers in the gaps.

現在請練習上一頁的表格填空題，將答案填入空格中。

Do not worry about spelling while you listen and write, but after you finish the listening practice, give yourself a few minutes to consider your spelling.

邊聽邊寫的時候不用在意拼字，但在聽力播放結束後，記得花幾分鐘檢查一下。

＊Answer Key p. 23

Task Practice | 題型練習

PART 1 ◀)) MP3 08

Questions 1-5

Complete the form below.

*Write **NO MORE THAN TWO WORDS AND/OR A NUMBER** for each answer.*

Event Booking Form

Date of event:	**July 9** (Example)
Name:	Mary **1** ....
Phone:	**2** ....
Event type:	**3** .... –(award ceremony)
No. of guests (max).	**4** ....
Food / beverage:	**5** .... and open bar

Questions 6-10

Complete the table below.

Write **NO MORE THAN TWO WORDS AND/OR A NUMBER** *for each answer.*

Venue	Description	Seating Capacity	Pricing per event
Main Dining Room	– conference setting – guests can see the **6** .... – antique furniture	250	**7 $**................. (not including deposit)
Theatre	– famous for **8** .... – balcony – hand-painted sets	350	$600 (not including deposit)
9	– includes Noble Room and Maple Hall – wall is removable	**10**	$400 (not including deposit)

Answer Key | 答案

Pre-Lesson Skills Practice

Skill 1 Writing letters or numbers

1	Taylor	**3**	Imogen	**5**	6740284462
2	30 // thirty	**4**	Axton		

Skill 2 Predicting

1 D	**4** B	**7** D	**10** A
2 F	**5** G	**8** G	
3 E	**6** C	**9** A	

Skill 3 Identifying parts of speech

1 V	**3** Adj	**5** N
2 Adj	**4** Prep	

Skill 4 Spelling common words

1 brown	**4** children	**7** public	**10** award
2 modern	**5** furniture	**8** February	
3 ceremony	**6** Wednesday	**9** eastern	

Listening Strategies ❶ Form Completion

1.1

❶ No more than three. Yes, it can also include or be a number.

❷ 1, 4, 6, 7, and possibly 5 (e.g. *last spring*)

❸ 2

❹ 3 and possibly 5 (e.g. *summer of 2019*)

❺ Possible answers:

Phone   What's your (phone/cell/mobile) number? //
         Could I get your (phone/cell/mobile) number?

Address   What's your address? // Could I get your address? // Where do you live? //
         Where are you staying?

Experience   What volunteer experience do you have? // Have you volunteered before? //
         Do you have any experience (volunteering)?

When   When did you do that? // When was that?

Tasks What tasks did you do? // What did you do? // What did that involve?

Animal preferences What animals do you prefer (working with)? //

What animals could you work with? //

Can you work with both dogs and cats?

1.2

1 Beasley

2 913 6726

3 40 Tattersall Road

4 soup kitchen

5 (last) February

6 picked up litter

7 dogs (only) // (only) dogs

Listening Strategies ❷ Table Completion

2.1

❶ It goes left to right.

❷ Only one word. Yes, it could be one word and a number or only a number.

❸ 8   Noun // Adjective

9   Number + Noun

10 Number

2.2

8   General

9   8 August // August 8

10 10:30

Task Practice

PART 1

1 Swaine

2 624 875 6637

3 work (event)

4 200 // two hundred

5 full dinner

6 stage

7 500

8 (unique) atmosphere

9 East Wing

10 200 // two hundred

LESSON 2

Multiple Choice with a Single Answer

單選題

Multiple Choice with a Single Answer
單選題

Lesson Overview

In this lesson, you will become familiar with the ***multiple choice with a single answer*** questions. You will learn how to approach this task and will become aware of common problems that IELTS candidates encounter in this question.

We will be working with IELTS Listening Part 1 and Part 2 for this task type.

♦ **Listening Part 1**
– Questions 1-10
– A conversation between two speakers
– The topic is non-academic, e.g. job interview, booking accommodations, etc.
– Form completion task is common in Part 1, but any question type is possible

♦ **Listening Part 2**
– Questions 11-20
– A monologue (a single speaker)
– Like Part 1, features a non-academic topic
– Any question type is possible

本課內容

在這堂課中,我們將會介紹「單選題」。你會學到這種題型的答題技巧,以及一般考生最常遇到的問題。

我們會透過 IELTS 聽力測驗 Part 1 和 Part 2 來練習這種題型。

聽力測驗 Part 1
– 第 1～10 題
– 兩人對話
– 非學術的對話主題,如:工作面試、預訂住宿等
– 表單填空題在 Part 1 相當常見,但也可能是其他題型

聽力測驗 Part 2
– 第 11～20 題
– 單人獨白
– 和 Part 1 一樣是非學術的主題
– 可能是任何題型

<table>
<tr><td>

Lesson Vocabulary Bank:
Schools / Education / Learning / Art

</td><td>

課程字彙庫：

校園 / 教育 / 學習 / 藝術

</td></tr>
</table>

🔊 MP3 09

- commission 動 委託 名 委託；委員會
  [kə`mɪʃ(ə)n]

- curricular 形 課程的
  [kə`rɪkjələ(r)]

- curriculum 名 課表
  [kə`rɪkjələm]

- cutting-edge 形（技術等）最尖端的
  [ˌkʌtɪŋ `edʒ]

- designate 動 指派
  [`dezɪgneɪt]

- designation 名 指定，任命
  [ˌdezɪg`neɪʃ(ə)n]

- enquire 動 詢問
  [ɪn`kwaɪə(r)]

- enquiry 名 詢問；調查
  [ɪn`kwaɪəri] [`ɪnkwəri]

- enquirer 動作者 調查者
  [ɪn`kwaɪərə(r)]

- except 動 把…除外 介 除了…之外
  [ɪk`sept] [ek`sept]

- exceptional 形 例外的
  [ɪk`sepʃ(ə)n(ə)l] [ek`sepʃ(ə)n(ə)l]
  (↔ unexceptional 非例外的)

- exception 名 例外
  [ɪk`sepʃ(ə)n] [ek`sepʃ(ə)n]

- facilitate 動 促進
  [fə`sɪlɪteɪt]

- facility 名 設施
  [fə`sɪləti]

- facilitator 動作者 促進者；協調人
  [fə`sɪlɪteɪtə(r)]

- fall behind the times 片 過時

- hands-on 形 實作的
  [ˌhændz `ɒn]

- major 形 主要的
  [`meɪdʒə(r)]

- majority 名 大多數
  [mə`dʒɒrəti]

- medium 名〔藝術〕材料；表現手法
  [`miːdɪəm]

- prefer 動 偏好
  [prɪ`fɜː]

- preference 名 偏好
  [`pref(ə)r(ə)ns]

- range (from A to B) 動 從 A 到 B
  [reɪndʒ]

- range 名 範圍；類別
  [reɪndʒ]

＊本書音標採用 IPA 音標系統

o refer (sb to...) 動 (將某人) 介紹給…
[rɪˋfɜː]

o referral 名 推薦；介紹
[rɪˋfɜːr(ə)l]

o renovate 動 翻新；修復
[ˋrenəveɪt]

o renovation 名 翻新
[renəˋveɪʃ(ə)n]

o renovator 動作者 修復者
[ˋrenəveɪtə(r)]

o sculpt 動 雕刻
[skʌlpt]

o sculpture 名 雕塑
[ˋskʌlptʃə(r)]

o sculptor 動作者 雕刻家
[ˋskʌlptə(r)]

o simplify 動 簡化
[ˋsɪmplɪfaɪ]

o simple 形 簡單的
[ˋsɪmp(ə)l]

o simplification 名 簡化
[ˌsɪmplɪfɪˋkeɪʃ(ə)n]

o state-of-the-art 形 最先進的
[ˌsteɪt əv ðɪ ˋɑːt]

o technophobe 名 科技恐懼者
[ˋteknə(ʊ)fəʊb]

o user-friendly 形 容易使用的
[ˌjuːzə ˋfrendli]

Pre-Lesson Skills Practice | 高分技巧訓練

Skill 1 **Identifying keywords**

技巧 1：找出關鍵字

Remember that you will be given time before each part of the IELTS listening test to read the next set of questions. At this time, you should always underline words that indicate important information about the answers. This could include:

在 IELTS 聽力測驗的每個部分開始之前，你會有一點時間先瀏覽接下來的題目。這時候你一定要將可以幫助作答的關鍵字畫底線。關鍵字可能包含：

- **Words about topics / the relationship between people and ideas**
  - Pay attention to any words that tell us the topic of the listening and the relationship between the people and ideas in it. Sometimes that will be nearly every word in the sentence. But look closely at what information each word or phrase is giving you.

關於主題以及說話者資訊的字詞

- 注意有些字詞會點出主題，或顯示出說話者和內容有何關係。有時候幾乎整句話都是重點，但你可以仔細檢視每個字詞所提供的資訊。

- **Wh-words**
  - who, what, where, when, why, how

Wh 疑問詞

- who, what, where, when, why, how

- **Modals**
  - can, could, should, ought to, must, have to, will
  - Modals go together with verbs and give us more information about them and the speaker's attitude about what they are saying.

情態助動詞

- can, could, should, ought to, must, have to, will
- 情態助動詞會搭配動詞使用，補充更多資訊，也顯示出說話者的態度。

- **Negatives**
  - won't, will not, isn't, is not, etc.

否定詞

- won't, will not, isn't, is not, etc.

● Verb tenses

❶ There <u>is</u> a pond in this park.

❷ There <u>was</u> a pond in this park.

The second sentence means there isn't a pond in this park anymore. That's important!

❸ There <u>is going to</u> be a pond in this park.

❹ There <u>hasn't been</u> a pond in this park for 30 years.

In the third sentence, we can assume there are plans to build a pond and that it will happen. In the fourth, there is no pond now. There was one, but something happened to it about 30 years ago. Between then and now = no pond.

During the test, when you're listening to the speakers, you should listen for the above words and ideas as well.

Let's try an example. In the sentence below, the keywords have been underlined. What do these words tell us about the speaker and the situation?

動詞時態

① There <u>is</u> a pond in this park.（公園裡<u>有</u>個池塘。）

② There <u>was</u> a pond in this park.（公園裡<u>曾經</u>有個池塘。）

③ There <u>is going to</u> be a pond in this park.（公園裡<u>將會</u>有個池塘。）

④ There <u>hasn't been</u> a pond in this park for 30 years.（公園裡30年來都<u>沒</u>有池塘。）

從第三句話可以推測未來有建造池塘的計畫，而且確定會進行。第四句話則表示現在沒有池塘，雖然過去曾經有，但30年前曾經發生了什麼事，從那時候至今都沒有池塘。

聽力播放時，別忘了要注意聽以上這類的關鍵字。

我們來練習一下。下面這個句子中，畫底線的關鍵字提供了關於說話者和情境的哪些資訊？

<u>So far</u>, <u>I</u>'ve <u>applied</u> for <u>two jobs</u>.

We would underline these words because they tell us:

- The speaker wants a job. They either have no job now or they're looking for a new one.
- How many jobs the speaker has applied for.
- The speaker plans to continue applying for more jobs. ('So far…')
- The speaker applied to these jobs quite recently, or recently enough that they are still thinking about this topic.

The phrase 'so far' does not occur with the simple past tense. (✗ So far, I applied to…). If you ever see or hear it, it is not standard. 'So far' implies an unfinished action. The simple past tense describes a finished action. The two contradict each other.

這些字被畫上底線，因為它們提供了以下資訊：

- 說話者想找工作。他不是現在沒工作，就是想換一個新的。
- 說話者已應徵的工作數量。
- 從 So far...（目前為止…）可知說話者打算繼續應徵工作。
- 過去完成式 I've applied 暗示說話者最近剛應徵工作，時間接近到他還在想著這件事。

特別注意 so far 不會搭配過去簡單式（✗ So far, I applied to...）。如果你曾經看過或聽過這樣的用法，那其實不太標準。so far 暗示的是未完成的動作，但過去簡單式是當下已結束的動作，兩者互相矛盾。

Read each sentence or question. Underline the keywords. Check your answers before moving on to questions 11-13 in the next section.

請閱讀以下句子，將關鍵字畫底線。完成後請先確認答案，再練習接下來的第 11～13 題。

1 I haven't bought my textbooks yet.

2 When is the earliest possible date for enrolment?

3 Only returning students are eligible for these benefits.

4 We've already got a swimming pool.

5 I won't write the title page until I've done the whole essay.

6 Our bank is located in China and across the whole of Europe.

7 He enquired about the way to the station.

8 Unlike all the other professors, she doesn't give extra credit assignments.

9 Most nights, I study in the library.

10 The majority of clients can receive a discount.
＊Answer Key p. 42

What do we learn from the underlined words in these three sentences provided above?
從前面的其中三個句子中，我們可以從畫底線的字詞得到什麼資訊？

11 I haven't bought my textbooks yet.

....

12 I won't write the title page until I've done the whole essay.

....

13 Unlike all the other professors, she doesn't give extra credit assignments.

....
＊Answer Key p. 42

| Skill 2 | **Recognising general paraphrasing** | 技巧 2：辨識一般改述 |

The IELTS has no specific vocabulary or grammar components, but it certainly tests your vocabulary and grammar!

IELTS 沒有獨立的單字和文法大題，但在題目中一定會考驗你的字彙能力和文法程度！

One way the IELTS tests your vocabulary is by using different words than those in the questions. Using different words to say something is called **paraphrasing**.

IELTS 考驗字彙能力的一種方法是把題目的內容用其他字詞表達。用不同的話敘述同一件事就是 paraphrasing（改述）。

Some common ways to paraphrase include using:

❶ **Synonyms**

the big dog → the large dog

❷ **Examples**

a country in Europe → Germany

❸ **Definitions**

a coastal city → a city situated near the sea

❹ **Descriptions**

a multi-functional cell phone app → an app that can not only show you what you would look like with different hairstyles, but also suggests what hair colour and style would look best on you

「改述」通常會運用：

① 同義詞：the big dog（那隻大狗）→ the large dog（那隻大狗）

② 舉例：a country in Europe（歐洲的一個國家）→ Germany（德國）

③ 定義：a coastal city（沿海城市）→ a city situated near the sea（在海邊的城市）

④ 描述：a multi-functional cell phone app（一款多功能手機軟體）→ an app that can not only show you what you would look like with different hairstyles, but also suggests what hair colour and style would look best on you（一款能讓你模擬自己不同髮型看起來如何，還能推薦最適合髮色和髮型的手機軟體）

Listen to the recording and compare each sentence to the sentences below. Circle **Same** *if they match in meaning, or* **Different** *if they don't. You may listen more than once.*

請聆聽音檔，判斷音檔中的句子和下列句子意思是否相同。意思相同，請圈 Same；意思不同，請圈 Different。你可以多次聆聽。

🔊 MP3 10

Example: [Same / (Different)] So far, I've applied for two jobs.

1   [Same / Different] I haven't bought my textbooks yet.

2   [Same / Different] When is the earliest possible date for enrolment?

3   [Same / Different] Only returning students are eligible for these benefits.

4 [Same / Different] We've already got a swimming pool.

5 [Same / Different] I won't write the title page until I've done the whole essay.

6 [Same / Different] Our bank is located in China and across the whole of Europe.

7 [Same / Different] He enquired about the way to the station.

8 [Same / Different] Unlike all the other professors, she doesn't give extra credit assignments.

9 [Same / Different] Most nights, I study in the library.

10 [Same / Different] The majority of clients can receive a discount.

＊Answer Key p. 42

Skill 3　Understanding stems

技巧 3：了解題幹

Some questions on the IELTS are phrased as full questions (e.g. *When should students turn in their applications?*) but other questions are phrased as unfinished sentences (e.g. *Students should turn in their applications...*).

IELTS 中有些題目是問句的形式，例如：When should students turn in their applications?（學生何時應提交申請？）有些則是還沒結束的句子，例如：Students should turn in their applications...（學生應提交申請…）。

This second type of question, the 'unfinished sentence' style, is called a **stem**. When you see a stem on the IELTS, you should try to understand the full Wh- or Yes/No question that it might represent.

第二種類型的題目，也就是還沒結束的句子，就稱為「題幹」。看到 IELTS 中的題幹時，要試著判斷它可能對應的 Wh 問句或 Yes/No 問句是什麼。

Here are some examples:
－ The fundraiser will begin...

以下是一些例子：
－ 募款活動將開始於…

→ When will the fundraiser begin? Where will it begin?

→ 募款活動何時開始？在哪裡開始？

- Mark already asked the professor...

- Mark 已經問教授⋯

  → What did Mark already ask the professor?

  → Mark 已經問了教授什麼？

- Darla thinks the new system is...

- Darla 認為新系統⋯

  → What does Darla think about the new system?

  → Darla 認為新系統怎麼樣？

*Look at the stems (sentence beginnings) below and write the questions they are asking. (Hint: First words would be **who**, **what**, **where**, **when**, **why**, or **how**.)*

請看以下題幹（句子的開頭），並寫下題目可能怎麼問。（提示：問句的開頭會是 who, what, where, when, why 或 how）

Example: The man lives in... → <u>Where does the man live?</u>

1 The best way to find a job is...

  ....

2 The woman described the health course as...

  ....

3 When opening a bank account, you should...

  ....

4 Tom is talking to the teacher in order to...

  ....

5 Della first travelled to New York together with...

  ....

＊Answer Key p. 42

Listening Strategies ❸
Multiple Choice with a Single Answer

聽力答題策略 ❸
單選題

Look at the two examples of single-answer multiple choice questions below.

請先看以下兩組「單選題」的例題。

---

1 *Choose the correct letter, **A**, **B**, or **C**.*

1 Start times for evening classes range from

   A 6:45-8:15 PM.
   B 6:45-8:30 PM.
   C 7:45-10:00 PM.

2 The man thinks a language class

   A might be dull.
   B is preferable to a hands-on class.
   C would be useful.

3 What is the man's opinion about the college's website?

   A It is easy to use.
   B It has too many links and buttons.
   C His friend would be interested in it.

4 The instructor for woodworking has been teaching at the college for

   A 3 years.
   B 15 years.
   C 30 years.

5 The woodworking class ends at

   A 7:30 PM.
   B 9:30 PM.
   C 9:00 PM.

2 *Choose the correct letter, **A**, **B**, or **C**.*

1 Alterations are being made to the campus because

    A the curriculum is too old-fashioned.

    B the library and classrooms are not clean and well-maintained.

    C many of the facilities are outdated.

2 What does the speaker say about the gymnasium?

    A New tennis courts are being added to it.

    B It is located on the road just outside the school gates.

    C The school has already begun renovating it.

3 What is the ideal number of students in each dormitory room?

    A Five

    B Three

    C Two

4 How will the garden be altered?

    A Artwork will be installed.

    B More trees will be planted.

    C Seating will be expanded.

LESSON **2** Multiple Choice with a Single Answer

Tips

Do NOT always choose the first answer you hear. It is likely you will hear all the answer choices, not only the correct one. Be especially mindful of words like *only*, *some*, *always*, and *not*, as these words will often accompany one of the wrong answers or give you the clue as to the correct answer.

千萬不要一聽到某個選項中出現的字詞，就直接當成答案，因為你很有可能會聽到所有選項中的關鍵字。記得留意 only（只有）、some（一些）、always（總是）、not（不），這些字常常會有陷阱，但也經常是正確答案的線索。

Notice any question that is not phrased as a full question (has no question mark). Quickly consider

特別注意不是用問句形式呈現的題目（沒有問號），在聆聽之前，

the question it is asking before you listen.

請先快速想一下這些問題在問什麼。

3.1

Study the multiple choice questions above on p. 36. Answer the following questions.

請觀察第 36 頁的單選題，並回答以下問題。

❶ What are the keywords in each question or question stem? Underline them.

❷ What questions are Questions 1, 2, 4, 5 asking? Write them.

....

❸ What are the keywords in each answer? Underline them.

❹ What are some possible paraphrases for the keywords you underlined in the questions and answers?

....

＊Answer Key p. 43

① 每一題的關鍵字是什麼？請畫底線。

② 第 1、2、4、5 題要問的問題是什麼？請寫下來。

③ 每個選項中的關鍵字是什麼？請畫底線。

④ 你在題目和選項中畫底線的關鍵字可以怎麼改述？

3.2　🔊 MP3 11

Now, listen to the recording of the multiple choice task on p. 36. As you listen, circle one answer.

＊Answer Key p. 44

現在請練習第 36 頁中的單選題，並選出一個答案。

3.3

Study the multiple choice questions above on p. 37. Answer the following questions.

請觀察第 37 頁的單選題，並回答以下問題。

❶ What are the keywords in each question or question stem? Underline them.

① 每一題的關鍵字是什麼？請畫底線。

❷ What question is Question 1 asking? Write it.

....

❸ What are the keywords in each answer? <u>Underline them.</u>

❹ What are some possible paraphrases for the keywords you underlined in the questions and answers?

....

＊Answer Key p. 44

❷ 第 1 題要問的問題是什麼？請寫下來。

③ 每個選項中的關鍵字是什麼？請畫底線。

④ 你在題目和選項中畫底線的關鍵字可以怎麼改述？

3.4   ◀) MP3 12

Now, listen to the recording of the multiple choice task on p. 37. As you listen, circle one answer.

＊Answer Key p. 44

現在請練習第 37 頁中的單選題，並選出一個答案。

Task Practice　　　　　　　　　　題型練習

PART 1　　🔊) MP3 13

Questions 1-6

*Choose the correct letter, **A**, **B**, or **C**.*

Schedule and Details for Arts Education Conference

1　The speaker is interested in conference events for

　A　Saturday afternoon.

　B　Saturday morning.

　C　Sunday morning.

2　The 'Unwanted Objects' lecture begins at

　A　2:45.

　B　3:30.

　C　5:00.

3　When are most of the academic papers presented on Saturday?

　A　in the morning

　B　around lunchtime

　C　in the afternoon

4　Paintings by students can be seen in the

　A　Yellow Room.

　B　Green Room.

　C　Red Room.

5　The youth orchestra

　A　won a regional competition earlier this year.

　B　has represented the region in a national competition.

　C　has won several contests.

6   Where will the 2 PM concert take place?

   A   in the theatre

   B   in the atrium

   C   on the lawn

PART 2   ◀)) MP3 14

Questions 1-5

*Choose the correct letter, **A**, **B**, or **C**.*

1   Shelly believes the main benefit to volunteering is

   A   increasing self-esteem.

   B   meeting new people.

   C   gaining new skills.

2   When approached by library users, volunteers

   A   can direct them to the restrooms.

   B   should avoid bothering library staff.

   C   handle the issue themselves.

3   The volunteer sign-in sheet is

   A   in the back of the library.

   B   on the second floor.

   C   in the front of the library.

4   Who will answer volunteers' questions during their shifts?

   A   the circulation supervisor

   B   the Children's Section clerk

   C   the designated staff person

5   Who is allowed to use the break lounge?

   A   Volunteers only

   B   Paid library staff and volunteers

   C   Paid library staff only

Answer Key | 答案

Pre-Lesson Skills Practice

Skill 1 Identifying keywords

Suggested underlining:

1 I <u>haven't bought</u> my <u>textbooks</u> <u>yet</u>.
2 <u>When</u> is the <u>earliest</u> possible <u>date</u> for <u>enrolment</u>?
3 <u>Only</u> <u>returning</u> <u>students</u> are <u>eligible</u> for these <u>benefits</u>.
4 We've <u>already</u> <u>got</u> a <u>swimming pool</u>.
5 I <u>won't write</u> the <u>title page</u> <u>until</u> I've <u>done</u> the <u>whole</u> <u>essay</u>.
6 Our <u>bank</u> is <u>located</u> in <u>China</u> and <u>across</u> the <u>whole</u> of <u>Europe</u>.
7 He <u>enquired</u> about the <u>way</u> <u>to</u> the <u>station</u>.
8 <u>Unlike</u> <u>all</u> the <u>other professors</u>, she <u>doesn't</u> give <u>extra credit</u> assignments.
9 <u>Most nights</u>, I <u>study</u> <u>in</u> the <u>library</u>.
10 The <u>majority</u> of <u>clients</u> <u>can receive</u> a <u>discount</u>.

....

11 The topic is related to school, university or general education (*textbooks*). The speaker does not have their textbooks at this time but intends to buy them, probably in the near future (*haven't bought / textbooks / yet*).
12 The topic is related to school, university or general education, or the speaker is writing something for a publication (*essay*). The speaker intends to write a title page, but they will do it after they complete their essay (*won't write / until / done / whole essay*).
13 The professor does not give extra credit assignments (*doesn't / extra credit*), but he or she is the only professor who does not give credit assignments (*unlike all / other professors*).

Skill 2 Recognising general paraphrasing

1	Same	4	Different	7	Different	10	Same
2	Same	5	Different	8	Same		
3	Different	6	Same	9	Different		

Skill 3 Understanding stems

1 What is the best way to find a job?
2 How did the woman describe the health course?
3 What should you do when opening a bank account?
4 Why is Tom talking to the teacher?
5 Who did Della first travel to New York with?

Listening Strategies ❸ Multiple Choice with a Single Answer

3.1

❶ Some possible underlining:
  1 <u>Start times</u> for <u>evening classes</u> range from
  2 The <u>man</u> <u>thinks</u> a <u>language class</u>
  3 <u>What</u> is the <u>man's</u> <u>opinion</u> about the <u>college's website</u>?
  4 The <u>instructor</u> for <u>woodworking</u> <u>has been teaching</u> at the <u>college for</u>
  5 The <u>woodworking</u> class <u>ends at</u>

❷ 1 What is the range of start times for evening classes?
  2 What does the man think about a language class?
  4 How long has the woodworking instructor been teaching at the college?
  5 When does the woodworking class end?

❸ Some possible paraphrases:
  2 might be <u>dull</u> // is <u>preferable</u> to a hands-on class // would be <u>useful</u>
  3 It is <u>easy</u> to use // It has <u>too many links and buttons</u> // His <u>friend</u> would <u>be interested in</u> it

❹ Some possible paraphrases:
  1 Start times for evening classes range from → Evening classes begin anywhere from...
     6:45 PM → a quarter to seven   7:45 PM → a quarter to eight
     8:15 PM → a quarter past eight   10:00 PM → ten at night
     8:30 PM → half past eight // half-eight
  2 The man thinks a language class → A language course seems…
     might be dull → could be boring
     is preferable to a hands-on class → is better than a class where you use your hands
     would be useful → would be practical
  3 opinion → I think…
     college's website → college's web page
     easy to use → user-friendly // intuitive
     has too many links and buttons → is too confusing
     His friend would be interested in it → his friend might want to try it
  4 The instructor for woodworking has been teaching at the college for → woodworking
     teacher has been here for
     The numbers in the options will likely not be paraphrased. However, listen closely for
     distractors.
  5 ends at → runs until // finishes at
     7:30 PM → half past seven // half-seven
     9:30 PM → half past nine // half-nine

3.2

1 B   **2** C   **3** A   **4** A   **5** B

3.3

❶ Some possible underlining:

1 Alterations are being made to the campus because
2 What does the speaker say about the gymnasium?
3 What is the ideal number of students in each dormitory room?
4 How will the garden be altered?

❷ Why are alterations being made to the campus?

❸ Some possible underlining:

1 the curriculum is too old-fashioned // the library and classrooms are not clean and well-maintained // many of the facilities are outdated
2 New tennis courts are being added to it // It is located on the road just outside the school gates // The school has already begun renovating it
4 Artwork will be installed // More trees will be planted // Seating will be expanded

❹ Some possible paraphrases:

1 Alterations → changes // renovations // [something] is being built // [something] is being knocked down

  is old-fashioned → fall behind the times // outdated

  not clean → dirty

  not well-maintained → in bad condition // hasn't been cared for // in ill repair

  facilities → gym // classrooms // whiteboards // computers // equipment
2 the gymnasium → the gym // the sports centre

  It is located... → you can/will find it... // you can/will see it...

  has already begun renovating it → started renovating it recently
3 the ideal number of students → It's best to have no more than ... students
4 Artwork → sculptures // murals // statues // sculpted hedges // lawn ornaments // rock garden

  Seating will be expanded → Seats will be added // They will add benches

3.4

1 C   **2** C   **3** C   **4** A

Task Practice

PART 1

1	A	**3**	C	**5**	A
2	B	**4**	A	**6**	A

PART 2

1	B	**3**	C	**5**	B
2	A	**4**	C		

Classifying / Sentence Completion

分類題 / 句子填空題

LESSON 3

Classifying / Sentence Completion
分類題 / 句子填空題

Lesson Overview

In this lesson, you will become familiar with the *classifying* question and the **sentence completion** question. You will learn how to approach these tasks and will become aware of common problems that IELTS candidates encounter in these questions.

We will be working with IELTS Listening Part 3 for these two task types.

♦ **Listening Part 3**
- Questions 21-30
- A dialogue (two or three speakers)
- Unlike Parts 1 and 2, features an academic topic
- Any question type is possible

本課內容

在這堂課中，我們將會介紹「分類題」和「句子填空題」。你會學到這兩種題型的答題技巧，以及一般考生最常遇到的問題。

我們會透過 IELTS 聽力測驗 Part 3 來練習這兩種題型。

聽力測驗 Part 3
- 第 21～30 題
- 多人對話
- 學術的對話主題
- 可能是任何題型

| Lesson Vocabulary Bank: Textbooks / Academic research / Language learning | 課程字彙庫：教科書 / 學術研究 / 語言學習 |

🔊 MP3 15

○ assess 動 評估
[əˋses]

○ assessed 形 估計的
[əˋsest]

○ assessment 名 評估
[əˋsesmənt]

○ assessor 動作者 估價員
[əˋsesə(r)]

○ compile 動 編纂；匯集
[kəmˋpaɪl]

○ compilation 名 編纂；匯集
[ˌkɒmpəˋleɪʃ(ə)n]

○ comprehend 動 理解
[ˌkɒmprɪˋhend]

○ comprehensible 形 容易理解的
[ˌkɒmprɪˋhensɪb(ə)l]
(↔ incomprehensible 無法理解的)

○ comprehension 名 理解力
[ˌkɒmprɪˋhenʃ(ə)n]

○ deduce 動 推論
[dɪˋdjuːs]

○ deductive 形 推斷的
[dɪˋdʌktɪv]

○ deduction 名 推論；扣除
[dɪˋdʌkʃ(ə)n]

○ define 動 定義
[dɪˋfaɪn]

○ defined 形 定義的
[dɪˋfaɪnd]

○ definition 名 定義
[defɪˋnɪʃ(ə)n]

○ differ 動 與⋯不同
[ˋdɪfə(r)]

○ different 形 不同的
[ˋdɪf(ə)r(ə)nt]

○ difference 名 差異
[ˋdɪf(ə)r(ə)ns]

○ educate 動 教育
[ˋedʒukeɪt]

○ educational 形 教育的
[edʒuˋkeɪʃ(ə)n(ə)l]
(↔ noneducational 非教育的)

○ education 名 教育
[edʒuˋkeɪʃ(ə)n]

○ educator 動作者 教育者
[ˋedʒukeɪtə(r)]

○ experiment 動 實驗
[ɪkˋsperɪm(ə)nt] [ekˋsperɪm(ə)nt]

○ experimental 形 實驗性的
[ɪkˌsperɪˋment(ə)l] [ekˌsperɪˋment(ə)l]

○ experiment 名 實驗
[ɪkˋsperɪm(ə)nt]

LESSON **3** Classifying / Sentence Completion

＊本書音標採用 IPA 音標系統

- experimentation 名〔總稱〕實驗
  [ɪkˌsperɪmen`teɪʃ(ə)n]

- experimenter 動作者 實驗者
  [ɪk`sperɪmentə(r)]

- impact 動 對…產生影響
  [ɪm`pækt]

- impactful 形 有影響力的
  [ɪm`pæktfl]
  （↔ unimpactful 沒有影響力的）

- impact 名 影響
  [`ɪmpækt]

- pollute 動 汙染
  [pə`lu:t]

- polluted 形 受汙染的
  [pə`lu:tɪd]
  （↔ unpolluted 未受汙染的）

- pollution 名 汙染
  [pə`lu:ʃ(ə)n]

- pollutant 動作者 汙染物
  [pə`l(j)u:t(ə)nt]

- statistical 形 統計的
  [stə`tɪstɪk(ə)l]

- statistics 名 統計學
  [stə`tɪstɪks]

- statistician 動作者 統計學家
  [ˌstætə`stɪʃ(ə)n]

- quote statistics 片 統計資料

- supplement 動 補充
  [`sʌpləment]

- supplemental 形 補充的
  [ˌsʌplə`ment(ə)l]

- supplement 名 補充物；副刊
  [`sʌpləm(ə)nt]

- supplementation 名〔總稱〕營養補充品
  [ˌsʌpləmen`teɪʃ(ə)n]

| **Pre-Lesson Skills Practice** | 高分技巧訓練 |

Skill 1 Spelling academic words

技巧 1：拼寫學術字彙

- Remember that spelling counts on the IELTS. Aside from common words, you also need to spell some words that are more academic. You should pay attention to these kinds of words when practising.

  別忘了拼字在 IELTS 中很重要。除了常見的字彙，你也需要會拼一些比較學術的字彙。練習的時候請多注意這類的字。

- Listen closely for the plural '-s' or '-es' at the end of words.

  記得聽清楚字尾有沒有複數形的 s 或 es。

Listen to each short extract. Spell the indicated words.

請聆聽音檔，音檔會先唸一個單字，再唸一個造句，最後重複一次單字。請將單字拼寫出來。

🔊 MP3 16

1 ....
2 ....
3 ....
4 ....
5 ....

6 ....
7 ....
8 ....
9 ....
10 ....

＊Answer Key p. 67

Skill 2 Recognising academic paraphrasing

技巧 2：辨識學術改述

The IELTS uses paraphrasing to assess the range and depth of not only your vocabulary, but also your grammar.

IELTS 測驗會改述題目，以考驗你的字彙和文法程度。

LESSON 3 Classifying / Sentence Completion

Recognising when paraphrasing is being used during the listening test means you understand when the speaker is preparing to give the answer to a question. It also means you recognise when the correct answer is spoken, and it means that you don't become tricked by other words and incorrectly choose them for the answer.

在聽力測驗中，辨識出題目的改述可以幫助你知道說話者可能會在哪裡說出答案。仔細判斷，就能避開混淆的字詞，選出正確答案。

In Lesson 2, we learnt about some different ways the IELTS paraphrases the ideas in its questions. Do you remember four common ways IELTS paraphrases? (Answer: synonyms, examples, definitions, descriptions)

我們在第 2 課學到 IELTS 測驗會用不同的字詞改述題目。你還記得四種常見的改述方式嗎？（答案是：同義詞、舉例、定義、描述）

Let's practise paraphrasing to get more familiar with how it works. Consider the word 'exam' in an academic context, i.e. related to schools and universities. Think about the following questions and write your ideas.

我們現在再來練習一下改述。以 exam 這個字用在學術內容中為例（和校園相關的用法）想想以下問題，把你的答案寫下來。

❶ What are some synonyms for 'exam' in an academic context?

....

❷ What are some examples of exams?

....

❸ How about a definition?

....

❹ And could you try a description?

....

Answers:

❶ Synonyms for 'exam' might be: test, examination, paper (in British English), or assessment.

❷ Examples might include: the IELTS, the SAT, the GRE, the LSAT, a final, a midterm, a college entrance exam.

❸ A definition could be: A formal test of a person's knowledge or proficiency in a particular subject or skill.

❹ A description of an exam: A situation where you answer questions on paper or online. Most people study for it. You wait for the results, and you often feel some stress or tension, since exam scores usually impact your future in some way.

All of these answers above could be paraphrases for 'exam.'

① 同義字：test、examination、paper〔英〕、assessment。

② 舉例：IELTS、SAT、GRE、LSAT（法學院入學考試）、a final（期末考）、a midterm（期中考）、a college entrance exam（大學入學考試）。

③ 定義：A formal test of a person's knowledge or proficiency in a particular subject or skill. （測驗一個人在特定領域或技術中是否具備知識、能力的正式考試。）

④ 描述：A situation where you answer questions on paper or online. Most people study for it. You wait for the results, and you often feel some stress or tension, since exam scores usually impact your future in some way. （你會用紙本或在線上回答問題，大部分的人會為了考試做準備。等待考試結果時可能會感到緊張，因為考試結果或多或少會影響你的未來。）

以上這些都可能是改述 exam 這個字的方法。

Let's try another. Consider the word 'deduce.'

我們再來試試看另一個字。以 deduce 這個字為例。

---

❶ What are synonyms for 'deduce?'

....

❷ And its definition?

....

Answers:

❶ Synonyms for 'deduce,' or very closely related words, might be: reason (verb), conclude, work out, gather, and infer. (Notice that the first four of these words all have different meanings in other contexts!)

答案：

① 同義字：意思非常接近的有動詞的 reason、conclude、work out、gather、infer（注意，前四個字都還有其他的意思）。

❷ A definition would be: To use the knowledge and information you have in order to understand something or form an opinion about it (*from Longman Dictionary of Contemporary English*).

② 定義：To use the knowledge and information you have in order to understand something or form an opinion about it.（運用已有的知識和資訊去理解某些事物，或是對其產生個人的意見）。

All of these answers above could be paraphrases of 'deduce.'

以上這些都可能是改述 deduce 這個字的方法。

Read each sentence in 1-5 and underline keywords. Listen and circle the sentence that has exactly the same meaning as the spoken sentence. Listen once more to check your work.

請先閱讀第 1～5 題中各個選項的句子，將關鍵字畫底線。接著聆聽音檔，圈出與題目意思完全相同的答案。你可以再次聆聽檢查答案。

◀》 MP3 17

Example:

A Giving <u>the essay</u> to <u>a classmate</u> to <u>correct your mistakes</u> is the most important <u>final step</u>.

B <u>An essay</u> <u>should not have</u> <u>mistakes</u>.

(C) After <u>finishing</u> <u>an essay</u>, <u>proofreading</u> for <u>errors</u> is crucial.

1　**A**　The lecture was as boring as I anticipated.

　　B　The lecture was unexpectedly interesting.

　　C　I proved that the lecture was dull.

2　**A**　The professor said that a survey could supplement a review of the literature.

　　B　The professor said that the students could either use a questionnaire or review the literature.

　　C　The professor said that the students could give out a questionnaire on the topic of writing literature reviews.

3　**A**　After discovering the cause of death for the fish, we analysed the level of toxins in the river and found them to be high.

　　B　We deduced that fish cannot survive in environments that are too polluted.

　　C　Our deduction that water pollution had killed the fish came from discovering a large amount of chemical toxins in the river.

4　**A**　The research was carried out very carefully, and the sample and data collection were excellent.

　　B　Each part of the research is explained clearly and with adequate details, particularly the sections on sample and data collection.

　　C　The researchers looked at the data and concluded that each component of research should be very clear and thorough.

5　**A**　The Scandinavian literature course will end this term, but the one on Italian cinema will still be offered.

　　B　There will be fewer courses on Scandinavian literature next term, but the one on Italian cinema will still be offered.

　　C　Next term, there will be more specialised courses on Italian cinema, but there will only be one course on Scandinavian literature.

＊Answer Key p. 67

Tips **Improve spelling**

補充：提升拼字能力

There are many methods for improving your spelling. However, there is no single 'best' way in general because every learner is different. The 'best way' for you may not be the best way for your classmate. The best thing you can do is find a combination of study methods that works for you.

提升拼字能力的方法很多，不過並沒有唯一「最好」的方法，因為每個學習者都不一樣，適合別人的方法不一定適合你。你能做到的是找出各種適合你的學習方法搭配使用。

Some methods that could improve spelling include:

提升拼字能力有以下這些方法：

- **Cover, copy, compare (CCC)**
  This method may be good for people who learn by doing. Make a list of 10 vocabulary words going down the left side of your paper. Study the first word. Fold your paper from the right so that the word list is covered. Write the first word from memory. Compare your attempt to the correct spelling. If you spelt it incorrectly, fold the paper again and try again. Repeat going down the list.

遮住、拼寫、比較

這個方法適合喜歡用實作學習的人。在一張紙的左邊往下列出 10 個單字，先看第一個字，接著將紙從右邊摺過來遮住單字，然後憑印象寫一次。對照你寫的內容和單字正確的拼法，如果拼錯了，就再試一次。就這樣依序往下重複練習每個單字。

- **Word Study**
  This method may be useful for people who feel especially lost with English spelling and vocabulary or who lack a strong English foundation. Word study is an approach to vocabulary, spelling, and phonics that involves students studying and thinking about the way words work. It deals with how letters match with sounds, how letters are grouped, and how groups of letters or morphemes (pieces of words) make meaning.

字彙分析

這個方法適合拼字能力還有待加強或是英文基礎不夠紮實的人。字彙分析包含學單字、拼法、發音，讓學習者認識並思考一個單字是怎麼組成的。這牽涉到字母和聲音的連結、字母之間怎麼組合，還有組合起來的字母是什意思。

Word study is a well-established approach to vocabulary teaching and learning, and there are

字彙分析在教學和自學都是個很完善的方法，也有很多教材可用

many materials available that you could use to improve your spelling. Word study begins at a very young age for English-speaking students and progresses to more advanced levels, so find the material that corresponds to your specific English level.

來協助你提升拼字能力。字彙分析從英文學習者年紀很小時就適用，逐步進階，所以你很容易找到適合自己程度的教材來練習。

- **'Air' writing**

This method may be useful for people who learn by seeing and doing. Look closely at a vocabulary word. While looking at the word, 'write' it in the air with your finger, on your hand, etc. You can repeat several times. Then, when you feel confident, really write the word on paper from memory.

空氣拼字法

這個方法適合喜歡用視覺和實作學習的人。仔細看一個單字，接著同時用手指在空中或手掌上「寫」這個字。你可以重複好幾次，等你有信心可以拼對的時候，再實際拿紙筆寫出來。

- **See and spell**

This method may be useful for people who learn by listening. Look closely at a vocabulary word, and spell the word out loud while looking. Repeat while looking at the word 3 more times. The fifth time, close your eyes and spell aloud from memory.

朗讀拼字法

這個方法適合喜歡用聽覺學習的人。仔細看一個單字，接著邊看邊大聲拼出來，然後再重複三次。第五次的時候，閉上眼睛然後憑記憶拼出來。

- **Graded readers**

This method is useful for any learner. Graded readers are short books made for language learners. They come in a wide range of language levels. Some of them are fiction, while others are non-fiction. They include features like comprehension questions, on-page translation of difficult terms, and vocabulary glossaries. They can be purchased through bookstores or may also be available in public or university libraries.

分級讀本

這個方法適合所有學習者。分級讀本是專為語言學習者編寫的輕薄書籍，可以細分成各種程度。內容很多是小說，也有非小說類，編寫時會納入閱讀測驗、生字註解，還有單字表。很多書店都買得到，市立圖書館或學校的圖書館也會有。

- **Language-learning apps**

  This method is useful for any learner. Language-learning apps have become very popular. For example, Duolingo is a popular language-learning app that is free for download. These apps are designed to be educational while still fun to use.

單字學習 app

這個方法適合所有學習者。現在語言學習 app 非常流行，例如 Duolingo 就是個非常熱門的免費 app。這些 app 都設計得既有助於學習，又相當有趣。

Tips **Reading for interest**

補充：課外閱讀

Reading for interest a few hours per week is the one thing every English student should be doing, especially if you're going to take the IELTS. When reading for interest:

每個英文學習者每週都應該按照自己的興趣課外閱讀幾小時，尤其是想要參加 IELTS 測驗的考生。課外閱讀的時候：

- Do not choose to read IELTS materials or other test materials. That is reading for study, not reading for interest.

不要選擇 IELTS 或其他語言檢定考試的閱讀素材。那些是針對考試去閱讀，而不是因興趣而讀。

- Consider your true, genuine interests. Are you fascinated by history? Celebrity gossip? Art? Travel? Science? Fashion and beauty? Whatever you truly like to learn about, start learning about it in English through websites, magazines, etc.

仔細想想你真正的興趣。你喜歡歷史嗎？還是名人八卦、藝術、旅行、科學、時尚？從現在開始，用英文閱讀任何你有興趣的內容，來源包含網路、雜誌等。

- Become comfortable being uncomfortable. You probably will not understand 100% of the words and grammar structures when reading English materials not designed for English learners, and although it will feel uncomfortable at first, that is okay.

慢慢適應不自在的感覺。閱讀不是刻意為英文學習者編寫的內容時，你很可能無法 100% 理解其中的單字和文法結構。雖然一開始會因此感到不太自在，但這都沒有關係。

- Reading for interest is not a test. The goal is not to understand everything as deeply as you would

依照興趣課外閱讀並不是在考試。這麼做的目標不是要你像用

if you were reading in your native language. The goal is to expose yourself to real English every day for roughly 20 minutes and learn about some new, interesting ideas at the same time—even if you only understand 20%.

母語閱讀時一樣深入了解所有內容，而是要讓你每天多接觸很自然的英文，一天大約 20 分鐘，然後順帶學到一些新奇、有趣的東西，即使你只了解閱讀內容的 20% 也沒關係。

| Listening Strategies ❹
Classifying | 聽力答題策略 ❹
分類題 |

Look at the example of a classifying question below.

請先看以下「分類題」的例題。

Whose book is each statement referring to?

*Write the correct letter, **A**, **B**, or **C** next to questions 1-5.*

NB *Any answer may be used more than once.*

> **A** Travers and Polski
> **B** Conway
> **C** Millican

1   The book was unexpectedly interesting.   ....

2   The book held students' attention by being funny.   ....

3   The book's structure distracted the students.   ....

4   The book is very well-organised.   ....

5   The book is longer than it needs to be.   ....

Tips

There will almost always be an 'NB' (nota bene: 'note well,' or 'pay attention') beneath classifying questions. The NB in this case reminds you that you need to use some answers more than once.

分類題下面幾乎都會有一個 NB（注意）的提示，用於提醒你有些答案選項可以使用超過一次。

The questions will be heard in order, but the answer choices will probably not. In the classifying question above, for instance, you might hear the name

題目會按照順序出現，但答案選項則不一定。舉例來說，以上的例題中，你可能會先聽到 Conway

'Conway' before you hear 'Travers and Polski.'

題個名字，再聽到 Travers and Polski。

The questions will almost certainly be paraphrased, so prepare yourself by thinking of one or two other ways to say the key points in each question.

題目幾乎一定會改述，所以瀏覽題目時記得先想想看每個關鍵字是否可以用別的方式表達。

| 4.1 |

Study the classifying question above. Answer the following questions.

請觀察上一頁的分類題，並回答以下問題。

❶ What are the keywords in each question? Underline them.

❷ What are some possible paraphrases for the keywords you underlined in the questions?

① 每個題目中的關鍵字是什麼？請畫底線。

② 你在題目中畫底線的關鍵字可以怎麼改述？

....

＊Answer Key p. 68

| 4.2 |　🔊) MP3 18

Now, listen to the recording of the classifying task on p. 61. As you listen, write one answer next to each statement.

現在請練習上一頁的分類題，將答案寫在題目旁。

＊Answer Key p. 68

Listening Strategies ❺
Sentence Completion

Look at the example of a sentence completion task below.

請先看以下「句子填空題」的例題。

Complete the sentences below.

*Write **NO MORE THAN TWO WORDS AND/OR A NUMBER** for each answer.*

- Jack feels overwhelmed at the amount of **1** .... on his topic.

- To make his topic less broad, the tutor suggests that Jack apply **2** .... to it.

- Jack discovered that teenagers who overuse mobile phones are more likely to experience **3** .... and tiredness.

- One study indicated that children 8 and under spend around **4** .... each day being entertained by electronics.

- Students' **5** .... has become shorter since the rise in popularity of smartphones.

LESSON 3 Classifying / Sentence Completion

Tips

Read directions carefully, as you will not receive a point if you write too many words or an inappropriate answer. As with all listening tasks, the questions will almost certainly be paraphrased, so prepare yourself by thinking of one or two other ways to say the key points in each question. As with all completion tasks, the answer must be spelt correctly.

一定要仔細閱讀題目說明,如果答案字數太多或不符合要求,就無法得到分數。和所有聽力題一樣,題目幾乎都會改述,所以瀏覽題目時記得先想想看關鍵字詞是否有其他說法。和所有填空題一樣,答案拼字一定要正確。

5.1

Study the sentence completion task above. Answer the following questions.

❶ What are the keywords in each question? Underline them.

❷ What are some possible paraphrases for the keywords you underlined in the questions?

....

❸ What word form (noun, verb, adjective, etc.) is needed for each gap? Can you predict anything else about each gap?

....

＊Answer Key p. 68

請觀察上一頁的句子填空題，並回答以下問題。

① 每一題的關鍵字是什麼？請畫底線。

② 你在題目中畫底線的關鍵字可以怎麼改述？

③ 每個空格應填入什麼樣的答案？（例如：名詞、動詞、形容詞等）你能預測其他任何關於答案的資訊嗎？

5.2   ◀)) MP3 19

Now, listen to the sentence completion task on p. 63. As you listen, write the answers in the gaps.

＊Answer Key p. 69

現在請練習上一頁的句子填空題，將答案填入空格中。

Task Practice   題型練習

PART 3   ◀)) MP3 20

Questions 1-5

Write **NO MORE THAN ONE WORD** *for each answer.*

- Professor Bates wants to avoid too much repetition of **1** .... during students' presentations.

- The importance of **2** .... information for humans explains the frequent mention of subtitles in Elsa's research.

- The small number of participants in the Huang and Eskey study possibly led to the surprising **3** ....

- Regular subtitles differ from bimodal subtitles in the number of **4** .... shown on the screen.

- 'Real-time difficult word subtitles' display the **5** .... of a difficult word beneath other subtitles.

Questions 6-10

Who will be responsible for each task?

*Write the correct letter, **A**, **B**, or **C** next to questions 6-10.*

A	Elsa
B	John
C	Katya

6   administering the survey face to face   ....

7   writing the methods section   ....

8   writing the results section   ....

9   creating visuals   ....

10   compiling the literature review   ....

Answer Key | 答案

Pre-Lesson Skills Practice

Skill 1 Spelling academic words

1	references	**4**	statistics	**7**	assessment	**10** faculty
2	attendance	**5**	architecture	**8**	management	
3	knowledge	**6**	experimental	**9**	psychology	

Skill 2 Recognising academic paraphrasing

Some possible underlining:

1 **A** The <u>lecture</u> was <u>as boring as</u> I <u>anticipated</u>.

    (**B**) The <u>lecture</u> was <u>unexpectedly</u> <u>interesting</u>.

    C I <u>proved</u> that <u>the lecture</u> was <u>dull</u>.

2 (**A**) The <u>professor</u> said that a <u>survey</u> could <u>supplement</u> a <u>review of the literature</u>.

    B The <u>professor</u> said that the <u>students</u> could either use a <u>questionnaire</u> or <u>review the literature</u>.

    C The <u>professor</u> said that the <u>students</u> could give out a <u>questionnaire</u> on the topic of <u>writing literature reviews</u>.

3 **A** <u>After discovering</u> the <u>cause</u> of <u>death</u> for the <u>fish</u>, we <u>analysed</u> the <u>level</u> of <u>toxins in the river</u> and found them to be <u>high</u>.

    B We <u>deduced</u> that <u>fish</u> <u>cannot survive</u> in <u>environments</u> that are too <u>polluted</u>.

    (**C**) Our <u>deduction</u> that <u>water pollution</u> had <u>killed</u> the <u>fish</u> <u>came from discovering</u> a large amount of <u>chemical toxins in the river</u>.

4 **A** The <u>research</u> was <u>carried out</u> very <u>carefully</u>, and the <u>sample and data collection</u> were <u>excellent</u>.

    (**B**) Each part of the <u>research</u> is <u>explained clearly</u> and with <u>adequate details</u>, <u>particularly</u> the sections on <u>sample and data collection</u>.

    C The <u>researchers</u> <u>looked at</u> the <u>data</u> and <u>concluded</u> that <u>each component</u> of <u>research</u> should be very <u>clear</u> and <u>thorough</u>.

5 (**A**) The <u>Scandinavian literature course</u> <u>will end</u> <u>this term</u>, but the one on <u>Italian cinema</u> <u>will still be offered</u>.

    B There will be <u>fewer courses</u> on <u>Scandinavian literature</u> <u>next term</u>, but the one on <u>Italian cinema</u> <u>will still be offered</u>.

    C <u>Next term</u>, there will be <u>more specialised courses</u> on <u>Italian cinema</u>, but there will only be <u>one course</u> on <u>Scandinavian literature</u>.

Listening Strategies ❹ Classifying

4.1

❶ Some possible underlining:

1　The book was <u>unexpectedly interesting</u>.
2　The book <u>held students' attention</u> by being <u>funny</u>.
3　The book's <u>structure</u> <u>distracted</u> the students.
4　The book is very <u>well-organised</u>.
5　The book is <u>longer than it needs to be</u>.

❷ Some possible paraphrases:

1　unexpectedly interesting → surprisingly interesting // more interesting than expected
2　held students' attention → kept students' interest // kept students interested
　　funny → humorous // made us laugh
3　structure ... distracted → had a distracting structure // wasn't laid out well
4　well-organised → organised very well // organised logically // We like the organisation of the book
5　longer than it needs to be → too long // should be shorter

4.2

1　C	3　B	5　A
2　A	4　A	

Listening Strategies ❺ Sentence Completion

5.1

❶ Some possible underlining:

- Jack <u>feels overwhelmed</u> at the <u>amount</u> of ... on <u>his topic</u>.
- To <u>make</u> his <u>topic</u> <u>less broad</u>, the <u>tutor</u> <u>suggests</u> that Jack <u>apply</u> ... to it.
- Jack <u>discovered</u> that <u>teenagers</u> who <u>overuse</u> <u>mobile phones</u> are <u>more likely</u> to <u>experience</u> ... and <u>tiredness</u>.
- One <u>study</u> indicated that <u>children 8 and under</u> <u>spend</u> around ... <u>each day</u> being <u>entertained</u> by <u>electronics</u>.
- <u>Students'</u> ... has become <u>shorter</u> <u>since the rise in popularity</u> of <u>smartphones</u>.

❷ Some possible paraphrases:

- feels overwhelmed → It's too much to handle
- make topic less broad → narrow down this topic
- teenagers who overuse mobile phones → teens who spend too much time on their cell phones

experience tiredness → feel tired // feel fatigued

children 8 and under → children up to age 8

- shorter → shrunk
- rise in popularity → become more popular

❸ 1 Noun. It's related to a study topic.

2 Noun. It's something that can be used to make a topic less broad.

3 Noun. It's something negative since 'overuse' implies using too much. It doesn't mean 'tiredness' because that's already given. It happens when you use your mobile phone too much.

4 Noun or number with noun. It could be a noun phrase like 'a lot of time' (since we 'spend time' in English) or it could be a number of minutes or hours.

5 Noun. It's something we measure with the words 'short' and 'long.' It's something affected by smartphones.

5.2

1 information	**4** four hours // 4 hours
2 question words	**5** attention span
3 stress	

Task Practice

PART 3

1 content	**4** languages	**7** C	**10** B
2 visual	**5** definition	**8** C	
3 results	**6** A	**9** A	

Notes Completion

筆記填空題

LESSON 4

Notes Completion
筆記填空題

Lesson Overview

本課內容

In this lesson, you will become familiar with the ***notes completion*** question on the IELTS. You will learn how to approach the task and will become aware of common problems that IELTS candidates encounter in these questions.

在這堂課中,我們將會介紹「筆記填空題」。你會學到這種題型的答題技巧,以及一般考生最常遇到的問題。

We will be working with IELTS Listening Part 4 for this task type.

我們會透過 IELTS 聽力測驗 Part 4 來練習這種題型。

♦ Listening Part 4

- Questions 31-40
- A monologue (a lecture)
- The topic is academic
- Notes completion is the most common task for Part 4, but any completion task is possible
- Generally said to be the most challenging part of the Listening Test, and for many people, of the entire IELTS

聽力測驗 Part 4

- 第 31～40 題
- 單人獨白(一場講座、演說)
- 學術的主題
- 筆記填空題在 Part 4 最常見,但也可能是任何填空題型
- 一般認為是聽力測驗中最困難的部分,對許多人而言,甚至是 IELTS 測驗中最困難的

Lesson Vocabulary Bank: Fashion / History / Culture

課程字彙庫：時尚 / 歷史 / 文化

🔊 MP3 21

○ accessorise 動 為…添加配件
[ək`sesəraɪz]

○ accessory 名 附件，配件
[ək`ses(ə)ri]

○ ancestral 形 祖先的；祖傳的
[æn`sestr(ə)l]

○ ancestor 名 祖先
[`ænsestə(r)]

○ authoritative 形 權威的
[ɔ:`θɒrətətɪv] [ɔ:`θɒrə‚teɪtɪv]

○ authority 名 權力，威信
[ɔ:`θɒrəti]

○ decorate 動 裝飾
[`dekəreɪt]

○ decorative 形 裝飾性的
[`dek(ə)rətɪv]

○ decoration 名 裝飾
[dekə`reɪʃ(ə)n]

○ decorator 動作者 裝修工
[`dekəreɪtə(r)]

○ depict 動 描述
[dɪ`pɪkt]

○ depiction 名 描述
[dɪ`pɪkʃ(ə)n]

○ differentiate (between...) 動 區別
[‚dɪfə`renʃɪeɪt]

○ domesticate 動 馴化
[də`mestɪkeɪt]

○ domestic 形 國內的，家庭的
[də`mestɪk]

○ endanger 動 危害
[ɪn`deɪndʒə(r)] [en`deɪndʒə(r)]

○ endangered 形 瀕臨絕種的
[ɪn`deɪndʒəd]

○ evolve 動 進化
[ɪ`vɒlv]

○ evolved 形 演化的
[ɪ`vɒlvd]

○ evolution 名 演化，進化
[i:və`lu:ʃ(ə)n] [evə`lu:ʃ(ə)n]

○ extinct 形 滅絕的
[ɪk`stɪŋkt] [ek`stɪŋkt]

○ extinction 名 絕種
[ɪk`stɪŋ(k)ʃ(ə)n] [ek`stɪŋ(k)ʃ(ə)n]

○ go/become extinct 片 滅絕

○ insulate 動 隔離
[`ɪnsjʊleɪt]

○ insulated 形 隔熱的；絕緣的
[`ɪnsjʊleɪtɪd]

○ insulation 名 隔絕
[‚ɪnsjʊ`leɪʃ(ə)n]

○ insulator 動作者 絕緣體
[`ɪnsjʊleɪtə(r)]

LESSON 4 Notes Completion

＊本書音標採用 IPA 音標系統

○ labour 動 致力於 名 勞工；勞動
[ˈleɪbə(r)]

○ labourer 動作者 勞動者
[ˈleɪb(ə)rə(r)]

○ limit 動 名 限制
[ˈlɪmɪt]

○ limited 形 有限的
[ˈlɪmɪtɪd]

○ process 動 加工；處理 名 過程
[ˈprəʊses]

○ processed 形 加工的
[ˈprəʊsest]

○ processor 動作者〔電腦〕處理器
[ˈprəʊsesə(r)]

○ realistic 形 實際的
[rɪəˈlɪstɪk]

○ reduce 動 減少
[rɪˈdjuːs]

○ reduced 形 降低的
[rɪˈdjuːst]

○ reduction 名 降低，減少
[rɪˈdʌkʃ(ə)n]

○ royal 形 皇家的
[ˈrɔɪəl]

○ royalty 名 皇室
[ˈrɔɪəlti]

○ sacred 形 神聖的
[ˈseɪkrɪd]

○ spiritual 形 精神上的
[ˈspɪrɪtʃuəl]

○ spirituality 名 神聖；靈性
[ˌspɪrɪtʃuˈæləti]

○ standardise 動 標準化
[ˈstændədaɪz]

○ standard 形 標準的 名 標準
[ˈstændəd]

○ supply 動 名 供應
[səˈplaɪ]

○ supplier 動作者 供應者
[səˈplaɪə(r)]

○ symbolise 動 象徵
[ˈsɪmbəlaɪz]

○ symbolic 形 象徵的
[sɪmˈbɒlɪk]

○ symbol 名 象徵
[ˈsɪmb(ə)l]

○ take ... for granted 片 將…視為當然

○ threaten 動 威脅
[ˈθret(ə)n]

○ threatened 形 受到威脅的
[ˈθret(ə)nd]

○ threatening 形 脅迫的
[ˈθret(ə)nɪŋ]

○ threat 名 威脅
[θret]

Pre-Lesson Skills Practice | 高分技巧訓練

Skill 1 Focused listening with paraphrasing

技巧 1：注意聽改述

Sometimes, you will not know the meaning of some words spoken on the listening test. A common mistake people make is to underline words they do not know. How can it help you to underline and pay attention to words you do not know? It can't! Underline what you do understand.

有時候你會不知道測驗中聽到的字是什麼意思。考生常犯的錯誤是把不認識的字畫底線當成關鍵字。如果你不認識那個字，畫上底線也沒什麼幫助。找關鍵字時，記得找你認識的字。

Other times, you may know the meaning, but you may miss the details the speaker is saying. In such cases, focus on what you have heard; you can still catch the important words and phrases that point you to the correct answer.

有時候則是你知道意思，但沒有聽清楚說話者提到的細節。這時你只要專注在有聽到的內容，還是有可能找到關鍵字詞幫助你正確作答。

To avoid being tricked into choosing the wrong answers:

如何避免掉入聽力測驗的陷阱中：

● Continue to develop your vocabulary through targeted practices and reading. The more vocabulary you know, the more easily you can identify paraphrases.

透過刻意練習和閱讀，持續增加字彙量。你認識愈多字，就愈容易聽出改述的內容。

● Practise listening frequently, and not just with IELTS materials. Use any English resources you can find and use English subtitles, such as TV shows, movies, news, internet materials, and anything else of interest to you. This can help you develop a key skill: hearing and understanding the words people say in English.

多練習聽力，而且不要只侷限用 IELTS 模擬測驗練習。多聽各式各樣可以同時看英文字幕的內容，例如電視節目、電影、新聞、網路影音，以及其他你有興趣的東西。這樣可以幫助你建立重要的技巧：聽懂實際對話中的英文。

LESSON 4 Notes Completion

● Practise listening for verb tenses. For example, if a speaker is talking about the past, don't be tricked into choosing an answer that refers to the future.

多練習聽動詞時態。舉例來說，如果說話者在講過去發生的事，就別選到未來式的答案。

Let's try some examples with our eyes before we use our ears. What is the same about these two sentences' meanings, and what is different?

在聽音檔練習之前，我們先用看的練習一下。以下兩個例句的意思有哪裡相同、哪裡不同？

---

❶ Renovations will begin on the eastern side of the school starting next month.

❷ The school started to renovate the eastern side of the building last month.

The same:

- They both refer to the eastern side of the school building.
- They both deal with renovations to that side of the school.

相同：
- 兩者都是關於學校建築的東側。
- 兩者都是關於翻修學校建築的東側。

'Renovations' are any actions we take to make an old building or piece of furniture look new and nice again. It is similar to 'restoration.' Notice that the verb form, 'renovate,' is used in sentence ❷.

renovations 是指老建築翻修或家具翻新，讓它們看起來重獲新生。意思和 restoration 很接近。注意第二句中用了動詞 renovate。

Different:

- In sentence ❶, the renovations have not begun yet (will begin). The eastern side of the building is still old and needs repairs.
- In sentence ❷, the renovations have already begun.
- In sentence ❶, the time referenced is next month (the future).

不同：
- 第一句中，翻修還沒開始，建築的東側還很老舊、需要整修。
- 第二句中，翻修已經開始。
- 第一句中提到的時間是下個月（未來）。
- 第二句中提到的時間是上個月（過去）。

– In sentence ❷, the time referenced is last month (the past).

We can see these two sentences are talking about the same topic, but their meanings are very different.

我們可以發現這兩個例句說的是一樣的主題，但內容非常不同。

Let's try another. What is the same about these two sentences' meanings, and what is different?

我們再來練習一下，以下兩個例句的意思有哪裡相同、哪裡不同？

❶ The repairs being made to the office will limit access to the storage room for roughly two weeks.

❷ In about half a month, there will be a second entrance to the storage room.

The same:
– They both refer to the storage room.
– Both sentences are talking about the future.
– The time period referred to in both sentences is about two weeks / half a month.

相同：
– 兩者都提到儲藏室。
– 兩者都在說未來的事。
– 兩者提到的時間都是兩週／半個月。

Different:
– Sentence ❶ mentions repairs to the office, while sentence ❷ does not.
– Sentence ❶ tells us that it will be more difficult to enter the storage room. We don't know why there will be this 'limit' to accessing this room. Maybe fewer people than usual can enter it, or perhaps anyone can enter it, but only at lunchtime, for example. Sentence ❷ has no mention of this situation.

不同：
– 第一句提到辦公室整修，第二句沒有提到。
– 第一句提到儲藏室出入會變困難。我們無法得知變困難的原因，舉例來說，可能是有人數限制，或是任何人都可以進出，但僅限午休時間等。第二句沒有提到這樣的狀況。

Again, these sentences have some similarities, but there are enough differences. If you don't understand

同樣地，這兩個例句雖然有一些相似之處，但其實很不一樣。如

LESSON **4** Notes Completion

the differences between them, you might choose the wrong paraphrases in the test.

果你無法判斷兩句的差異，就很可能在考試時選到錯誤的改述。

---

*Listen to each sentence. Write **S** beside the sentences that have the same meaning as the sentence you hear. Write **D** beside sentences that have different meanings from the sentence you hear. You may listen more than once.*

請聆聽音檔，如果聽到的句子和題目意思相同，答案請寫 S；如果意思不同，答案請寫 D。你可以多次聆聽。

🔊 MP3 22

Example A:

___S___ One other possible advantage of online social networking is that it may be good for the self-esteem of its users.

Example B:

___D___ In 1975, the school grounds were modernised, with the basketball courts on the campus' eastern edge being completely renovated.

1 .... Business schools tend to specialise in one area to be different from their competitors.

2 .... England's economy in the 1600s was largely supported by the oil and gas industry, an enterprise based in its north.

3 .... In the 19th and early 20th centuries, egret plumes were in high demand among French and German interior decorators whose clients wanted these attractive items for use in flower arrangements.

4 .... One of the main difficulties facing tourism in Kenya is the fact that many of the roads to its popular destinations are currently unpaved, which makes them especially hard to reach during the rainy season.

＊Answer Key p. 88

Skill 2   Listening and reading at the same time

技巧 2：同時聽讀

Being able to listen and read at the same time is an important skill on the IELTS, particularly because you only hear each recording once and have to think about paraphrases at the same time.

能夠同時聽和讀是作答 IELTS 的重要技巧，因為聽力測驗只會播放一次，而且你必須邊聽邊思考題目可能改述的方式。

Listen to the sentences below. Replace the underlined keywords with the paraphrased words used by the speaker. Do not change the grammar of the sentence. You may pause the recording to write, and you may listen more than once.

請聆聽音檔，將以下句子畫底線的關鍵字換成聽到的內容。不用改變句子的文法。你可以暫停音檔寫答案，也可以重複聆聽。

🔊 MP3 23

Example:

Original sentence:

One other possible <u>advantage</u> of online social networking is that it may <u>be good for</u> the self-esteem of its users.

Sentence after listening:

One other possible <u>benefit</u> of online social networking is that it may <u>have a positive impact on</u> the self-esteem of its users.

1   Business schools <u>tend to</u> specialise in <u>one area</u> to <u>be different</u> from their <u>competitors</u>.

   ....

2   One of the main <u>difficulties</u> facing <u>tourism</u> in Kenya is the fact that <u>many</u> of the roads to its <u>popular destinations</u> are currently unpaved, which makes them <u>especially</u> hard to <u>reach</u> during the rainy season.

   ....

* Answer Key p. 88

LESSON 4 Notes Completion

Underline the keywords in the sentences below. Listen again to the sentences. Replace the keywords with the words used by the speaker.

先將以下句子中的關鍵字畫底線，再聆聽音檔，將不同之處換成聽到的內容。

🔊 MP3 24

3   England's economy in the 1600s was largely supported by the oil and gas industry, an enterprise based in its northernmost regions.

....

4   In the 19th and early 20th centuries, egret plumes were in high demand among French and German milliners whose clients wanted these attractive items for use in flower arrangements.

....

＊Answer Key p. 88

| Listening Strategies ❻
 Notes Completion | 聽力答題策略 ❻
 筆記填空題 |

Look at the example of a notes completion task below.

請先看以下「筆記填空題」的例題。

Complete the notes below.

*Listen and write **NO MORE THAN TWO WORDS** for each answer.*

The History of Shoes

Early Human History

– Shoes were usually made of **1** .... natural resources.
– 7000 or 8000 B.C.: The earliest known shoes were sandals made from sagebrush bark.
– 4000 B.C.: Murals from Ancient Egypt show people wearing thong sandals, the ancestor of today's flip-flop sandal.
– 3300 B.C.: Ötzi the Iceman's shoes had bearskin bases, deerskin side panels, and an adjustable **2** .... of bark-string.

Middle Ages - Early Modern Period

– Shoe design became more complex and similar to today's footwear, e.g. the espadrille sandal, which can lace around the **3** ....
– Craftsmen assembled the turnshoe **4** ....

1400s - 1500s

– The pattens shoe is thought to be the ancestor of the modern high-heeled shoe.
– Turkish chopines, 17 to 20 centimetres high, became a status symbol.

- High heels became popular with **5** .... who wanted to increase their height and look more imposing.
- By 1580, both sexes were wearing high heels.

  'Well-heeled' described someone with power or **6** ....

1600s - 1700s

- Since the late 1600s, most leather shoes have had a sewn-on sole.

  This feature is **7** .... for high quality dress shoes today.
- Before 1800, welted rand shoes were usually made with the left and right foot identical.

  Each **8** .... had only two possible widths.

1800s - Present

- Before 1850, most shoemakers used the same hand tools their Ancient Egyptian peers worked with.
- 1845: The rolling machine saved shoemakers time and **9** .... when preparing sole leather.
- 1846: Howe's sewing machine was at first meant for use in the **10** ....

Tips

Notes completion is the most common task for Part 4. Unlike Parts 1-3, there is no break in Part 4. You will be given a longer time before the track begins to look at all ten questions.

Do NOT skim the questions slowly for deep comprehension in this short time. You might be tempted to, but it will not help you. Instead, follow the instructions in '6.1' below and always remember them

筆記填空題是 Part 4 最常出現的題型。和 Part 1〜3 不同，Part 4 要一次作答 10 題，中間沒有間斷，所以你一開始會有多一點時間瀏覽所有問題。

千萬不要花時間慢慢從頭到尾瀏覽問題，你可能會很想這麼做，但這對作答並沒有什麼幫助。請運用接下來「6.1」的策略，每次

before you do Part 4 Practice Tests.

Do not worry about spelling while the track is playing. Instead, write quickly while 'keeping your ears open' to what is being spoken at the same time.

Do spell carefully after the whole test is finished, when you transfer answers to the answer sheet.

Do not be surprised by how much the speaker talks in Part 4. A common error of unpractised IELTS candidates is expecting answers to always come quickly after each other. In Part 4, they do not. If you glance at a script from Lesson 4, you will see a huge amount of 'extra' words. Many of these extra words are tricks. They are distractors, or 'the wrong answers.'

The answer choices will almost certainly be paraphrased, so prepare yourself by thinking of one or two other ways to say the key points in each answer choice.

練習 Part 4 時都記得要這麼做。

聽力播放期間,不用太在意拼字。你應該做的是快速做筆記,同時仔細聽清楚播放內容。

聽力播放結束後,再將答案填入答案紙,這時就一定要仔細檢查拼字。

別被 Part 4 相當長的播放內容嚇到。沒有充分準備的考生往往誤以為答案會一個接著一個快速出現,但在 Part 4 並非如此。若你稍微看一眼 Part 4 的錄音逐字稿,會發現有很多答案之外的「多餘」內容。這些內容常常是題目的陷阱,讓你選到錯誤的答案。

答案幾乎一定會改述,所以瀏覽題目時記得先想想看每個關鍵字是否可以用別的方式表達。

LESSON 4 Notes Completion

6.1

Study the notes completion task on p. 81. Answer the following questions.

請觀察第 81 頁的筆記填空題,並回答以下問題。

❶ What is the word limit? Can the answer be a number?

....

① 字數限制幾個字?答案可以是數字嗎?

❷ Look at the title: what is the lecture about? Look at the bold headings (subheadings): how has this speaker organised their lecture?

....

❸ Set a timer for 1 minute. When it starts, quickly skim the task. Underline any keywords that will help you listen for the answer. STOP at 1 minute.

＊Answer Key p. 88

If you finished skimming the whole task, good. If you didn't, that's okay:

- Later, when you listen to the recording, very quickly glance at the remaining questions while the announcer says, 'Now listen and answer questions 1-10.'
- Note the section they are in (e.g. 9-10 are in section '1800s - Present').
- Then very quickly underline the words before the answer gap, starting with **the first verb** that you see. If you don't have time to think about the verb, just underline **five words before the gap**.

When the track begins, you MUST be back at the beginning of the notes, ready to catch the first question.

6.2 ◀》 MP3 25

Now, listen to the recording of the notes completion task on p. 81. As you listen, write the answers in the gaps. When finished, do NOT look at the answers yet.

② 先看大標題：講座是關於什麼？再看每個段落的標題：講者每個段落要講什麼？

③ 計時 1 分鐘，快速瀏覽題目，將有助於你聽到答案的任何關鍵字畫底線。

如果你有瀏覽完所有題目，非常好！如果沒有，也沒關係：

- 接下來開始聆聽音檔時，聽到「Now listen and answer questions 1-10」，快速瞥一眼剩下的題目。
- 確認每一題出現在哪個段落（例如：第 9～10 題在「1800s - Present」這一段）。
- 快速將空格前面的字從你看到的第一個動詞開始畫底線，如果你沒有時間判斷動詞，那就將空格前面五個字畫底線。

當聽力開始播放時，你一定要回到筆記填空題的最開頭，準備好作答第 1 題。

現在請練習第 81 頁的筆記填空題，將答案填入空格中。聽力播放結束後，請先不要對答案。

If you struggled a lot:

- Turn to the script for this track. Listen to the track again while you read along at the same time.
- Turn back to the notes completion task. Listen again, this time with NO SCRIPT. Check your work or give it a second try.

∗ Answer Key p. 88

如果你覺得這部分非常困難：

- 翻到書末這一題的逐字稿，邊看逐字稿邊再聽一次音檔。
- 翻回到前面的筆記填空題，再聽一次音檔，這次不要對照逐字稿。檢查你的答案，或再寫一次題目。

LESSON 4

Notes Completion

Task Practice　｜　題型練習

PART 4　🔊 MP3 26

Complete the notes below.

*Write **NO MORE THAN ONE WORD AND/OR A NUMBER** for each answer.*

Human Use of Feathers

Types of feathers

- Contour: on bird's outside, wings, tail. Humans perceive them as 'beautiful.'
- Down: at base of contour feathers. Insulate birds from cold. Fluffier and
  1 .... than contour feathers.

Practical use of feathers

- Used in pillows since 400 C.E.
- Before mid-1800s, goose feathers used in tools for **2** ....
- Most common uses: **3** .... objects and personal decoration.

Symbolic use of feathers

- Associated with spirituality.
- Ancient Egypt: Ostrich feather symbolised truth. Often shown with Ma'at (goddess of truth and justice).
- Amazon's indigenous people: feathers for religion and ritual.

  Tapirapé society: feathered masks used during dry-season rituals.

  Yanomamö men: feathered armbands look like **4** ...., associating wearer with bird spirits.

Feathers in fashion

- Roughly **5** .... birds killed annually to satisfy demand.
- Frank Chapman, 1886: observed 542 feathered women's hats in New York City out of 700 hats.
- Drastic overhunting of birds worldwide threatened or exterminated many species.

  Great Egret and Snowy Egret plumes used as fashion decoration on women's **6** ....

Protection of endangered bird species

- Plummeting bird numbers lead to bird protection laws.
- *Federal Migratory Bird Treaty Act*, 1918: **7** .... how many months per year that sportsmen could shoot migratory birds.
- 1937, 1973: Similar treaties signed protecting migratory birds.
- United States: Laws prohibit clothes or **8** .... from being made with certain wild birds' feathers.

Fashion changes help endangered birds

- 1920s: Hair cut too short for large hats.
- 1930s - 1950s: Feathers appeared again, but were not **9** .... for hat.
- 1960s: Hats went out of style.
- Today: Technology gives **10** .... appearance to fake feathers.

Answer Key 答案

Pre-Lesson Skills Practice

Skill 1 Focused listening with paraphrasing

1 S   **2** D   **3** D   **4** S

Skill 2 Listening and reading at the same time

1 Business schools <u>typically</u> specialise in <u>a specific sector</u> to <u>differentiate themselves</u> from their <u>competition</u>.

2 One of the main <u>challenges</u> facing <u>the tourism industry</u> in Kenya is the fact that <u>a great number</u> of the roads to its <u>main tourist attractions</u> are currently unpaved, which makes them <u>particularly</u> hard to <u>access</u> during the rainy season.

3 England's economy in the 1600s was largely supported by the <u>wool</u> industry, an enterprise based in its <u>east and south</u>.

4 In the 19th and early 20th century, egret plumes were in high demand among <u>European</u> and <u>American</u> milliners whose clients coveted these attractive items for use in <u>hats</u>.

Listening Strategies ❻ Notes Completion

6.1

❶ One or two words. There is no mention of numbers, so no, these questions cannot be answered with numbers.

❷ It's about the history of shoes. The lecture is organised by time period.

❸ Some possible underlining:

<u>made of</u> // <u>natural resources</u> // <u>adjustable</u> // <u>of bark-string</u> // <u>lace around</u> // <u>assembled the turnshoe</u> // <u>became popular with</u> // <u>look more imposing</u> // <u>someone with power</u> // <u>for high quality dress shoes</u> // <u>only two possible widths</u> // <u>saved shoemakers time</u> // <u>sewing machine</u> // <u>meant for use in</u>

6.2

1 unprocessed // raw   6 wealth
2 net   7 standard
3 ankle   8 size
4 inside-out // inside out   9 labour // labor
5 royalty   10 home

Task Practice

PART 4

1 softer
2 writing
3 sacred
4 wings
5 5 million // 5,000,000

6 hats
7 limited
8 accessories
9 foundation
10 realistic

LESSON 5

Short Answer / Matching from a List

簡答題 / 列表配合題

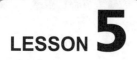
Short Answer / Matching from a List
簡答題 / 列表配合題

Lesson Overview

本課內容

In this lesson, you will become familiar with the **short answer** question and the **matching from a list** question on the IELTS. You will learn how to approach the tasks and will become aware of common problems that IELTS candidates encounter in these questions. You will also practise the notes completion question at the end of this lesson.

在這堂課中,我們將會介紹「簡答題」和「列表配合題」。你會學到這兩種題型的答題技巧,以及一般考生最常遇到的問題。在本課的「題型練習」,你也會再次複習「筆記填空題」。

We will be working with IELTS Listening Part 1 and Part 2 for these two task types.

我們會透過 IELTS 聽力測驗 Part 1 和 Part 2 來練習這兩種題型。

♦ Listening Part 1
- Questions 1-10
- A conversation between two speakers
- The topic is non-academic, e.g. job interview, booking accommodations, etc.
- Form completion task is common in Part 1, but any question type is possible

聽力測驗 Part 1
- 第 1～10 題
- 兩人對話
- 非學術的對話主題,如:工作面試、預訂住宿等
- 表單填空題在 Part 1 相當常見,但也可能是其他題型

♦ Listening Part 2
- Questions 11-20
- A monologue (a single speaker)
- Like Part 1, features a non-academic topic
- Any question type is possible

聽力測驗 Part 2
- 第 11～20 題
- 單人獨白
- 和 Part 1 一樣是非學術的主題
- 可能是任何題型

| Lesson Vocabulary Bank:
Fitness / Health / Workplace | 課程字彙庫：
健身 / 健康 / 職場 |

🔊 MP3 27

○ academic 名〔人〕學者
[͵ækə`demɪk]

○ appreciate 動 欣賞；感謝
[ə`pri:ʃɪeɪt]

○ appreciative 形 有欣賞力的；感激的
[ə`pri:ʃ(ɪ)ətɪv]

○ appreciation 名 欣賞；感激
[ə͵pri:ʃɪ`eɪʃ(ə)n]

○ certify 動 證實
[`sɜ:tɪfaɪ]

○ certified 形 經認證的
[`sɜ:tɪfaɪd]

○ certification 名 檢定；證書
[͵sɜ:tɪfɪ`keɪʃ(ə)n]

○ custodial 形 監管的
[kʌ`stəʊdɪəl]

○ custodian 名 監護人；管理人
[kʌ`stəʊdɪən]

○ distinctive 形 獨特的
[dɪ`stɪŋ(k)tɪv]

○ distinct 形 明顯的
[dɪ`stɪŋ(k)t]

○ environmentalist 名 環保主義者
[ɪn͵vaɪrən`ment(ə)lɪst]

○ exhibit 動 展示，陳列 名 展示品
[ɪg`zɪbɪt]

○ exhibition 名 展覽
[͵eksɪ`bɪʃ(ə)n]

○ facility 名 設施
[fə`sɪləti]

○ identify 動 辨識，認出
[aɪ`dentɪfaɪ]

○ identifiable 形 可識別的
[aɪ͵dentɪ`faɪəb(ə)l]

○ identification 名 識別；身分證明
[aɪ͵dentɪfɪ`keɪʃ(ə)n]

○ lifeguard 名 救生員
[`laɪfgɑ:d]

○ marina 名 碼頭；船塢
[mə`ri:nə]

○ multimedia 名 多媒體
[͵mʌltɪ`mi:dɪə]

○ pushy 形 有衝勁的
[`pʊʃi]

○ publicise 動 宣傳，公布
[`pʌblɪsaɪz]

○ public 形 大眾的
[`pʌblɪk]

○ publicity 名 知名度
[pʌb`lɪsəti]

＊本書音標採用 IPA 音標系統

○ recreate 動 再創造
[ri:krɪˋeɪt]

○ sedentary 形 久坐的
[ˋsed(ə)nt(ə)ri]

○ replicate 動 複製
[ˋreplɪkeɪt]

○ shortage 名 短缺
[ˋʃɔ:tɪʤ]

○ replicate 形 複製的
[ˋreplɪkət]

○ touch lives 片 扣人心弦

○ replica 名 複製品
[ˋreplɪkə]

Pre-Lesson Skills Practice | 高分技巧訓練

Skill 1 **Focused listening for verb tenses**

技巧 1：注意聽動詞時態

Being able to identify the verb tense a speaker is using (and understanding the meaning of it) can help you avoid the wrong answers on the IELTS. And in real-world scenarios, it helps you understand more of what is being said. That's definitely a bonus!

聽出說話者使用的時態和背後的意義，能夠讓你在 IELTS 測驗中避開錯誤的答案，也能幫助你在現實生活中更聽得懂別人說的英文！

You are already familiar with at least some of common verb tenses and how they work (*I go, I went, I have gone, I'm going, I will go*), which is great. Many of the IELTS listening questions will test your ability to hear and understand these.

你應該很熟悉許多常見動詞的時態了，例如動詞 go（去）：I go、I went、I have gone、I'm going、I will go。IELTS 聽力測驗常常會考驗你是否知道這些基本動詞的時態。

However, the most difficult questions on the IELTS will test how well you can understand more complex tenses and grammar.

然而，IELTS 測驗中最困難的題目考的是你是否會運用更複雜的時態和文法。

First, let's look at some examples of verb tenses and the different kinds of jobs they do.

首先，讓我們來看看不同的動詞時態，了解它們的用途。

Present simple

現在簡單式

Present simple can describe an action that happens regularly.

現在簡單式可以表達規律的動作或習慣。

Example: My father cooks.

例：My father cooks.（我爸爸會煮飯。）

Does this sentence mean my father is cooking right now, at this moment? No. Don't be fooled by the name of this verb tense. 'Present simple' does not always mean an action is happening in this present moment.

這個句子表示「我爸爸現在正在煮飯」嗎？並不是，別被這個時態的名字誤導了。「現在簡單式」並不是都用於現在發生的事。

Instead, this sentence is expressing a fact about my father, something that is generally true but not always happening. My father knows how to cook. Sometimes he cooks meals, but other times my mother does. (*She cooks, too!*)

這個句子說明了有關「我爸爸的事」，表示那是真實的事，但不表示動作一直進行。My father cooks. 意思是 My father knows how to cook.（我爸爸知道怎麼煮飯。）他有時候會煮飯，但有時候可能換成媽媽煮（所以也可以說 She cooks.）。

Present continuous

Present continuous can describe an action happening at this moment, but it can also describe a planned action that will happen in the future.

Example: My father is <u>cooking</u>.

現在進行式

現在進行式可以表達正在進行的動作，也可以用於未來已經規劃好、確定會發生的事。

例：My father is <u>cooking</u>.（我爸爸正在煮飯 / 將會煮飯。）

Does this sentence mean my father is cooking right now, at this moment? Maybe! It might also refer to a planned action in the foreseeable future. We need more information (i.e. we need context) to be able to answer accurately.

這個句子表示「我爸爸現在正在煮飯」嗎？有可能！但這句也可以表示未來的規劃，我們需要更多資訊（前後文）來判斷是哪種意思。

Take a moment to add information to the sentence. Your extra information should make the sentence refer to the present moment (right now).

請幫這個句子增加一些資訊，讓它的意思一定是指動作現在正在發生。

My father is cooking.

....

What did you write? Some possible answers include:

你的答案是什麼？以下是一些可能的答案：

○ My father is cooking right now / at this moment.
○ Sorry, my father can't talk to you. He's busy. He's cooking.

○ My father is cooking right now / at this moment.（我爸爸現在正在煮飯。）
○ Sorry, my father can't talk to you. He's busy. He's cooking.（不好意思，我爸爸現在不能來和你說話，他正忙著煮飯。）

Now add different information to the sentence. This time, the information should make the sentence refer to a plan in the future.

現在請幫這個句子增加一些不同的資訊，這次讓它的意思變成在說明未來的規劃。

My father is cooking.

....

What did you write? Some possible answers include:

你的答案是什麼？以下是一些可能的答案：

○ My father is cooking tomorrow / tonight / next weekend.
○ Sorry, my father won't be able to join you tomorrow. He's cooking for my mom's birthday.

○ My father is cooking tomorrow / tonight / next weekend.（我爸爸明天 / 今晚 / 下週末會煮飯。）
○ Sorry, my father won't be able to join you tomorrow. He's cooking for my mom's birthday.

○ A: Hey, are you going to a restaurant for your birthday?

B: No. My father's cooking.

（不好意思，我爸爸明天不能加入你們。他要煮我媽媽的生日大餐。）

○ A: Hey, are you going to a restaurant for your birthday?（你生日會去餐廳慶生嗎？）

B: No. My father's cooking.（不會，我爸爸會負責煮大餐。）

Note that 'are you going...' refers to the future in this question, not the present moment.

注意上面問句中的 are you going 問的是未來，不是現在。

Past simple

過去簡單式

The past simple expresses a completed, finished action.

過去簡單式用於表達過去結束的動作。

Example: I studied for three hours today.

例：I studied for three hours today.（我今天讀了三小時的書。）

Does this sentence mean the speaker is studying at this moment? No. Does it sound like she intends to study more? No. It sounds like she is finished for today.

這個句子表示「我正在讀書」嗎？不是。那有「我打算要讀書」的語意嗎？也沒有。這句話的意思是已經讀完書了。

Example: I used to study every day.

例：I used to study every day.（我之前每天讀書。）

Does this sentence mean the speaker studies every day now? No. The speaker doesn't study every day anymore.

這個句子表示「我現在每天讀書」嗎？並不是，這句話言下之意是「我現在已經沒有每天讀書了」。

Note that 'used to' is a special usage you will encounter often. For instance, 'He used to be a doctor.' 'I used to run every morning.' It describes

請注意 used to 是個很常見的用法。例如 He used to be a doctor.（他曾是個醫生。）、I used to run

a past situation that is no longer true or an action that occurred repeatedly in the past but does not anymore.

every morning.（我之前每天早上慢跑。）used to 表達的是「過去習慣或狀況，但現在已經不是如此」。

Present perfect

The present perfect can describe an action that started in the past and continues into the present.

Example: I've <u>studied</u> for three hours today.

Does this sentence mean the speaker is studying right now? Possibly. Does it sound like she intends to study more today? Maybe.

Another similar usage of present perfect is an action that occurred in the past but could still happen again within a time period (e.g. *today, during this class, or this week*). The present perfect can also express an action that occurred in the recent past and is still affecting the present in some way.

Example: I've only <u>eaten</u> one meal today—breakfast.

Does the speaker seem to think he can still eat another meal today? Yes. Maybe it's early in the day!

Compare to 'I only <u>ate</u> one meal today—breakfast.' By using the simple past tense, this speaker shows that he seems to think his time for eating is finished.

現在完成式

現在完成式表達從過去開始至今的動作。

例：I've <u>studied</u> for three hours today.（我今天已經讀了三小時的書。）

這個句子表示「我現在正在讀書」嗎？有可能。那有「我今天會繼續讀書」的語意嗎？也有可能。

現在完成式也可以表達過去發生的動作，未來一段時間內（例如今天、課堂上、這週）可能再次發生。或是過去近期發生的動作，持續影響至今。

例：I've only <u>eaten</u> one meal today—breakfast.（我今天目前只吃了早餐。）

這個句子有「我之後還可能再吃別餐」的語意嗎？有可能，或許說這句話時，時間還很早。

如果這句話是用過去簡單式 I only <u>ate</u> one meal today—breakfast.（我今天只吃了早餐。）語意就會是

Maybe it's 11:59 PM, or maybe he doesn't want to eat another meal.

「今天可以用餐的時間已結束，我只吃了早餐」，或許說這句話的時間是晚上 11:59，也或許只是因為說話者不想再吃東西。

Example: Be careful! I've broken a cup!

例：Be careful! I've broken a cup!
（小心！我打破了一個杯子。）

Why does the speaker warn us to be careful? He broke the cup recently, and there's probably still broken glass that could cut you.

為什麼這句話的說話者要提醒大家小心？因為他剛打破杯子，別人可能會被碎片割傷，也就是說「打破杯子」這個過去發生的動作可能持續影響至今。

Present perfect continuous

The present perfect continuous expresses an action that started in the past and is still continuing to this present moment.

現在完成進行式

現在完成進行式表達從過去開始持續至今的動作，強調的是此刻仍進行中。

Example: I've been studying for three hours.

例：I've been studying for three hours.（我已經讀了三小時的書。）

Does this sentence mean the speaker is studying right now? Yes! Does it sound like she intends to study more? Possibly. We need more information. It could be 'I've been studying for three hours. That's enough. Time to relax for today' or 'I've been studying for three hours! I wish I could quit, but the test is tomorrow morning!'

這個句子表示「我正在讀書」嗎？沒錯！那有「我會繼續讀書」的語意嗎？有可能，我們需要更多資訊才能判斷。有可能是 I've been studying for three hours. That's enough. Time to relax for today.（我已經讀了三小時的書！夠了，該休息了。）也可能是 I've been studying for three hours! I wish I could quit, but the test is tomorrow morning!（我已經讀了三

小時的書！好想休息，但明天早上要
考試。）

Sometimes, we can use either present perfect or present perfect continuous, and the meaning is the same. 'I've lived here for 20 years' has the same meaning as 'I've been living here for 20 years.'

有時候，我們用現在完成式和現在完成進行式的意思是一樣的，例如 I've lived here for 20 years. 和 I've been living here for 20 years. 都是指「我在這裡住了二十年。」

(Past modal + have + past participle)

Modals are special types of verbs that must go together with main verbs. They can be used in the 'perfect' verb tense construction. Modals tell us more specific information, and most modals carry a different meaning. A few have similar or identical meanings, such as 'ought to' and 'should.'

(過去式助動詞 + 完成式)

助動詞必須跟著動詞一起使用，可以用於完成式的句型結構中。讀者能透過助動詞得到更多補充資訊。大部分的助動詞都有不同的意思，但有些助動詞意思很接近，例如 ought to 和 should。

● **Should have / ought to have done...**
Something would have been a good idea, but you didn't do it. For instance, 'I should have / ought to have brushed my teeth this morning.'

Should have / ought to have done... （應該要…）
某件事應該要做，但你沒做。像是 I should have / ought to have brushed my teeth this morning. （我今天早上應該要刷牙的。）

Example: I should have brought flowers.

例：I should have brought flowers. （我應該帶花來的。）

Did the speaker bring flowers? No. Does he seem to wish he had brought flowers? Yes.

說話者有帶花嗎？沒有。他是不是希望自己有帶花來？是。

● **Shouldn't have done...**
Something was a bad idea, but you did it anyway.

Shouldn't have done... （不該…）
某件事不該做，但你做了。例

For instance, 'I shouldn't have played video games all night.' (Note that 'oughtn't to have' is much less common than 'shouldn't have.')

如 I shouldn't have played video games all night.（我不該整晚打電動的。）特別注意，雖然也可以說 oughtn't to have，但這個用法比 shouldn't have 少見很多。

● **Could have done...**
Something was possible, but you didn't do it. For instance, 'I could have been a professional musician.'

Could have done...（本來可以…）
某件事本來有可能，但你沒有去做。像是 I could have been a professional musician.（我本來可以當個職業音樂家的。）

Example: You did this math problem correctly. You could also have used a different method to find the answer.

例：You did this math problem correctly. You could also have used a different method to find the answer.（這題數學你答對了，但你也可以用另一種方法解題。）

Does the speaker seem to think your method wasn't good? No. The speaker is just stating another possibility. If the speaker thought your method was inferior, they would say, 'You should have used a different method to find the answer.'

說話者有表達「你用的方法不好」嗎？沒有。說話者只是指出另一種可能性。如果說話者真的認為方法不好，會說 You should have used a different method to find the answer.（你應該要用另一種方法解題的。）

● **Couldn't have done...**
Something was impossible. Even if you had wanted to do it, you couldn't have. For instance, 'I couldn't have stopped that train accident.'

Couldn't have done...（當時不可能…）
某件事不可能做到，即使當時希望能達成，也沒有辦法。例如 I couldn't have stopped that train accident.（我當時不可能阻止得了那起火車事故。）

- **Would have done...**

You wanted or intended to do something, but you didn't do it. This is used with hypothetical past situations, expressing a situation that would have been different under different conditions. For instance, 'I would have called you if my phone hadn't been broken.'

Example: Bob would have been a good teacher.

Was Bob a teacher? No. Does the speaker believe Bob could still become a teacher? No. If the speaker thought this was possible, he would say, 'Bob would be a good teacher.'

- **Wouldn't have done...**

You did something, but you're imagining the past if the conditions were different.

Example: I wouldn't have called you if I'd known you were asleep.

Did the speaker call you? Yes. Did they know you were asleep? No. If they had known, they would not have called you.

Would have done...（當時可以…）

你想要做某件事，但實際上沒有做。用於假設的過去情境，意思是如果當時情況不同，結果可能會不同。像是 I would have called you if my phone hadn't been broken.（要是那時我的手機沒壞，我就會打給你。）

例：Bob would have been a good teacher.（Bob 當時可以成為一位好老師的。）

Bob 是個老師嗎？不是。說話者認為 Bob 還可以成為老師嗎？不認為。如果說話者認為有可能的話，會說 Bob would be a good teacher.（Bob 會是一位好老師。）

Wouldn't have done...（當時就不會…）

你做了某件事，但如果當時情況不同，你可能就不會做。

例：I wouldn't have called you if I'd known you were asleep.（要是我知道你在睡覺，就不會打給你。）

說話者實際上有打電話給你嗎？有。他知道你在睡覺嗎？不知道。如果當時他知道，就不會打給你了。

LESSON **5** Short Answer / Matching from a List

We can also use this to compare someone's real reactions during a past event to another person's hypothetical reactions.

這個用法也可以用於比較某人在過去事件中的真實反應和另一個人可能會有的反應。

Example: If I were you, I <u>wouldn't have been</u> rude to the doctor.

例：If I were you, I <u>wouldn't have been</u> rude to the doctor.（我是你的話，就不會對醫生那麼無禮。）

Was the speaker rude to the doctor? No. Is the speaker talking to someone who was rude to the doctor? Yes.

說話者有對醫生很無禮嗎？沒有。那他說話的對象對醫生很無禮嗎？沒錯。

Note that this is not an inclusive list of verb tenses or modal phrases. There are simply more than we have the time and room for here. There are whole grammar books on these topics!

以上並不是英文所有的動詞時態或助動詞。實際上還有非常多用法，但我們在此只能提到一些重點。要完整討論的話，還有專門的文法書呢！

Listen to each sentence. Pay special attention to the verb tenses. Answer each question with the best option: **Yes** *or* **No**. *You may listen more than once.*
請聆聽音檔，特別注意動詞的時態，並用 Yes 或 No 回答以下問題。你可以多次聆聽。

🔊 MP3 28

Example: Does the speaker buy a pastry for breakfast every morning? ____No____

1　Is it raining? ....

2　Is the speaker at the library? ....

3　Does the speaker live in this city now? ....

4　Is the speaker in Thailand? ....

5　Is the speaker in Taipei? ....

6 Is the speaker's room clean? ....

7 Is there a lovely garden behind the building? ....

8 Is the floor wet now? ....

9 Did the speaker meet someone at the bus station? ....

10 Does the park have more visitors now than in the past? ....

＊Answer Key p. 114

Skill 2 **Spelling non-academic words**   技巧 2：拼寫非學術字彙

Listen and spell the indicated word.
請聆聽音檔，音檔會先唸一個單字，再唸一個造句，最後重複一次單字。請將單字拼寫出來。

🔊》 MP3 29

1 ....   **4** ....   **7** ....

2 ....   **5** ....   **8** ....

3 ....   **6** ....

Follow-up Activity 補充練習

Listen to the sentences above again. Write each full sentence to practise spelling, grammar, and listening ability.

請再次聆聽上面的題目，將聽到的造句寫下來，練習拼字、文法，以及聽力技巧。

1 ....

2 ....

3 ....

4 ....

5 ....

6 ....

7 ....

8 ....

∗ Answer Key p. 114

Listening Strategies ❼
Short Answer

聽力答題策略 ❼
簡答題

Look at the example of a short answer task below.

請先看以下「簡答題」的例題。

Answer the questions below.

*Write **NO MORE THAN TWO WORDS OR A NUMBER** for each answer.*

1 When did the new sports centre open?   ....

2 Who created the café reading lounge?   ....

3 What does Greg recommend for Sara's children?   ....

4 How many times per week did David used to play racquetball?   ....

> **Tips**

As with all completion tasks, read the directions carefully. If you break the rules of the question, e.g. writing too many words, you will not receive a point.

和所有填空題一樣,一定要仔細閱讀題目說明。如果答案不符合題目要求(例如寫太多字),就得不到分數。

The question words 'who, what, where, when, why,' and 'how' are crucial in these questions. They tell you what kind of word you are listening for, such as a person, a place, a time period, etc.

題目中的疑問詞 who(誰)、what(什麼)、where(哪裡)、when(何時)、why(為何)和 how(如何)非常重要,等於提示你要注意聽哪類的字詞,例如人物、地點、時間等。

Read the questions carefully and understand exactly what they are asking. There will be extra words (distractors, 'wrong answers') spoken.

仔細閱讀題目,理解題目在問什麼。要注意音檔中會設計很多陷阱來混淆你判斷正確答案。

LESSON 5 Short Answer / Matching from a List

7.1

Study the short answer questions above. Answer the following questions.

❶ What is the word limit? Can the answer be a number?

....

❷ What are the keywords in each question? Underline them.

❸ What are some possible paraphrases for the keywords you underlined in the questions?

....

❹ Which questions are referring to the past?

....

＊Answer Key p. 114

請觀察上一頁的簡答題，並回答以下問題。

① 字數限制幾個字？答案可以是數字嗎？

② 每一題的關鍵字是什麼？請畫底線。

③ 你在題目中畫底線的關鍵字可以怎麼改述？

④ 哪些問題問的是過去的事？

7.2　◀） MP3 30

Now, listen to the recording of the short answer task on p. 107. As you listen, write the answers in the gaps.

＊Answer Key p. 115

現在請練習上一頁的簡答題，將答案填入空格中。

Listening Strategies ❽
Matching from a List

聽力答題策略 ❽
列表配合題

Look at the example of a matching from a list task below.

請先看以下「列表配合題」的例題。

What does the speaker say about each of the following exhibits and events?

*Choose **FIVE** answers from the box and write the correct letter, **A-G**, next to questions 1-5.*

Comments

A was publicised in the media

B includes some items given by locals

C includes an interactive element

D requires an additional fee

E includes items from both the past and present

F features filmed interviews with experts

G is located in a different building

Exhibits

1 Oh Captain, My Captain!   ....

2 180 Days Alone   ....

3 Happy Ocean, Happy Earth   ....

4 Monsters of Yesteryears   ....

5 A Tradition Unbroken   ....

Tips

The matching from a list task and the classifying task (see Lesson 3) are very similar. They are actually in the same 'family' of question types. Unlike in the classifying task, the answer choices in the matching from a list task are used **only once**.

There are also obviously more answer choices than a classifying task. This means that some of the answer choices will not be used. The keywords in the unused answer may be mentioned, though, in the recording. If they are mentioned, they will be distractors, or 'tricks.' To avoid being tricked by distractors, practise listening for:

- negatives like 'not'
- contrast words like 'but'
- adjectives that indicate negativity, including 'too + adjective'
- adverbs like 'already'
- verb tenses like the simple past, such as 'used to'

列表配合題與分類題（請見第 3 課）非常相似，可以把它們視為同類的題型。但和分類題不同的是，列表配合題的每個答案選項只會使用一次。

此外，列表配合題的答案選項也比較多，有些選項並不會用到。你可能還是會聽到這些選項中的關鍵字，但它們只是用來混淆你的陷阱。為了避免掉入陷阱，要多練習注意聽以下字詞：

- 否定詞，例如 not（不）
- 轉折詞，例如 but（但是）
- 帶有負面語意的形容詞，包含 too + 形容詞（太過於⋯）
- 副詞，例如 already（已經）
- 時態，例如過去簡單式，像是 used to...（過去會⋯）

8.1

What should an IELTS candidate do before listening to a matching from a list task? Circle the letter of the correct actions. Some actions are not appropriate for this question.

A underline keywords in the answer choice box
B underline keywords in the questions
C consider possible paraphrases for keywords in the answer choice box

IELTS 考生在聆聽列表配合題前應該做些什麼？請圈出正確的答案，有些作法不適合這種題型。

A 將答案選項中的關鍵字畫底線
B 將題目中的關鍵字畫底線
C 想想看答案選項中的關鍵字可以怎麼改述

D consider possible paraphrases for keywords in the questions

     ＊Answer Key p. 115

D 想想看題目中的關鍵字可以怎麼改述

Look at the matching from a list task on p. 109 for 30 seconds. Do the correct actions from the list above.

請用 30 秒瀏覽第 109 頁的列表配合題，並練習以上正確的作法。

8.2   ◀)) MP3 31

Now, listen to the recording of the matching from a list task on p. 109. As you listen, write one answer next to each question.

     ＊Answer Key p. 115

現在請練習第 109 頁的列表配合題，將答案寫在題目旁。

LESSON 5 Short Answer / Matching from a List

Task Practice | 題型練習

PART 1   🔊 MP3 32

Questions 1-5

Complete the notes below.

Write **NO MORE THAN TWO WORDS AND/OR A NUMBER** for each answer.

Farewell Party for Mary

Date: **1** ....

Venue: the **2** ....

Invitations

Who to invite:

- regional manager and husband
- the **3** ....
- the Front Desk team
- the **4** ....
- the new gardener

Date for sending invitations: **5** ....

Questions 6-10

Answer the questions below.

Write **NO MORE THAN TWO WORDS AND/OR A NUMBER** *for each answer.*

6 Where will Jean collect money for the gift?   ....

7 How much money will be suggested for the collection?   ....

8 How long has Mary worked at the hotel?   ....

9 What department provides the party fund?   ....

10 What will guests be asked to bring?   ....

PART 2   🔊 MP3 33

What does the speaker say about each Work Group?

Choose **FIVE** *answers from the box and write the correct letter,* **A-G**, *next to questions 1-5.*

Comments

A has the most people

B has the most interaction with the campers

C contains workers from multiple groups

D must present extra documents today

E keeps camp equipment in good condition

F wears a different uniform

G reports directly to the groundskeeper

Work Groups

1 Group A   ....

2 Group B   ....

3 Group C   ....

4 Group D   ....

5 Group E   ....

Answer Key　｜　答案

Pre-Lesson Skills Practice

Skill 1　Focused listening for verb tenses

1	Yes	**4**	No	**7**	No	**10**	Yes
2	No	**5**	Yes	**8**	Yes		
3	Yes	**6**	No	**9**	No		

Skill 2　Spelling non-academic words

1	February	**3**	snake	**5**	housekeeping	**7**	accounting
2	manager	**4**	fund	**6**	snack	**8**	August

Follow-up Activity

1 I went to Thailand in February.
2 She is the manager of the restaurant.
3 Did you see that yellow snake in the garden?
4 The fund was established to help the poor.
5 The housekeeping staff keeps the hotel neat and clean.
6 Fruit is a healthy snack to eat between meals.
7 The accounting department handles the money.
8 I'm going to England next August.

Listening Strategies ❼ Short Answer

7.1

❶ No more than two. Yes.

❷ Some possible underlining:

　1 <u>When</u> did the <u>new sports centre</u> <u>open</u>?

　2 <u>Who</u> <u>created</u> the <u>café reading lounge</u>?

　3 <u>What</u> does <u>Greg</u> <u>recommend</u> for <u>Sara's children</u>?

　4 <u>How many times</u> <u>per week</u> did <u>David</u> <u>use to</u> <u>play racquetball</u>?

❸ Some possible paraphrases:

　1 When → In what year // What month // What day

　　new sports centre → new gym // new sports club // new sports hall // new health club

　　open → first open its doors ('Open' is the most natural verb to use here.)

2 Who created → Whose idea [was it] // Who started // Who was the creator/founder of
café reading lounge → café reading room // café reading area

3 recommend → advise // suggest // think [the children] would/should/ought to

4 How many times per week → How often per week / each week / on a weekly basis
play racquetball → meet for racquetball // have a game of racquetball

❹ 1, 2, 4

7.2

1 (in) August

2 café manager // (the) manager

3 swimming classes

4 2 // two

Listening Strategies ❽ Matching from a List

8.1

A, C

8.2

1 G

2 A

3 F

4 C

5 E

Task Practice

PART 1

1 13(th) February

2 Dining Hall

3 housekeeping staff

4 kitchen staff

5 4(th) February

6 break room

7 2 dollars // two dollars // $2

8 25 years // twenty-five years

9 Accounting

10 snacks

PART 2

1 G

2 D

3 B

4 C

5 F

LESSON 6

Multiple Choice with More Than One Answer

多選題

Multiple Choice with More Than One Answer
多選題

Lesson Overview

In this lesson, you will become familiar with the *multiple choice with more than one answer* questions on the IELTS. You will learn how to approach the task and will become aware of common problems that IELTS candidates encounter in these questions. You will also practise the form completion, table completion and multiple choice with single answer questions at the end of this lesson.

We will be working with IELTS Listening Part 1 and Part 4 for this task type.

♦ **Listening Part 1**
− Questions 1-10
− A conversation between two speakers
− The topic is non-academic, e.g. job interview, booking accommodations, etc.
− Form completion task is common in Part 1, but any question type is possible

♦ **Listening Part 4**
− Questions 31-40
− A monologue (a lecture)
− The topic is academic

在這堂課中,我們將會介紹「多選題」。你會學到這種題型的答題技巧,以及一般考生最常遇到的問題。在本課的「題型練習」,你也會再次複習「表單填空題」、「表格填空題」和「單選題」。

我們會透過 IELTS 聽力測驗 Part 1 和 Part 4 來練習這種題型。

聽力測驗 Part 1
− 第 1∼10 題
− 兩人對話
− 非學術的對話主題,如:工作面試、預訂住宿等
− 表單填空題在 Part 1 相當常見,但也可能是其他題型

聽力測驗 Part 4
− 第 31∼40 題
− 單人獨白(一場講座、演說)
− 學術的主題

- Notes completion is the most common task for Part 4, but any completion task is possible
- Generally said to be the most challenging part of the Listening Test, and for many people, of the entire IELTS

- 筆記填空題在 Part 4 最常見，但也可能是任何填空題型
- 一般認為是聽力測驗中最困難的部分，對許多人而言，甚至是 IELTS 測驗中最困難的

<table>
<tr><td>

Lesson Vocabulary Bank:
Food / Diets / Nutrition

</td><td>

課程字彙庫：
食物 / 飲食 / 營養

</td></tr>
</table>

🔊 MP3 34

- allergic 形 過敏的；對…反感的
  [ə`lɜ:ʤɪk]

- allergy 名 過敏；厭惡
  [`æləʤi]

- allergen 動作者 過敏原
  [`æləʤ(ə)n]

- be allergic to... 片 對…過敏

- aubergine 名 茄子
  [`əʊbəʒi:n]
  (美 eggplant)

- cancel 動 取消
  [`kæns(ə)l]

- cancellation 名 取消
  [ˌkænsə`leɪʃ(ə)n]

- consume 動 消耗；花費
  [kən`sju:m]

- consumption 名 消耗量
  [kən`sʌm(p)ʃ(ə)n]

- consumer 動作者 消費者
  [kən`sju:mə(r)]

- conventional 形 慣例的，傳統的
  [kən`venʃ(ə)n(ə)l]
  (↔ unconventional 非傳統的)

- convention 名 大會；慣例
  [kən`venʃ(ə)n]

- counterbalance 動 使平衡；抵消
  [ˌkaʊntə`bæl(ə)ns]

- counterbalance 名 抗衡；抵消
  [`kaʊntəˌbæl(ə)ns]

- dairy 形 乳製的 名 乳製品
  [`deəri]

- fortify 動 增強；加固…的結構
  [`fɔ:tɪfaɪ]

- fortified 形 加強的
  [`fɔ:tɪfaɪd]

- fortification 名〔複數〕防禦工事
  [ˌfɔ:tɪfɪ`keɪʃ(ə)n]

- incentivise 動 激勵
  [ɪn`sentɪvaɪz]

- incentive 名 鼓勵；刺激
  [ɪn`sentɪv]

- interchange 動 交換
  [ˌɪntə`tʃeɪn(d)ʒ]

- interchangeable 形 可互換的
  [ˌɪntə`tʃeɪn(d)ʒəbl]

- interchange 名 交換；交流道
  [`ɪntətʃeɪn(d)ʒ]

- level off 片 保持穩定

- loudspeaker 名 擴音器，喇叭
  [ˌlaʊd`spi:kə(r)]

- marine 形 海洋的
  [mə`ri:n]

- majority 名 多數
  [mə`ʤɒrɪti]

- maximise 動 最大化
  [`mæksɪmaɪz]
- maximum 形 最大的 名 最大值
  [`mæksɪməm]

- minimise 動 最小化
  [`mɪnɪmaɪz]
- minimum 形 最小的 名 最小值
  [`mɪnɪməm]

- monitor 動 監控 動作者 監控人員
  [`mɒnɪtə(r)]

- stimulate 動 刺激，促進
  [`stɪmjʊleɪt]
- stimulating 形 刺激性的；啟發性的
  [`stɪmjʊleɪtɪŋ]
- stimulus 名 刺激
  [`stɪmjʊləs]

- vary 動 變化
  [`veəri]

- varied 形 各式各樣的
  [`veərɪd]
- variability 名 變化性
  [veərɪə`bɪləti]
- variable 動作者 〔數〕變項；可變因素
  [`veərɪəb(ə)l]

- veal 名 小牛肉
  [vi:l]

- vehicular 形 車輛的
  [və`hɪkjələ(r)]
- vehicle 名 車輛；交通工具
  [`vi:ɪk(ə)l]

- vend 動 販賣
  [vend]
- vendor 動作者 小販；供應商
  [`vendə(r)] [`vendɔ:(r)]

- waive 動 放棄；免除（費用等）
  [weɪv]
- waiver 名 放棄；棄權
  [`weɪvə(r)]

Pre-Lesson Skills Practice | 高分技巧訓練

Skill 1　Following a list

技巧 1：聽出順序

The IELTS listening task you will practise in Lesson 6 requires your ears, eyes, and English vocabulary skills to work together at the same time under pressure.

第 6 課要練習的題型需要你在時間壓力下，同時運用聽力、閱讀和單字能力。

Why? Because you must be able to follow a list as a speaker paraphrases some or all of the items in that list out of order.

為什麼？因為你必須看著一串選項，同時聽說話者什麼時候會提到選項中的內容。說話者可能會改述部分或所有的選項內容，而且不會照順序提到。

Let's study a simple example in written form first to get a better idea of what this means. Take a moment to read the four answers choices A-D below. Then answer the question.

我們先用看的來練習一下，讓你更了解上面提到的是什麼意思。請閱讀以下題目，然後回答問題。

Question: What is the speaker excited to do in Italy?

Answer Choices:

A　make coffee
B　eat pasta
C　sit at an espresso bar
D　try cheesecake

Text:

One country I would love to visit is Italy. Why? For one thing, the food is world-famous. The pasta, for instance, is said to taste much better than pasta in my country. I want to see if it's true! Desserts are also a big attraction for me. My husband's excited about trying Italy's cheesecake, but tiramisu is what I want to try because it's made with coffee. I love coffee and make it every morning at home, but one dream I have is going to an Italian espresso bar and drinking espresso—that's a tiny cup of strong coffee–while standing up at the bar like an Italian!

Answer: B

答案：B

If you chose **B**, eat pasta, you're correct. However, that was not the point of this exercise. **What did you do to answer this question?**

如果你選了 B「吃義大利麵」，你就答對了。不過，答案不是這個練習的重點。重點是：你怎麼回答這個問題的？

Did you read the answer choices A-D, find the keywords in the text, read closely, and decide if they were true? Or did you read the text and check out the keywords on the left when you came to them? Or did you read the entire text and then go back to look at each answer choice?

你是先看完選項、去文章中找到關鍵字，然後確認哪個選項正確；還是一邊看文章，碰到關鍵字的時候一邊對照選項；還是先看完整段文章，最後再看每個選項？

Whichever method you used, your eyes had to move up and down the answer column because the answer keywords are not in the same order as they are presented in the text. Answer B is also paraphrased, so you had to identify the paraphrasing:

無論你是用哪種方法，你的目光都會在四個選項之間上下移動，因為選項的順序和關鍵字出現在文章中的順序並不一樣。以下是每個選項的關鍵字出現在文章中的部分，正確答案 B 經過改述，所以你還需要能辨識改述：

A make coffee → *I love coffee and make it every morning at home*
B eat pasta → *I want to see if it's [the pasta is much better in Italy] true!*
                (The speaker must eat the pasta in Italy to see if it truly is better.)
C sit at an espresso bar → *while standing up at the espresso bar like an Italian!*
D try cheesecake → *My husband's excited about trying Italy's cheesecake*

While reading, this is not such a problem. However, imagine doing this same exercise without the text, and only **listening once**. That is what you must do in the IELTS tasks we will practise in Lesson 6.

用看的話，感覺這個練習不會太困難。不過，想像一下同樣的題目，但沒有文字，而是用聽的，而且只能聽一次。這就是你在考試時會遇到的狀況。

Let's practise with our ears now, starting with a warm-up.

接下來，讓我們實際用聽的練習一下，先從一個簡單的暖身開始。

Look at the list of words below for 20 seconds. Number the words in order as you hear them. You may listen more than once.

請先用 20 秒瀏覽以下單字，接著聆聽音檔，依照你聽到的順序將單字編號。你可以多次聆聽。

🔊 MP3 35

....	Specialist	....	Wallet
....	Between	....	Table
....	Atmosphere	....	Impactful
....	Elephant	....	Interactive
....	Standard	....	Sacred
....	Sedentary	....	Published

＊Answer Key p. 135

Now let's increase the difficulty. Instead of single words, let's follow a list containing phrases.

現在我們要提高難度。接下來不再是聽單字，而是要聽出各項敘述的順序。

For 30 seconds, look at the list of phrases below related to an unforgettable travel experience. Listen to a speaker describing an unforgettable travel experience. As you listen, number the following phrases from her talk in the order that you hear them. Note that there will be no paraphrasing in this exercise, and two of the phrases will be unused. You will hear an example first.

請先用 30 秒瀏覽以下各項敘述，內容都和一次難忘的旅行經驗有關。接著聆聽這段旅行經驗分享，依照你聽到的內容將敘述依序編號。請注意：這個練習中沒有改述，而且有 2 項敘述不會出現。你會先聽到一個範例。

🔊 MP3 36

.... ready to hit the beaches

.... arriving at the port

.... a few nights in Bangkok

...1....... last year was unusual (*Example*)

.... a few days in Bangkok

.... they looked like paradise

.... arriving at the airport

＊Answer Key p. 135

Skill 2 Recognising paraphrasing in a list

技巧 2：辨識改述內容的順序

You've practised moving your eyes across a list while listening to a speaker. Let's now add a challenging feature of the IELTS exam: paraphrasing. The speaker will now use different words to express the ideas in the list.

你已經練習過如何一邊瀏覽一串選項、一邊聽音檔了。接下來，我們要加入 IELTS 測驗中很具有挑戰性的元素 —— 改述。下面的練習中，說話者將會改述選項的內容。

For 30 seconds, look at the list of phrases below related to an unforgettable meal. Listen to a speaker describing an unforgettable meal he has eaten. As you listen, number the following ideas from his talk in the order that you hear them. One answer is extra and will not be used. You may listen more than once.
NB *The ideas will be paraphrased in the recording.*

請先用 30 秒瀏覽以下各項敘述，內容都和一次難忘的用餐經驗有關。接著聆聽這段用餐經驗分享，依照你聽到的內容將敘述依序編號。有 1 項敘述不會出現。你可以多次聆聽。你會先聽到一個範例。

注意：音檔中的內容經過改述。

🔊)) MP3 37

.... The duck was accompanied by a side of thin pancakes.

.... It tasted bad.

.... I had never heard of this idea before.

.... They explained to me that duck has more fat than chicken.

.... We could walk right past them and go to our seats without waiting.

...1...... Wherever I go, I usually look for the best possible meal. **(Example)**

.... My co-workers reserved a table for us at a well-known duck restaurant.

＊Answer Key p. 135

Listening Strategies ❾
Multiple Choice with More Than One Answer

聽力答題策略 ❾
多選題

Look at the examples of multiple choice questions excerpt from a Part 1 conversation and a Part 4 monologue below.

請先看以下兩組「多選題」的例題。第一組是 Part 1 的對話題，第二組是 Part 4 的獨白題。

---

1 *Questions 1-2*

Which **TWO** reasons does Alina give for visiting the farmer's market?

A Her family can meet the farmers.

B It is close to her house.

C Her children like it.

D It helps the environment.

E It is cheaper than the conventional supermarket.

Questions 3-5

Which **THREE** kinds of items does Alina come to the farmer's market for specifically?

A baked goods

B fruit and/or vegetables

C almonds

D milk

E meat and/or poultry

F spices

2 *Questions 1-2*

Which **TWO** statements about fish production are true?

A   There will probably not be increases in total marine fish catch in the future.

B   Aquaculture involves seeking out areas where fish or aquatic plants live.

C   World fisheries production stopped growing in the 1970s.

D   Fish production declined dramatically in the 1950s and 1960s.

E   Marine fisheries are an important source of food security in Asia.

Tips

The main difference between this version of multiple choice and the kind we did in Lesson 2 is that this type requires you to pick 2 or 3 answers from a list of 5 to 7 options.

這一課介紹的多選題和第 2 課的單選題不同,多選題是要從 5～7 個選項中選出 2～3 個答案。

Usually, most or all of the options will be mentioned in the recording to distract you. They may also appear in a different order in the recording than in your exam paper. For example, you may hear option E before option A.

一般來說,為了混淆考生,幾乎每一個選項的關鍵字都會出現在音檔中。而且選項很可能不會依照順序出現,例如你可能會先聽到選項 E,才聽到選項 A。

If this question occurs in Parts 1 or 3 (conversation) of the test, you may be cued as to which question you are on. If it occurs in Part 2 or 4 (monologue), you will have to listen closely for keywords or signposting (see Pre-Lesson Skills 'Identifying keywords' in Lesson 2).

如果在 Part 1 或 Part 3(對話題)遇到多選題,對話可能會暗示現在講的是哪一題的答案。不過如果是在 Part 2 或 Part 4(獨白題),你就得仔細聆聽關鍵字或指示字詞(請見第 2 課高分技巧訓練的「找出關鍵字」)。

This type of questions tests your ability to follow a conversation, listen for detail, identify synonyms and paraphrases, and avoid misdirection.

這種題目要測驗你理解對話的能力，是否能聽到細節、聽出同義字和改述的內容，以及是否能不被誤導。

9.1

Study the multiple choice questions above on p. 127. Answer the following questions.

請觀察第 127 頁的多選題，並回答以下問題。

❶ How many answers should you circle for each question?

① 每一題應該選出幾個答案？

···

❷ What are the keywords in each question? Underline them.

② 題目的關鍵字是什麼？請畫底線。

❸ What are the keywords in each answer choice? Underline them.

③ 每個選項中的關鍵字是什麼？請畫底線。

❹ What are some possible paraphrases for the underlined keywords?

④ 畫底線的關鍵字可以怎麼改述？

···

＊Answer Key p. 135

9.2   ◀)) MP3 38

Now, listen to the recording of the multiple choice task on p. 127. As you listen, circle the correct answers.

＊Answer Key p. 136

現在請練習第 127 頁的多選題，並圈出正確的答案。

9.3

Study the multiple choice task on p. 128. How would you prepare for this task?

＊Answer Key p. 136

請觀察第 128 頁的多選題。作答前你會做什麼？

9.4   ◀) MP3 39

Now, listen to the recording of the multiple choice task on p. 128. As you listen, circle the correct answers. You may listen more than once.

＊Answer Key p. 136

現在請練習第 128 頁的多選題，並圈出正確的答案。你可以多次聆聽。

Task Practice | 題型練習

PART 1   ◀)) MP3 40

Questions 1-3

Complete the form.

*Write **NO MORE THAN TWO WORDS AND/OR A NUMBER** for each answer.*

Restaurant Booking Form

Name: **1** ....

Date: 13 July

Guest no. **2** .... (Note: 1 high chair)

    Adults: 41

    Children: **3** ....

Questions 4-5

Which **TWO** kinds of items does the woman not want on her menu?

A pork

B spicy dishes

C shellfish

D pasta

E veal

Questions 6-7

Which **TWO** situations would result in an extra fee charged?

A not meeting the sales minimum

B cancelling eight days before the event

C playing music through loudspeakers

D specialty items from preferred vendors

E exceeding the guaranteed guest count list

Questions 8-10

Which **THREE** are benefits of being a Select Member?

A no cancellation fee

B gift card based on event cost

C free audio-visual equipment

D personalised event menu

E gift cards for online shopping

F free event consultation

PART 4   ◀)) MP3 41

Questions 1-2

Which **TWO** statements about sodium are true?

A Celery, beets, and milk do not contain sodium.

B Three-quarters of sodium intake in Europe comes from processed foods.

C Sodium is rarely added to natural foods during processing.

D People often refer to sodium as salt.

E Sodium is the same as salt.

Questions 3-4

*Choose one answer, **A**, **B**, or **C**.*

3 The proportion of chloride in table salt is

    A 10%.

    B 60%.

    C 90%.

4 The global daily average salt intake is

    A 1 gram.

    B less than 5 grams.

    C 9 to 12 grams.

Questions 5-7

Complete the table below.

Write **NO MORE THAN ONE NUMBER** for each answer.

Low Salt Content (per 100 grams of food)	Medium Salt Content (per 100 grams of food)	High Salt Content (per 100 grams of food)
Less than 0.3 g salt or 0.1 g sodium	0.3 g -1.5 g salt or **5** .... - 0.4 g sodium	Over 1.5 g salt or **6** .... g sodium
Sodium content per given amount of table salt		
1/4 teaspoon salt = 575 mg sodium		
1/2 teaspoon salt = 1,150 mg sodium		
3/4 teaspoon salt = **7** .... mg sodium		
1 teaspoon salt = 2,300 mg sodium		

Questions 8-10

Which **THREE** are problems of fortifying water with iodine?

A   high cost

B   lack of water sources

C   iodine's length of stability in water

D   lack of effectiveness

E   differences in water consumption worldwide

F   difficult to supervise and control

Answer Key | 答案

Pre-Lesson Skills Practice

Skill 1 Following a list

_7_	Specialist	_8_	Wallet
_4_	Between	_1_	Table
_10_	Atmosphere	_11_	Impactful
_9_	Elephant	_6_	Interactive
_12_	Standard	_5_	Sacred
_3_	Sedentary	_2_	Published

_4_	ready to hit the beaches	_3_	a few days in Bangkok
_5_	arriving at the port	_2_	they looked like paradise
✕	a few nights in Bangkok	✕	arriving at the airport
_1_	last year was unusual (*Example*)		

Skill 2 Recognising paraphrasing in a list

_4_	The duck was accompanied by a side of thin pancakes.
_6_	It tasted bad.
_5_	I had never heard of this idea before.
✕	They explained to me that duck has more fat than chicken.
_3_	We could walk right past them and go to our seats without waiting.
_1_	Wherever I go, I usually look for the best possible meal. (*Example*)
_2_	My co-workers reserved a table for us at a well-known duck restaurant.

Listening Strategies ❾
Multiple Choice with More Than One Answer

9.1

❶ **1-2** Two

  3-5 Three

❷ Some possible underlining:

  1-2 Which <u>TWO</u> <u>reasons</u> does <u>Alina</u> give for <u>visiting</u> the <u>farmer's market</u>?

  3-4 Which <u>THREE</u> kinds of <u>items</u> does <u>Alina</u> <u>come</u> to the <u>farmer's market</u> for <u>specifically</u>?

❸ Some possible underlining:

  1-2 A Her <u>family</u> <u>can meet</u> the <u>farmers</u>.

B It is <u>close to</u> her <u>house</u>.

C Her <u>children</u> <u>like</u> it.

D It <u>helps</u> the <u>environment</u>.

E It is <u>cheaper than</u> the <u>conventional supermarket</u>.

3-5 all options

❹ Some possible paraphrases:

1-2 visiting → coming to // shopping at

family → kids // children

meet → get to know

close to → near // just [a few] miles away from // right around the corner from

children → family // kids

like → enjoy // have fun at // find [it] interesting

helps the environment → lowers our carbon footprint // is more sustainable

cheaper than → costs less than // is more budget-friendly than // saves money over

conventional supermarket → regular supermarket / grocery store // big chain
supermarket / grocery store

3-5 baked goods → sourdough bread // wheat bread // rolls // buns // cakes // pies

fruit and/or vegetables → apples // peaches // carrots // potatoes

almonds → nuts

milk → cow's milk // soy milk // almond milk (Note: 'milk' is not likely to be paraphrased
if referring to cow's milk)

meat and/or poultry → beef // chicken // steak // turkey

spices → nutmeg // rosemary // thyme // basil

9.2

1-2 A, C [*in any order*]　　　　　　　　**3-5** B, E, F [*in any order*]

9.3

You should quickly skim the list and underline keywords: nouns, verbs, adjectives, and adverbs. Pay close attention to negatives (no, no longer). If there's a word you don't know (maybe 'aquaculture'), do not let it worry you. If time allowed, you might predict a few logical answers.

9.4

1-2 A, C [*in any order*]

Task Practice

PART 1

1 Queen
2 49 // forty(-)nine
3 7 // seven

4-5 C, E [*in any order*]
6-7 A, E [*in any order*]
8-10 C, D, F [*in any order*]

PART 4

1-2 B, D [*in any order*]
3 B
4 C
5 0.2

6 0.5
7 1,725 // 1725
8-10 A, C, F [*in any order*]

LESSON 7
Flow Chart Completion
流程圖填空題

LESSON 7

Flow Chart Completion
流程圖填空題

Lesson Overview

本課內容

In this lesson, you will become familiar with the *flow chart completion* task on the IELTS. You will learn how to approach the task and will become aware of common problems that IELTS candidates encounter in these questions.

在這堂課中,我們將會介紹「流程圖填空題」。你會學到這種題型的答題技巧,以及一般考生最常遇到的問題。

We will be working with IELTS Listening Part 3 and Part 4 for this task type.

我們會透過 IELTS 聽力測驗 Part 3 和 Part 4 來練習這種題型。

♦ **Listening Part 3**
- Questions 21-30
- A dialogue (two or three speakers)
- Unlike Parts 1 and 2, features an academic topic
- Any question type is possible

聽力測驗 **Part 3**
- 第 21~30 題
- 多人對話
- 學術的對話主題
- 可能是任何題型

♦ **Listening Part 4**
- Questions 31-40
- A monologue (a lecture)
- The topic is academic
- Notes completion is the most common task for Part 4, but any completion task is possible
- Generally said to be the most challenging part of the Listening Test, and for many people, of the entire IELTS

聽力測驗 **Part 4**
- 第 31~40 題
- 單人獨白(一場講座、演說)
- 學術的主題
- 筆記填空題在 Part 4 最常見,但也可能是任何填空題型
- 一般認為是聽力測驗中最困難的部分,對許多人而言,甚至是 IELTS 測驗中最困難的

Lesson Vocabulary Bank:
Environment / Scientific Processes /
Manufacturing

課程字彙庫：
環境 / 流程 / 製造

🔊 MP3 42

○ absorb 動 吸收
[əb`zɔ:b]

○ absorption 名 吸收
[əb`zɔ:pʃ(ə)n]

○ blend 動 混合 名 混合；混合物
[blend]

○ blender 動作者 攪拌器
[`blendə(r)]

○ cite 動 引用
[saɪt]

○ citation 名 引用
[saɪ`teɪʃ(ə)n]

○ component 名 元素；成分
[kəm`pəʊnənt]

○ compost 動 施肥 名 堆肥
[`kɒmpɒst]

○ conserve 動 節省；保存
[kən`sɜ:v]

○ conservation 名 保育；保存
[ˌkɒnsə`veɪʃ(ə)n]

○ discard 動 丟棄
[dɪ`ska:d]

○ discard 名 丟棄；丟棄物
[`dɪska:d]

○ distribute 動 分配；分發
[dɪ`strɪbju:t] [`dɪstrɪbju:t]

○ distribution 名 分配；分布
[ˌdɪstrɪ`bju:ʃ(ə)n]

○ distributor 動作者 批發商；經銷商
[dɪ`strɪbjʊtə(r)]

○ evaporate 動 蒸發
[ɪ`væpəreɪt]

○ evaporation 名 蒸發
[ɪˌvæpə`reɪʃ(ə)n]

○ extract 動 取出；提取
[ɪk`strækt]

○ extract 名 提取物
[`ekstrækt]

○ filter 動 過濾 名 過濾器
[`fɪltə(r)]

○ generalise 動 歸納；概括
[`dʒen(ə)rəlaɪz]

○ general 形 普遍的
[`dʒen(ə)r(ə)l]

○ generalisation 名 概括化；普遍化
[ˌdʒen(ə)rəlaɪ`zeɪʃ(ə)n]

○ harvest 動 收穫；採收 名 收穫，收成
[`ha:vɪst]

* 本書音標採用 IPA 音標系統

○ immerse 動 使沉浸；使浸泡
　[ɪˋmɜːs]

○ immersive 形 沉浸的
　[ɪˋmɜːsɪv]

○ immersion 名 沉浸
　[ɪˋmɜːʃ(ə)n]

○ publicise 動 宣傳；公告
　[ˋpʌblɪsaɪz]

○ public 形 公共的；公開的
　[ˋpʌblɪk]

○ recruit 動 招聘
　[rɪˋkruːt]

○ recruitment 名 招聘，招募
　[rɪˋkruːtm(ə)nt]

○ recruiter 動作者 招聘人員
　[rɪˋkruːtə(r)]

○ refer to X as Y 片 將 X 稱為 Y

○ utilise 動 利用
　[ˋjuːtɪlaɪz]

○ utilitarian 形 實用的；功利主義的
　[juˌtɪlɪˋteərɪən]

○ utility 名（水、電等）公共事業
　[juːˋtɪləti]

○ veer 動 轉向
　[vɪə(r)]

Pre-Lesson Skills Practice | 高分技巧訓練

Skill 1   Understanding shortened sentences

技巧 1：理解簡化語句

The IELTS listening tasks you will practise in Lesson 7 often require you to shorten a full sentence or long phrase into a very short phrase while keeping the original meaning. To receive marks for these questions, you must know how to omit the correct types of words in the original sentence.

These tasks also sometimes feature the **passive voice** instead of the active voice, so you should be able to understand and use this grammar. You must look at the words given in the answer choices to see if the passive voice is required on an IELTS listening task.

第 7 課介紹的題型常常會要你將句子或比較長的片語簡化成非常短的內容，同時維持原來的語意。要在這種題型中得到分數，你必須知道哪些字詞可以被省略，哪些要保留。

這種題型有時也會用到被動語態，所以你必須熟悉被動的用法。你要能從選項中判斷各個問題是否會需要用被動。

Types of Words

字詞的種類

Can you remember the **parts of speech** from Lesson 1? Here are some examples:

你還記得第 1 課提到的詞性嗎？以下有一些例子：

- **Nouns / pronouns**
  Mary, she, movie, it, Canada, thing

名詞 / 代名詞
Mary、she（她）、movie（電影）、it（它）、Canada（加拿大）、thing（東西）

- **Verbs**
  run, do, be, read, sleep, believe

動詞
run（跑）、do（做）、be（是）、read（讀）、sleep（睡）、believe（相信）

- **Adjectives**
  <u>cute</u>, <u>yellow</u>, <u>large</u>, <u>French</u>, <u>quiet</u>, <u>bored</u>

- **Adverbs**
  <u>quickly</u>, <u>often</u>, <u>yesterday</u>, <u>down</u>, <u>abroad</u>, <u>now</u>

- **Prepositions**
  in, of, by, about, through, with

- **Conjunctions**
  and, so, because, if, not only ... but also

  'not only ... but also' is an example of a correlative conjunction. These conjunctions work in pairs. Both parts of the conjunction must be present in the sentence in order for it to function. For instance, 'He enjoyed <u>not only</u> the food <u>but also</u> the scenery.'

- **Articles**
  a, an, the

- **Interjections**
  Ouch, Hi, Help!, Yay!, Eww (to show disgust), Huh?

形容詞
<u>cute</u>（可愛的）、<u>yellow</u>（黃色的）、<u>large</u>（大的）、<u>French</u>（法國的）、<u>quiet</u>（安靜的）、<u>bored</u>（無聊的）

副詞
<u>quickly</u>（迅速）、<u>often</u>（時常）、<u>yesterday</u>（昨天）、<u>down</u>（向下）、<u>abroad</u>（在國外）、<u>now</u>（現在）

介系詞
in（在⋯中）、of（屬於）、by（透過）、about（關於）、through（憑藉）、with（有⋯；帶著⋯）

連接詞
and（和）、so（所以）、because（因為）、if（如果；假如）、not only ... but also（不只⋯還⋯）

not only ... but also 是「相關連接詞」，這種連接詞會成對出現，才能充分表達語意，例如：He enjoyed <u>not only</u> the food <u>but also</u> the scenery.（他不只品嚐了美食，還欣賞了美景。）

冠詞
a、an、the

感嘆詞
Ouch（哎喲！）、Hi（嗨）、Help!（救命！）、Yay!（耶！）、Eww（嗯！）、Huh?（啊？）

Content Words and Function Words

Look again at the Parts of Speech examples in the list above. What is special about the words which are underlined?

The underlined words like 'French,' 'now,' or 'sleep' have a specific meaning. The other words (e.g. *it*, *an*, *of*, etc.) are 'grammar' words. That is, their purpose is to show the grammatical relationship between ideas in a sentence. They do not have much or any meaning alone.

- Words with specific meaning are called **content words**, while the 'grammar' words are called **function words**.

- If you must shorten a phrase or sentence on the IELTS Listening test, you will usually **keep most of the content words and drop all or most of the function words**. This does NOT mean that all content words must always be kept and that all function words must always be dropped, though.

Now, let's try some exercises. The following are sentences from a To-Do List. The sentences are too long for a To-Do List, however. Rewrite the sentences using only **THREE to FOUR words**. Keep the original sentence's meaning. The content words have been underlined to help you. Do not add new content words to the sentences.

實詞和虛詞

再看一次以上列出的詞性和例子，你看得出來畫底線的字詞有什麼特別的嗎？

畫底線的字詞，例如 French（法國的）、now（現在）或 sleep（睡）都有明確的意思，其他字詞（例如 it、an、of 等）則是「文法用字」，意思是它們的用途在於表達句子中字詞的文法關係，獨立存在的時候沒有意義，或意思較不明確。

有明確意思的字叫做 content words（實詞），表達文法關係的字則叫做 function words（虛詞）。

如果你必須在 IELTS 聽力測驗的答案中簡化片語或句子，通常都會留下大部分的實詞，刪去虛詞。不過這並不表示所有狀況下，實詞都要留下、虛詞都要刪去。

現在我們來練習看看。以下的句子來自一個待辦事項清單，不過句子太長了。請維持語意，用 3～4 個字改寫句子。句子中的實詞已經畫上底線幫助你判斷，請不要加入新的實詞。

LESSON **7** Flow Chart Completion

❶ I <u>need</u> to <u>take out</u> the <u>trash</u> <u>tonight</u>.

....

❷ <u>Jenny</u> <u>needs</u> me to <u>take</u> her to the <u>doctor's</u> <u>office</u>.

....

❸ I <u>have</u> to <u>water</u> the <u>flowers</u> in the <u>neighbour's</u> <u>garden</u>.

....

Answers:

❶ Take out trash (tonight)

In this case, we would cut 'need.' Why? For one thing, the definition of a To-Do List is a reminder of tasks that you need to do, so keeping this word is not necessary for meaning.

We would not cut 'out' in 'take out the trash' because 'take the trash' does not have exactly the same meaning as 'take out the trash' in English. ('Take out' is a special multi-word verb called a phrasal verb.) However, the meaning of 'take trash' would still be clear to a reader or listener.

❷ Take Jenny to doctor

Cut 'need' for the same reason as above. We should keep 'to' for best clarity since four words are allowed.

答案：

① Take out trash (tonight)

這題可以刪去實詞 need（需要）。為什麼？因為這是一個待辦事項清單，本來就是用於提醒你需要做的事，所以保留 need 是多餘的。

take out the trash 中的 out 會保留，因為 take the trash（拿垃圾）和 take out the trash（倒垃圾）意思不太一樣（take out 是個「片語動詞」）。不過，雖然 take out the trash 意思比較正確，但如果說成 take trash，讀者和聽者還是可以理解。

② Take Jenny to doctor

這題和前一句一樣可以刪去 need（需要）。既然可以寫 4 個字，就保留 take … to…（帶…去…）語意最完整。

❸ Water neighbour's flowers

We would cut 'garden' because it is not necessary for understanding. (You're unlikely to forget where your neighbour's flowers are.) Also, 'garden flowers' is not a natural phrase in English and thus sounds odd.

Now, can you shorten the same three sentences on the To-Do List using **no more than TWO words**?

❶ ....

❷ ....

❸ ....

Answers:

❶ Take trash / Trash tonight / Trash

Either of these shortened options would be clear on a real To-Do List.

❷ Jenny doctor

Both of these words are needed to maintain meaning.

❸ Neighbour's flowers

You might argue that 'flowers' would be enough of a reminder, but if two words are allowed, it is best to keep the word that tells us more about 'flowers.' If only ONE word was allowed, 'flowers' would be

③ Water neighbor's flowers

這題可以刪去實詞 garden（花園），刪去後並不會影響理解（畢竟你不太可能忘記鄰居的花在哪裡）。此外，garden flowers 這個說法在英文中不太自然。

接著，進一步將前面待辦事項清單的三個句子改寫為 2 個字以下。

答案：

① Take trash / Trash tonight / Trash

在現實生活的待辦事項清單中，以上這些簡化版本意思都夠清楚。

② Jenny doctor

只能寫 2 個字的話，一定要有這 2 個字才能表達意思。

③ Neighbor's flowers

你可能會覺得待辦事項清單上只要寫 flowers（花）就夠清楚了，不過既然可以寫 2 個字，最好還是保留 neighbor's（鄰居

the word to keep.

的）來補充說明。如果只能寫
1 個字，那就只留下 flowers。

Passive Voice

Another feature you will sometimes encounter on the IELTS Listening, especially in the types of tasks featured in Lesson 7, is the passive voice. To understand the passive voice, you must know the parts of a sentence and the job each part performs.

被動語態

在 IELTS 聽力測驗中，尤其是這一課要介紹的題型，很常遇到「被動語態」的用法。要了解被動語態，你必須熟悉英文句子的組成元素，以及它們個別的功能。

● Active voice

^SAndy ^Vwrote ^Othe introduction.

主動語態

^SAndy ^Vwrote ^Othe introduction.
（Andy 寫了引言。）

- Andy performed the action of the sentence. Andy is the **subject**.
- Wrote expresses the action of the sentence. Wrote is the **verb**.
- The introduction receives the action of the verb. The introduction is the **object**.

- Andy 負責執行這句中的動作（寫），是主詞。
- wrote（寫）是這句中的動作，是動詞。
- The introduction（引言）接受動詞的動作（被寫出來），是受詞。

Sentences in English typically follow this order: subject—verb—object. This is called the **active voice**.

英文句子一般會按照〈主詞＋動詞＋受詞〉的順序，這就是主動語態。

In an active voice sentence, the first thing we think about is the **subject**. The second thing we think of is **what the subject did**. Thus, there is emphasis on the subject—Andy, in this case.

在主動語態的句子中，讀者第一個想到的會是「主詞」，接著會想到「主詞做了什麼」。也就是說，主動語態強調的是主詞，在前面的例子裡就是 Andy。

In some situations, though, it is better to change the

有些狀況則比較適合改變一下順

order of these parts, shifting the emphasis to the object. This rearrangement results in the **passive voice**: object—verb—subject.

序，把重點放在受詞上，也就是將句子改為被動語態，變成〈受詞＋動詞＋主詞〉。

● Passive voice
^OThe introduction ^Vwas written by ^SAndy.

被動語態
^OThe introduction ^Vwas written by ^SAndy.（這個引言是 Andy 寫的。）

Notice that when we do this, the verb becomes 'be + past participle.' This is because objects have a different kind of relationship with the verb compared to subjects.

特別注意，改為被動的動詞會變成〈be＋過去分詞〉，因為受詞和動詞的關係不同於主詞和動詞的關係。

In the passive voice, the object of the sentence is placed at the front, taking attention away from the subject or dropping the subject completely.

被動語態中，受詞會放在句子的開頭，讓主詞的重要性降低，甚至省略主詞。

[Active voice]
^SThe police caught the thief.

〔主動語態〕
^SThe police caught the thief.（警察逮捕竊賊。）

[Passive voice]
^OThe thief was caught.

〔被動語態〕
^OThe thief was caught.（竊賊被逮捕。）

Not all sentences have a passive voice form because not all sentences have objects.

不過，不是所有句子都可以改成被動語態，因為並非所有句子都有受詞。

● ^SJohn ^Vjumped up from his chair.
　→ 'Up from his chair' does not receive the action of the verb. It simply tells us how John jumped. If we removed it from the sentence, the meaning would not change. An object cannot be

^SJohn ^Vjumped up from his chair.（John 從椅子上跳起來。）
→ up from his chair 只是補充說明動詞 jump（跳），並不是受詞，如果將整個片語刪去，句子的

removed.

意思不變。如果是受詞，就不能隨意刪去。

- ^SThis movie ^Vis popular.
  → The be verb in this sentence describes a state of being—not an action.

^SThis movie ^Vis popular.（這部電影很熱門。）

→ 句中的 be 動詞 is 敘述的是狀態，而不是動作，因此 popular（熱門的）也不是受詞。

Some verbs have multiple uses. Some of their uses may work in active voice sentences but not passive voice.

另外，有些動詞有許多用法，若是不及物的用法就只能用在主動語態，不能用在被動語態中。

- ^SChris ^Vdid well.
  → 'Did' does not take an object in this sentence.

^SChris ^Vdid well.（Chris 表現得很好。）

→ 這句中的 did（表現；行動）後面沒有受詞，不能改為被動。

- ^SHe ^Vdid ^Ohis homework.
  → 'Did' takes an object in this sentence.

^SHe ^Vdid ^Ohis homework.（他做了作業。）

→ 這句中的 did（做）後面有受詞 his homework（他的作業），可以改為被動。

Situations Which Often Use the Passive

常用被動語態的狀況

❶ You don't know who the subject is.

^OStonehenge ^Vwas built around 5,000 years ago.

→ No one knows for sure who built it.

① 主詞不明

^OStonehenge ^Vwas built around 5,000 years ago.（巨石陣大約建造於五千年前。）

→ 沒有人確定是誰建造的。

❷ The subject isn't important or is easy to guess.

^OThe thief ^Vwas caught.

→ Most likely, the police caught the thief.

② 主詞不重要，或顯而易見

^OThe thief ^Vwas caught.（竊賊被逮捕。）

→ 最有可能是被警察逮捕。

❸ **You don't want to emphasise the subject.**

^OA mistake ^Vwas made when your account was billed.

→ It was the speaker's fault or the fault of someone in their company.

❹ **You want to emphasise the object.**

^OHoney ^Vis produced by ^Sbees.

→ Honey is the main topic, not bees.

❺ **General truths or facts.**

^OA straight line ^Vcan be drawn between any two points.

→ This is a mathematical 'rule,' or fact.

On the IELTS Listening exam, you'll sometimes hear the passive voice when speakers describe the steps in a process—how something is done.

For example, 'First, the topic is assigned.' (Who assigns the topic? Probably the teacher, but that is not the focus in this situation.)

Rewrite this passive voice sentence to make it active voice.

③ 不希望強調主詞

^OA mistake ^Vwas made when your account was billed.（您的帳戶在結帳時發生錯誤。）

→ 很可能是說話者或說話者所屬公司中某人的失誤。

④ 希望強調受詞

^OHoney ^Vis produced by ^Sbees.（蜂蜜由蜜蜂製造。）

→ 重點在於 honey（蜂蜜），而不是 bees（蜜蜂）。

⑤ 客觀規則或事實

^OA straight line ^Vcan be drawn between any two points.（直線由任意兩個點連結而成。）

→ 這是個數學規則和事實。

在 IELTS 聽力測驗中，你可能會在步驟說明的內容聽到被動語態，解釋事情如何被完成。

例如：First, the topic is assigned.（首先，主題已指定。）主題被誰指定？很可能是老師，但這不是句子的重點。

請將這個句子改為主動語態。

LESSON **7** Flow Chart Completion

First, the topic is assigned.

....

Answers: The teacher assigns the topic.

Now you are familiar with the passive voice. Let's try to shorten the passive sentences.

Look at the passive voice sentence again, shorten this sentence to only **TWO words**.

First, the topic is assigned.

Answers: Topic assigned.

Let's do some exercises. Shorten the sentences below to **no more than THREE words**. The topic is a zoo's procedures for keeping its animals healthy.

❶ Most animals here at the zoo are fed daily.

❷ The cages are cleaned on a regular basis.

❸ The temperature in each animal's enclosure is carefully monitored to ensure they're in the right type of environment for optimal health.

答案：The teacher assigns the topic.

熟悉了被動語態之後，現在我們來簡化被動語態的句子。

再看一次這個被動語態的句子，將句子簡化成 2 個字。

答案：Topic assigned.

我們繼續來練習一下。請將以下句子簡化到 3 個字以下，句子是有關動物園維持動物健康的流程。

Answers:

❶ Animals fed daily

❷ Cages cleaned regularly

In this case, it is acceptable to change the word form of adjective 'regular' to adverb 'regularly.' This maintains the meaning and follows the word limit instructions. 'Cleaned regular basis' does not work as 'regular basis' requires 'on a' to have meaning.

❸ Temperatures (carefully) monitored / Enclosure temperatures monitored

We need to keep the idea of a plural somewhere, since we're not talking about only one enclosure.

答案：

① Animals fed daily

② Cages cleaned regularly

這句可以把形容詞 regular 改為副詞 regularly，才能維持語意又符合字數限制。cleaned regular basis 不成立，因為 on a regular basis（定期）這個片語必須完整寫出才有意義。

③ Temperatures (carefully) monitored / Enclosure temperatures monitored

這句簡化的重點是要能顯示出 enclosure（圍欄）不只一個，這裡的簡化方式是用複數的 temperatures（溫度）來表達是多個地點。

LESSON 7　Flow Chart Completion

*Sentences 1-4 below have been shortened for use in flow charts, which show the steps in a process. Choose the complete sentence **A**, **B**, or **C** that has the same meaning as the shortened sentence. The context of the sentence is given to help you.*

以下第 1～4 題的句子為了用於流程圖中，已經經過簡化。選項 A、B、C 是完整的句子，請選出與題目意思相同的答案。括號中補充了句子使用的情境以幫助你判斷。

1　Team rejects idea　[Context: Business]

　A　The idea is rejected by the team.

　B　The team is rejected by the idea.

　C　Teams reject ideas.

2　Case investigated and findings reported　[Context: Criminal investigation]

　A　The case investigates the findings and reports them.

　B　The case is investigated and the findings are reported.

　C　The findings are reported and investigated by Case.

3 Inspection first, then warehousing   [Context: Manufacturing]

    A After being sent to a warehouse, the product is inspected.

    B Inspection is the first step in warehousing.

    C After being inspected, the product is sent to a warehouse.

4 Action taken—issue resolved?   [Context: Problem-solving]

    A After action is taken, (you must) check to ensure whether the issue has been resolved or not.

    B Did you take action? Should you resolve the issue?

    C When resolving an issue, you must take action.

* Answer Key p. 166

Skill 2   Understanding sequencing words
技巧 2：理解表達順序的字詞

- Sequencing words tell us the order of steps in a process: First, ... Next, ... After that, ... Then, ... Finally, ...

  表達順序的字詞可以幫助我們理解流程中的步驟，例如：First（首先）、Next（然後）、After that（接下來）、Then（接下來）、Finally（最後）。

- These basic sequencing words can take many forms:

  表達順序的字詞有很多講法：

First, ... （首先）	First of all, ... The first [step] is... [It] starts / begins with... The initial step is...
Next / After that / Then, ... （然後，接下來）	The next [step] is... The subsequent [step] is... Subsequently, ... Following this, ... The following [step] is...

Once [that step is done], ...
（一旦⋯就⋯）

After / When [that step is done], ...

Afterwards, ...

As [... begins to happen], ...

Meanwhile, ...
（同時）

While [that step is happening], ...

At the same time, ...

- 'Once' does not only mean 'next.' It is a step that should only be started when the goal of the previous step has been reached, e.g. *Only putting pasta into water once the water is boiling—not before!*

  Once（一旦⋯就⋯）必須用在某步驟或條件已達成的狀況。例如：Only putting pasta into water once the water is boiling—not before!（水滾後才把義大利麵放進去——不是水滾之前！）

- 'Meanwhile' introduces a point where two or more steps are being done at the same time.

  Meanwhile（同時）表達兩個或更多步驟同時進行的狀況。

Put the following sentences into the proper order. The first one has been done as an example.

請將句子依照順序編號，以下已經標示出了第 1 句（下一頁還有題目）。

.... Next, heat a nonstick skillet over a medium-low flame and toss in a pat of butter. Make sure the butter coats the pan.

.... As the eggs start to become firm, add chopped fresh herbs, or bits of ham or cheese.

...1... Scrambling eggs starts with beating your eggs in a bowl until they're completely blended. Add a little water, cream or milk to make them tender.

.... Finally, turn your eggs onto warmed plates and enjoy.

....   After they've begun to heat up a little, move the eggs across the pan slowly so that they cook evenly.

....   Then, pour the eggs into your butter-coated pan. Pause to let them heat slightly. Gentle heat is essential.

＊Answer Key p. 166

Listening Strategies ❿
Flow Chart Completion

聽力答題策略 ❿
流程圖填空題

Look at the two examples of flow chart completion tasks below.

請先看以下兩組「流程圖填空題」的例題。

---

1 *Complete the flow chart below.*

Write **NO MORE THAN TWO WORDS AND/OR A NUMBER** *for each answer.*

Organising a Community Clean-Up

┌───┐
Select Clean-Up Area

- Entire community or one neighbourhood
- Identifiable **1** .... helpful if announcing via newspapers or flyers
└───┘

↓

┌───┐
Contact City Maintenance

- Obtain maps, compost site hours, street sweeping dates
- Provide **2** .... with information or brochure about clean-up
└───┘

↓

┌───┐
Choose Date and Time

- Weekends popular
- **3** .... in advance ideal
- Autumn or spring best months
└───┘

↓

┌───┐
4 .... **Volunteers**

- 6-30 needed
└───┘

- Remind to bring equipment, i.e. gloves
- Need some volunteers with **5** ...., e.g. trucks, trailers, for transporting bags

↓

6 .... **Clean-Up**

- 3 weeks before clean-up
- Place door hangers / flyers in newspaper box or on front door knob

↓

Clean-Up Day

- Determine gathering site
- Review all clean-up **7** ....; thank special guests, sponsors and volunteers

2 *Complete the flow chart below.*

Write **NO MORE THAN THREE WORDS** *for each answer.*

The Process of Decaffeinating Coffee

Chemical Solvent Process	**Swiss 1** .... **Process**
Direct Method ► Solvent touches beans Indirect Method ► Solvent does not touch beans	
Direct method ► Beans steamed Indirect method ► **2**	Beans immersed in water solution 8 hours

↓　　　　　　　↓

Direct method
▶ Beans rinsed with chemical solvent—process complete
Indirect method
▶ Beans and water **3** ....

↓

Indirect method ▶ Solvent introduced to water

↓

Indirect method ▶ Water **6** .... beans; chemical solvents rinsed or evaporated

4 ....

↓

Green coffee extract passed through carbon filter

↓

Next batch of beans **5** .... with green coffee extract

Tips

Flow charts are used to describe a process, so listen for sequence words like 'first,' 'next,' and 'after.' These words will guide you through the chart.

流程圖的功能是說明過程，所以請特別注意表示順序的字詞，例如：first（首先）、next（接下來）、after（之後）。這些字詞會引導你了解整個流程。

Be aware that the steps and descriptions in flow charts often use abbreviated (or shortened) English grammar. This allows the words to fit into the small spaces. Speakers will still use proper grammatical English, though, so listen for keywords in the sentence that match the shortened sentence in the flow chart.

另外也要注意，流程圖常常因為空間限制，會使用縮寫或簡化過的英文，音檔中的說話者則是會維持正常的說法。所以請仔細聆聽句子中的關鍵字，與流程圖上的內容對照。

As with all completion tasks, read instructions carefully. If you write too many words, you will not

和所有的填空題一樣，請仔細閱讀題目說明。如果你不小心寫太

receive a mark for that answer.

If the task allows up to two words and the gap requires a noun, listen especially for an **adjective** before the noun. The adjective might be required for the answer to be correct. Use the context of the sentence to decide if the adjective is necessary.

Example: I can't meet you for breakfast because my car has a <u>flat tyre</u>.

If this were an IELTS answer, the adjective 'flat' would be required for the answer to be correct. The sentence would not be logical if it said, 'I can't meet you for breakfast because my car has a tyre.'

Remember this simple example and extend it to more complicated examples as you practise your IELTS listening.

| 10.1 |

Study the flow chart question on p. 157. Answer the following questions.

❶ Does this flow chart use the active voice or the passive voice?

....

多字，就得不到分數了。

如果答案可以填入 2 個字，而且包含名詞，請務必注意聽那個名詞前面的形容詞。答案有可能必須包含這個形容詞才正確，請從題目的上下文判斷。

例：I can't meet you for breakfast because my car has a <u>flat tyre</u>.（我沒辦法和你去吃早餐，因為我的車爆胎了。）

如果畫底線的地方是一題 IELTS 的題目，答案就必須包含形容詞 flat（洩氣的）才正確。如果漏掉形容詞，I can't meet you for breakfast because my car has a tyre. 意思會是「我沒辦法和你去吃早餐，因為我的車有輪胎。」

請記住這個簡單的例子，之後練習 IELTS 聽力測驗時也要應用在更複雜的題目上。

請觀察第 157 頁的流程圖填空題，並回答以下問題。

① 這個流程圖用了主動語態還是被動語態？

❷ What is the word limit? Can the answer be a number?

....

❸ What kind of word is required for each gap (noun, verb, etc.)?

....

❹ What are some possible paraphrases for the words near the gaps?

....

＊Answer Key p. 166

② 字數限制幾個字？答案可以是數字嗎？

③ 每個空格應填入什麼樣的答案？（例如：名詞、動詞等）

④ 空格前後的字詞可以怎麼改述？

| 10.2 | ◀) MP3 43

Now, listen to the recording of the flow chart task on p. 157. As you listen, write the answers in the gaps.

＊Answer Key p. 167

現在請練習第 157 頁的流程圖填空題，將答案填入空格中。

| 10.3 |

Study the flow chart question above on p. 158. Answer the following questions.

請觀察第 158 頁的流程圖填空題，並回答以下問題。

❶ Does this flow chart use the active voice or the passive voice?

....

❷ What is the word limit? Can the answer be a number?

....

❸ What kind of word is required for each gap (noun, verb, etc.)?

....

❹ What are some possible paraphrases for the words near the gaps?

....

＊Answer Key p. 167

① 這個流程圖用了主動語態還是被動語態？

② 字數限制幾個字？答案可以是數字嗎？

③ 每個空格應填入什麼樣的答案？（例如：名詞、動詞等）

④ 空格前後的字詞可以怎麼改述？

LESSON **7**

Flow Chart Completion

[10.4]　◀》 MP3 44

Now, listen to the recording of the flow chart task on p. 158. As you listen, write the answers in the gaps.

＊Answer Key p. 168

現在請練習第 158 頁的流程圖填空題，將答案填入空格中。

Task Practice | 題型練習

PART 3 ◀)) MP3 45

Questions 1-5

Complete the flow chart below.

Write **NO MORE THAN ONE WORD** *for each answer.*

How Arial revises a paper

First stage: 3-6 hours after completion

Check paper's **1** ....
↓
Check thesis: should be **2** ....
Avoid generalisation

↓

Second stage: 4-7 days after completion

Ensure paper has **3** .... throughout
↓
Check organisation of information, e.g. logical pattern, smooth **4** ....
↓
Check information: cite sources, ensure facts are **5** ....
↓
Check conclusion

PART 4   ◀) MP3 46

Questions 1-6

Complete the flow chart below.

*Write **NO MORE THAN THREE WORDS** for each answer.*

Tomato Harvesting and Cleaning
Ripe tomatoes harvested, cleaned, and sorted. **1** .... ones removed.

↓

Pulping
Tomatoes crushed to extract juice. **2** .... separated from juice.

↓

Tomato 3 .... **Production**
Tomato juice heated—excess water evaporated.

↓

Flavour Enhancement and Preservation
Vinegar added for acidity and preservation. Sugar and spices introduced (salt, onions, garlic).

↓

Flavour Integration
Mixture **4** .... to allow flavours to blend.

↓

5 .... Heating and Pasteurisation

Remaining microorganisms eliminated.

Safety and product stability ensured.

↓

Cooling

Rapid cooling to set ketchup's consistency.

↓

Packaging

Ketchup packaged into bottles, jars, or containers.

↓

Sealing and Labelling

Containers sealed to **6** ....

Labels affixed to containers.

↓

Distribution

Packaged ketchup products ready for distribution to consumers.

Answer Key 答案

Pre-Lesson Skills Practice

Skill 1 Understanding shortened sentences

1 A　　　　　　**2** B　　　　　　**3** C　　　　　　**4** A

Skill 2 Understanding sequencing words

　2　Next, heat a nonstick skillet over a medium-low flame and toss in a pat of butter. Make sure the butter coats the pan.

　5　As the eggs start to become firm, add chopped fresh herbs, or bits of ham or cheese.

　1　Scrambling eggs starts with beating your eggs in a bowl until they're completely blended. Add a little water, cream or milk to make them tender.

　6　Finally, turn your eggs onto warmed plates and enjoy.

　4　After they've begun to heat up a little, move the eggs across the pan slowly so that they cook evenly.

　3　Then, pour the eggs into your butter-coated pan. Pause to let them heat slightly. Gentle heat is essential.

Listening Strategies ❿ Flow Chart Completion

10.1

❶ Active voice

❷ One or two words. Yes, the answer could be or include a number.

❸ **1**　Noun // Adjective + Noun

　2　Noun // Adjective + Noun

　3　Noun (including -ing word) // Adjective + Noun // Number + Noun

　4　Verb

　5　Noun

　6　Verb

　7　Noun

❹ Some possible paraphrases:

　1　identifiable → recognisable // (well-)known

　　　helpful → be a big help // be a good idea // beneficial

　2　provide → give // offer

　　　information or brochure → reading materials // pamphlets // leaflets

　3　in advance → ahead of time // before [something] // beforehand // early

4 'Volunteers' is unlikely to be paraphrased, but the speaker will probably talk about fall or spring being the best months soon before the answer is given.

fall or spring → October or April

best months → months with the best weather // most pleasant months

5 e.g. trucks, trailers for transporting → large vehicles // transport vehicles

6 'Clean-up' is unlikely to be paraphrased, but before the answer is given, the speaker might talk about either '3 weeks before clean-up' or the trucks or trailers for transporting bags.

3 weeks before clean-up → 3 weeks prior to clean-up

e.g. trucks, trailers for transporting → large vehicles // transport vehicles

7 review → go over // look over // take a look at

thank → acknowledge // express gratitude to

10.2

1 boundaries

2 fact sheet

3 one month // 1 month

4 Recruit

5 support vehicles

6 Publicise // Publicize

7 instructions

10.3

❶ Mostly passive voice

❷ No more than three words. No, numbers are not allowed.

❸ 1 Adjective // Noun

2 Most likely a noun and a past participle

3 Past participle // Past participle + Adverb

4 Most likely a noun and a past participle

5 Past participle // Past participle + Adverb

6 Most likely a past participle and a preposition (such as 'by' or 'to')

❹ Some possible paraphrases:

1 process → method

2 The speaker will probably talk about the direct method before this answer is given. There is no likely synonym for 'steamed' in English, but we might expect the speaker to describe how the beans are steamed, or for how long.

3 rinsed → washed

water → water solution

4 The speaker may talk about the indirect method of the chemical solvent process before this answer.

5 next batch → subsequent batch

6 rinsed → washed away

evaporated → vaporised

10.4

1 Water

2 Beans soaked

3 separated

4 Beans discarded

5 washed and filtered

6 reintroduced to

Task Practice

PART 3

1 focus

2 specific

3 balance

4 transitions

5 accurate

PART 4

1 defective

2 seeds and skins

3 Paste

4 heated

5 Final

6 maintain freshness

LESSON 8

Summary Completion / Matching Tasks with Charts or Graphs

摘要填空題 / 圖表配合題

Summary Completion / Matching Tasks with Charts or Graphs
摘要填空題 / 圖表配合題

Lesson Overview

本課內容

In this lesson, you will become familiar with the **summary completion** and **questions with charts or graphs** on the IELTS. You will learn how to approach the two tasks and will become aware of common problems that IELTS candidates encounter in these questions.

在這堂課中,我們將會介紹「摘要填空題」和「圖表配合題」。你會學到這兩種題型的答題技巧,以及一般考生最常遇到的問題。

We will be working with IELTS Listening Part 3 and Part 4 for these two task types.

我們會透過 IELTS 聽力測驗 Part 3 和 Part 4 來練習這兩種題型。

♦ **Listening Part 3**
- Questions 21-30
- A dialogue (two or three speakers)
- Unlike Parts 1 and 2, features an academic topic
- Any question type is possible

聽力測驗 **Part 3**
- 第 21～30 題
- 多人對話
- 學術的對話主題
- 可能是任何題型

♦ **Listening Part 4**
- Questions 31-40
- A monologue (a lecture)
- The topic is academic
- Notes completion is the most common task for Part 4, but any completion task is possible
- Generally said to be the most challenging part of the Listening Test, and for many people, of the entire IELTS

聽力測驗 **Part 4**
- 第 31～40 題
- 單人獨白(一場講座、演說)
- 學術的主題
- 筆記填空題在 Part 4 最常見,但也可能是任何填空題型
- 一般認為是聽力測驗中最困難的部分,對許多人而言,甚至是 IELTS 測驗中最困難的

Lesson Vocabulary Bank: Technology / Workplace / Society

課程字彙庫：科技 / 職場 / 社會

🔊 MP3 47

○ antisocial 形 不愛社交的；反社會的
[ˌæntɪˈsəʊʃ(ə)l]

○ attribute X to Y 片 把 X 歸因於 Y

○ capable 形 有能力的
[ˈkeɪpəb(ə)l]

○ capability 名 能力
[ˌkeɪpəˈbɪləti]

○ condone 動 寬恕
[kənˈdəʊn]

○ customise 動 客製化，訂做
[ˈkʌstəmaɪz]

○ customised 形 客製化的
[ˈkʌstəmaɪzd]

○ customisation 名 客製化
[ˌkʌstəmaɪˈzeɪʃ(ə)n]

○ cyberbully 動 網路霸凌
[ˈsaɪbəbʊli] 動作者 網路霸凌者

○ cyberbullying 名 網路霸凌
[ˈsaɪbəˌbʊlɪŋ]

○ demographic 形 人口統計學的
[ˌdeməˈgræfɪk] 名（顧客等）族群

○ discriminate 動 辨別；歧視
[dɪˈskrɪmɪneɪt]

○ discriminatory 形 差別待遇的
[dɪˈskrɪmɪnət(ə)ri]

○ discrimination 名 辨別；歧視
[dɪˌskrɪmɪˈneɪʃ(ə)n]

○ filter 動 過濾 動作者 過濾器
[ˈfɪltə(r)]

○ fraudulent 形 欺騙的
[ˈfrɔːdjʊl(ə)nt]

○ fraud 名 欺騙；騙局
[frɔːd]

○ gadget 名 小工具，小機械
[ˈgædʒɪt]

○ globalise 動 全球化
[ˈgləʊbəlaɪz]

○ globalisation 名 全球化
[ˌgləʊb(ə)laɪˈzeɪʃ(ə)n]

○ hack 動 駭入，非法入侵
[hæk]

○ hacking 名 駭客入侵
[ˈhækɪŋ]

○ hacker 動作者 駭客
[ˈhækə(r)]

○ identity theft 片 盜用身分

○ interact 動 互動
[ˌɪntərˈækt]

○ interactive 形 互動的；交互作用的
[ˌɪntərˈæktɪv]

＊本書音標採用 IPA 音標系統

- interaction 名 互動；交互影響
  [ˌɪntərˋækʃ(ə)n]

- malware 名 惡意軟體
  [ˋmælweə(r)]

- media platform 片 媒體平台

- prevalent 形 盛行的，普遍的
  [ˋprev(ə)l(ə)nt]

- prevalence 名 流行，普遍
  [ˋprev(ə)l(ə)ns]

- produce 動 生產，製造
  [prəˋdjuːs]

- productive 形 有生產力的
  [prəˋdʌktɪv]
  (↔ unproductive　無產出的)

- productivity 名 生產力
  [ˌprɒdʌkˋtɪvɪti]

- racial 形 種族的
  [ˋreɪʃ(ə)l]

- race 名 種族
  [reɪs]

- receipt 名 收據
  [rɪˋsiːt]

- religious 形 宗教的
  [rɪˋlɪdʒəs]

- religion 名 宗教
  [rɪˋlɪdʒ(ə)n]

- revolutionise 動 徹底改革
  [revəˋluːʃ(ə)naɪz]

- revolutionary 形 革命性的
  [revəˋluːʃ(ə)n(ə)ri]

- revolution 名 革命
  [revəˋluːʃ(ə)n]

- savvy 形〔口語〕有知識的
  [ˋsævi] 名〔口語〕常識

- scam 動 詐騙，欺騙 名 騙局
  [skæm]

- scammer 動作者〔口語〕詐欺犯
  (= scam artist)

- streamline 動 簡化；使成為流線型
  [ˋstriːmlaɪn]

- virus 名 病毒
  [ˋvaɪrəs]

Pre-Lesson Skills Practice | 高分技巧訓練

Skill 1　Working with summary

技巧 1：練習摘要

- A summary is a short sentence or sentences that provide the main idea of a text without including the details.

summary（摘要）由一個或幾個簡短的句子組成，用於表達一段文字的主旨，並省略細節。

- Answer choices on the IELTS listening are often summaries of what the speakers are saying.

IELTS 聽力測驗很多題型中的選項常常就是音檔內容的摘要。

- To do well on these questions, you must be able to tell the difference between the main ideas and the details of information you hear.

要順利作答和摘要相關的題型，你必須會分辨聽到的內容哪些是主旨，哪些是補充細節。

- To differentiate between main ideas and details, you must use your knowledge of English vocabulary and grammar. Linking words are especially important in understanding the connection between ideas.

要分辨主旨和細節，就得運用你的英文字彙和文法能力。其中，表達轉折的字詞對於了解論點之間的關係格外重要。

Main Ideas vs. Details

主旨 vs. 細節

- **Main ideas** are what the sentence or passage is mostly about.

「主旨」是句子或段落要表達的重點。

- **Details** support the main idea. They often include:
  - Descriptions
  - Facts (such as background information)
  - Thoughts
  - Explanations
  - Dialogue
  - Actions

「細節」則是用於支持主旨的內容，通常包含：
- 描述
- 事實（背景資訊等）
- 想法
- 說明
- 對話

- Statistics

- 動作
- 統計數據

Read the following excerpt. In addition to its main idea, it contains details that support these key points. Underline the key point of the passage. Then consider the details. Which types of details are they? Look at the above list for help.

請閱讀以下文章節錄,其中除了主旨之外,還包含支持主旨的細節。將主旨畫底線,然後想想看這個段落中的細節屬於哪一類?(請參考以上的列表)

When I first began my university studies, I was unsure what subject I wanted to major in. I consulted with my parents, who suggested I go into finance, but this seemed dull to me. Numbers had never held my interest. My personal love had always been the outdoors, so I tried to think of a major that would let me spend plenty of time outside while still making enough money to support myself.

Answers:

- The main idea of the excerpt is in the last sentence: '...so I tried to think of a major that would let me spend plenty of time outside while still making enough money to support myself.'
- The supporting details in this excerpt are **background information** and **explanations**. They may be interesting, but if they were cut from the excerpt, the main point would not change.

答案:

- 這個段落的主旨是最後一句: ... so I tried to think of a major that would let me spend plenty of time outside while still making enough money to support myself. (⋯所以我試著找出可以讓我長時間待在戶外,未來又能有不錯收入的科系。)
- 這個段落的細節屬於「背景資訊」和「說明」。這些內容雖然有趣,不過如果省略也不會影響段落的主旨。

Read the following excerpt about Kerry and her major. Choose a summary from the options provided that summarises several sentences in the excerpt. Use parentheses to indicate which sentences are summarised by each numbered choice, as in the example.

請閱讀以下關於 Kerry 選擇科系的文章節錄，在文中用括號標示出下方選項 1～4 是哪一段內容的摘要。文章中已經標示出了 Summary 4。

(Summary 4 When I first began my university studies, I was unsure what subject I wanted to major in. I consulted with my parents, who suggested I go into finance, but this seemed dull to me. Numbers had never held my interest. My personal love had always been the outdoors, so I tried to think of a major that would let me spend plenty of time outside while still making enough money to support myself.) After a few months of indecision, I consulted with my professor. Surprisingly enough, she suggested nursing! When I asked her why, she explained that nurses work long shifts three to four days a week, leaving extra long weekends to pursue whatever I like. That, of course, is if I have enough energy after 16 to 20 hours shifts! I thought about it for a while, and the idea became more and more appealing to me. I told my parents I was considering going into nursing, and they were pleased as could be. I looked into the option a bit more, talked to a nurse friend of mine and then to some of the nursing programme faculty. At last, I made up my mind. I entered the programme, studied hard, and got my certification. That was 10 years ago, and here I am today, a tired but happy registered nurse who spends her free days in the woods.

Summaries:

1 A professor suggested that the schedule of a nurse could possibly suit Kerry's needs.

2 Kerry joined the nursing programme, and today she is a nurse who is able to enjoy her hobby when not working.

3 Kerry liked the idea of becoming a nurse.

4 Kerry tried to think of a profitable major that would let her spend time outdoors.

∗ Answer Key p. 193

Skill 2　Identifying embedded questions

技巧 2：找出嵌入的問句

- Some questions on the IELTS don't look like traditional questions. That is, they are statements and contain no question marks. They contain gaps where one or more words are missing, and you must determine what word or words go in its place.

IELTS 測驗中有些題目不像一般的問句，會是一段敘述，結尾沒有問號。敘述中會有空格，你必須在空格中填入適當的字詞。

- To succeed at these questions, you must be able to look at the sentence and understand what question is contained—or embedded—in it.

要順利作答這種題型，你必須判斷敘述中嵌入的問句要問什麼。

- You do NOT need to write these embedded questions during the test, but it is important that you know what they are. Why? You must know what a question is before you can answer it.

考試時，你不用把嵌入的問句寫出來，不過釐清這些問句非常重要。畢竟回答問題前，一定要知道問題是什麼。

- To understand the embedded questions, the words near the gap are especially important.

要回答嵌入的問句，空格前後的字詞是重要的關鍵。

In the following, assume that the answer asks for only ONE word. What do we know about the missing word?

假設以下的空格只能填入 1 個字，我們可以推測出關於這個字的什麼資訊？

Sharon needs .... in her essay.

The word before the gap, *needs*, tells us the answer is a noun. 'Need' describes a lack of **something** or **someone**.

空格前的動詞 needs（需要）提示我們答案是個名詞，而且從 needs（需要）的意思可知是缺少了某個東西或人。

The phrase after the gap, *in her essay*, tells us that the missing noun is likely something and not

從空格後的片語 in her essay（在她的論文中）可知空格應該填入

someone. If we place the idea of 'people' in the gap, the answer is not logical:

✖ Sharon needs <u>Bob</u> in her essay.
✖ Sharon needs <u>students</u> in her essay.

You might argue that maybe Sharon needs to interview Bob or students to include their opinions in her essay. That would be more logical.

But remember: The answer is only ONE word. We cannot say 'Sharon needs <u>interview (v.)</u> in her essay' because that is not grammatical. Likewise, we cannot say 'Sharon needs <u>to interview people</u> in her essay' because the instructions call for only one word. Also, it would be more correct to say '<u>for</u> her essay' in this case.

Therefore, the missing word is a noun—a thing of some kind.

Choose the word below which introduces the embedded question in the sentence on p. 176. Then write the full question.

- Who—people
- What—things
- Where—places, locations

「東西」而不是「人」。如果填入「人」，答案會不合邏輯，例如：

✖ Sharon needs <u>Bob</u> in her essay.（Sharon 的論文裡需要 Bob。）
✖ Sharon needs <u>students</u> in her essay.（Sharon 的論文裡需要學生。）

你可能會覺得，說不定這個情境是 Sharon 需要訪談 Bob 或一些學生，把他們的想法納入她的論文中，這樣就合理多了。

但別忘了，空格限制只能填入 1 個字。我們不能說 Sharon needs <u>interview (v.)</u> in her essay，因為文法不正確。我們也不能說 Sharon needs <u>to interview people</u> in her essay，因為只能填入 1 個字，而且這個狀況下，後面的片語應該是 <u>for</u> her essay 比較正確。

因此，空格要填入一個名詞，而且是個「東西」。

請選出適合的疑問詞，寫出第 176 頁那個句子嵌入的問句。

- Who：人
- What：東西
- Where：場所、地點

LESSON **8** Summary Completion / Matching Tasks with Charts or Graphs

- When—time periods, years, hours
- Why—reasons
- How—manners, ways, methods

- When：一段時間、年代、幾點
- Why：原因
- How：方法、手段、技巧

Sharon needs .... in her essay.

→

....

Possible answers:

- What does Sharon need in her essay?
- What does Sharon's essay need?

參考答案：

- What does Sharon need in her essay?
- What does Sharon's essay need?（Sharon 的論文需要什麼？）

Note that it is very uncommon to use the awkward form 'Sharon's essay needs what?' or 'Sharon needs what in her essay?' in everyday English. However, it's fine if thinking this way helps you during these questions on the IELTS.

注意：日常英文中，問句不會寫成 Sharon's essay needs what? 和 Sharon needs what in her essay? 這種形式。不過如果對正確答題有幫助，考試時你可以這樣思考沒關係。

For this next example, also assume the question calls for only ONE word as the answer. What kind of word cannot be the answer?

下一個練習中，也請假設空格只能填入 1 個字。答案不可能是什麼樣的字詞？

The results of the study showed that .... people experienced low self-esteem after viewing social media.

Answer:

The phrase before the gap, *showed that*, and the

答案：

空格前的 showed that（顯示出）和

word after the gap, *people*, tell us that the missing word cannot be **an adverb**, **noun**, **preposition**, or a **base (infinitive form) of a verb**, such as 'learn.' These would all be ungrammatical.

空格後的 people（人）提示我們答案不可能是副詞、名詞、介系詞或動詞原形，例如 learn（學習）。填入這些，文法都不正確。

The word 'people' gives much more information. Brainstorm words that **could** go in the gap before 'people.' Write your ideas after the three examples.

people 這個字還提供我們很多線索。腦力激盪一下，想想什麼字可以放在這個的空格中，將你的答案寫下來（已提供三個範例）。

> *some, English, these,* ....
>
> ....

Answer:
Possible words could be **adjectives** such as 'young,' 'shy,' 'many,' or **determiners** like 'three' or 'those.'

答案：
可能填入的字包含 young（年輕的）、shy（害羞的）、many（很多的）等形容詞，還有 three（三個）、those（那些）等指示詞。

Now write the full question or questions that could be embedded in the sentence. Start with an appropriate question word: who, what, where, etc.

現在請寫出這個句子可能嵌入的問句，記得以適合的疑問詞（who、what、where 等）開頭。

> The results of the study showed that .... people experienced low self-esteem after viewing social media.
>
> → ....

Possible answers:
– How many people experienced low self-esteem after viewing social media?

參考答案：
– How many people experienced low self-esteem after viewing

- What kind of people experienced low self-esteem after viewing social media?
- Which people experienced low self-esteem after viewing social media?

social media?（有多少人在看社群網站之後感到沒自信？）

- What kind of people experienced low self-esteem after viewing social media?（什麼樣的人在看社群網站之後感到沒自信？）

- Which people experienced low self-esteem after viewing social media?（哪些人在看社群網站之後感到沒自信？）

Write the full questions that are embedded in each sentence.
寫出以下句子中嵌入的問句。

1   The proposed project will cost ....

→ ....

2   Carl's .... suggested he change his major.

→ ....

3   John was on holiday in .... when he first thought of becoming an entrepreneur.

→ ....

4   Many people experience feelings of .... when they move abroad.

→ ....

∗ Answer Key p. 193

Skill 3 Understanding graph and chart language

技巧 3：理解圖表用詞

Some questions on the Listening part of the exam require you to understand the type of language associated with charts: fractions, percentages, and phrases that express them.

作答聽力測驗的某些題目時，你必須熟悉有關圖表的常見說法，包含比例、百分比，以及各種相關表達方式。

If you are taking the Academic IELTS, you have likely studied these words and phrases for the Writing portion of the test (Task 1).

如果你是應考 IELTS 測驗的學術組，你應該已經在準備寫作測驗 Task 1 的時候學過這些字詞了。

The table below presents the most common percentages, fractions, and associated phrases you will encounter on the IELTS Listening. However, you could hear any percentage on the test, so keep your ears open!

以下表格列出 IELTS 聽力測驗中最常見的百分比、比例，以及相關片語。不過，你在考試中還是可能聽到任何其他比例，所以務必仔細聽。

Percentage （百分比）	Fraction （比例）	Phrases （相關片語）	
100%	–	• all	• the entirety
85-95%	–	• the (vast) majority	• most
75%	3/4	• three quarters	• three fourths
51-52%	–	• just over 50% / (a) half	• about half
50%	1/2	• half	
48-49%	–	• just under 50% / (a) half • nearly 50% / (a) half • about 50% / (a) half	• just below 50% / (a) half • almost 50% / (a) half
34-35%	–	• just over 33% / one third	• just above 33% / one third
33%	1/3	• a third	• one third

31-32%	–	• just under 33% / one third • nearly 33% / one third • about 33% / one third	• just below 33% / one third • almost 33% / one third
26-27%	–	• just over 25% / a quarter / one fourth • roughly 25% / a quarter / one fourth • more than 25% / a quarter / one fourth	
25%	1/4	• a quarter • one fourth	• one quarter
23-24%	–	• just under 25% / a quarter / one fourth • just below 25% / a quarter / one fourth • nearly 25% / a quarter / one fourth • almost 25% / a quarter / one fourth • about 25% / a quarter / one fourth	
11-12%	–	• just over 10% / one tenth	• approximately one tenth
10%	1/10	• one tenth	
8-9%	–	• just under 10% / one tenth • nearly 10% / one tenth • about 10% / one tenth	• just below 10% / one tenth • almost 10% / one tenth

There is no single definition of 'vast majority' or 'grand majority' that everyone agrees on. Some say the vast majority is 75% or more. Others feel that it is 85% or more. The same goes for 'just under' or 'nearly' a number or percentage. The IELTS will NOT use this fact to trick you on the test.

vast majority 和 grand majority 所指的「大部分」到底是多少，並沒有絕對的答案，有人認為是 75% 以上，有人認為是 85% 以上。just under（略低於）和 nearly（幾近於）也是類似的狀況。IELTS 測驗並不會針對這點當作考題。

*Match the phrases or fractions on the left with their percentage values **A-H** on the right. There may be more than one correct answer. Mark an ✗ if there are no suitable answers.*

請將百分比 A～H 和對應的說法配對，將答案填入空格中。答案可能不只一個，如果沒有符合的答案，請打 ✗。

1	....	3/4	**A**	11%
2	....	about half	**B**	25%
3	....	the (vast) majority	**C**	30%
4	....	just under half	**D**	90%
5	....	just over a third	**E**	51%
6	....	about a tenth	**F**	9%
7	....	a quarter	**G**	34%
8	....	less than a third	**H**	48 %

∗ Answer Key p. 193

Look at the pie chart below. How could the following categories be described using phrases, fractions, and percentages?

請看以下的圓餅圖，這幾個分類要怎麼用片語、比例和百分比表示？

Example: Refrigeration + Air Conditioning:

just over 10% / about a tenth / a minority

9 Lighting and Other Appliances + Water Heating:

....

10 Space Heating + Lighting and Other Appliances:

....

11   Water Heating:

....

12   Lighting and Other Appliances:

....

How Energy Is Used in Homes (2009)

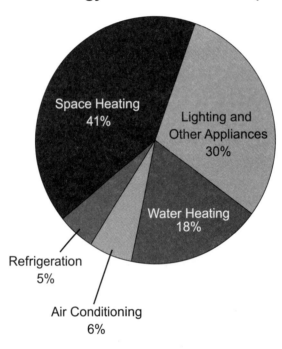

Source: U.S. Energy Information Administration,
Residential Energy Consumption Survey (RECS) 2009.

＊Answer Key p. 193

Listening Strategies ⑪
Summary Completion

聽力答題策略 ⑪
摘要填空題

Look at the example of a summary completion task below.

請先看以下「摘要填空題」的例題。

Complete the summary below.

*Write **NO MORE THAN TWO WORDS** for each answer.*

There are divided views on the presence of technology in every area of modern life. Proponents of technology in education say that it increases motivation and confidence because lessons can be **1** .... and adjusted to meet individual students' needs. Technology also allows for instant unlimited sources of **2** .... information. However, technology in schools may also have a detrimental impact on the development of **3** ...., and relationships will suffer as a result. Students can also be distracted by technology in school, and placing **4** .... on electronic devices is not effective enough because modern students probably know how to get past them.

> **Tips**

Summary completion tasks look similar to sentence completion tasks (see Lesson 3) at first glance, and indeed there are some similarities. Your pre-listening approach to both questions is the same. The main difference is that summary completion questions contain more distractors in the form of paraphrases. It is easy to lose your place because many sentences in the recording are combined (summarised) into one

摘要填空題和句子填空題（請見第 3 課）乍看之下很像，它們確實也有一些相似之處。在開始作答這兩種題型前，你要做的準備都一樣，最大的不同在於，摘要填空題會有更多改述題目的地方，讓你更難判斷出正確答案。音檔中的很多句子在題目會被摘

or two sentences in the question, and the words used by the speaker are paraphrased. The grammar of the sentences often changes as well.

要整合成一兩句話，用字也會經過替換，甚至連文法有時都會不同，所以作答時非常容易搞混。

Be aware of this as you practise.

練習時，一定要特別注意這幾點。

11.1

Study the summary completion question above. Answer the following questions.

請觀察上一頁的摘要填空題，並回答以下問題。

❶ What is the word limit? Can the answer be a number?

① 字數限制幾個字？答案可以是數字嗎？

....

❷ What kind of word is required for each gap (noun, verb, etc.)?

② 每個空格應填入什麼樣的答案？（例如：名詞、動詞等）

....

❸ Underline keywords near the gaps. What are possible paraphrases for them?

③ 將空格前後的關鍵字畫底線。這些字詞可以怎麼改述？

....

❹ What are the embedded questions for each gap?

④ 每個空格可能嵌入的問句是什麼？

....

＊Answer Key p. 193

11.2   ◀》 MP3 48

Now, listen to the recording of the summary completion task on p. 185. As you listen, write the answers in the gaps.

現在請練習上一頁的摘要填空題，將答案填入空格中。

＊Answer Key p. 194

Listening Strategies ⑫
Matching Tasks with Charts or Graphs

聽力答題策略 ⑫
圖表配合題

Look at the examples of matching tasks with charts below.

請先看以下「圖表配合題」的例題。

Questions 1-3

Label the chart below.

*Choose your answers from the list below and write the correct letter, **A-F**, in boxes 1-3.*

Average hours and minutes spent on media platforms per adult per day

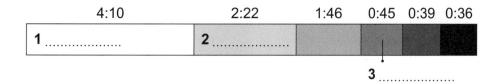

Media Platforms
A App / web on tablet
B Radio
C Live TV
D Time-shifted TV
E App / web on smartphone
F Internet on computer

Questions 4-6

Choose the correct letter, A-F.

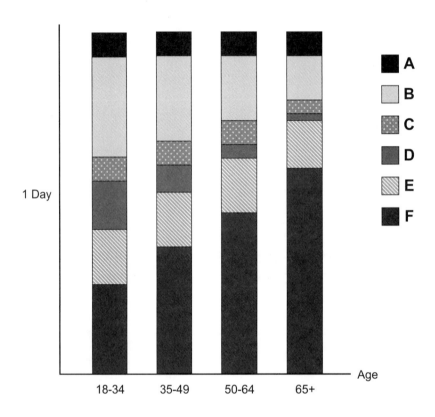

Share of Daily Time Spent by Platform

4　Internet on computer　　................

5　TV-connected devices　　................

6　Live + time-shifted TV　　................

Tips

Matching tasks with charts or graphs are less common in the IELTS listening than other question types, but they are certainly possible. Be aware that there are many types of charts or graphs, but

圖表配合題在 IELTS 聽力測驗中相對比較少見，但還是有可能出現。圖表有很多種，不過最常見的還是長條圖和圓餅圖。音檔中

bar charts and pie charts are the most common. Speakers might not give numbers for the data, instead using words like 'majority' or 'minority,' so be prepared for this.

不一定會直接講出數字，而是會用 majority（大多數）、minority（少數）這種敘述，因此請特別注意。

12.1

Study the matching tasks with charts on p. 187. Answer the following questions.

請觀察第 187 頁的圖表配合題，並回答以下問題。

❶ For Questions 1-3, think of some possible paraphrases for the times that correspond to the indicated questions.

① 第 1～3 題中對應的時間長度可以怎麼改述？

....

❷ For Questions 1-3, look for significant trends in the categories, e.g. large / short bars, similar bars.

② 第 1～3 題中的各個分類有什麼趨勢？（例如：多數、少數、相似等）

....

❸ For Questions 4-6, look for significant trends in the categories, e.g. large / short bars, similar bars.

③ 第 4～6 題中的各個分類有什麼趨勢？（例如：多數、少數、相似等）

....

＊Answer Key p. 194

12.2   ◀》MP3 49

Now, listen to the recording of the matching tasks with charts on p. 187. As you listen, write the answers in the gaps.

現在請練習第 187 頁的圖表配合題，將答案填入空格中。

＊Answer Key p. 195

Task Practice   題型練習

PART 3   🔊) MP3 50

Question 1

*Listen and choose one answer, **A**, **B**, or **C**.*

Which of the following describes Martin and Tessa's first chart?

Prevalence of Online Harm Among Adult Internet Users

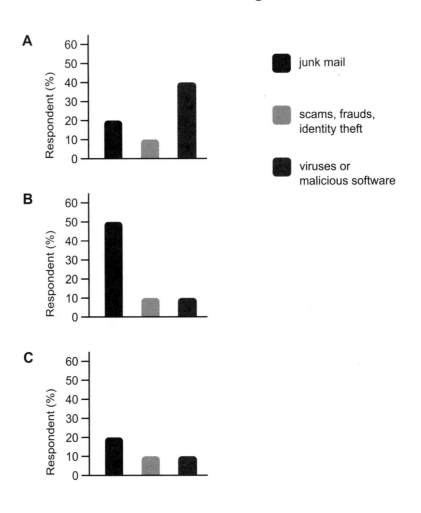

Questions 2-4

Label the chart below.

Possible Reasons for Cyberbullying

A financial status   **E** academic achievement

B personal conflicts   **F** religion

C race   **G** unknown

D appearance   **H** other

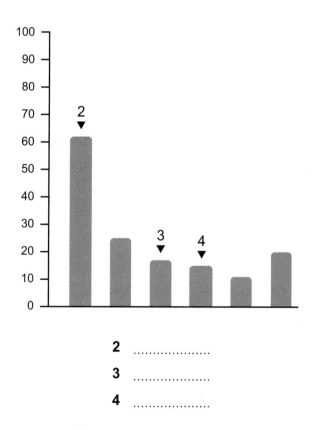

Teenagers' Reported Reasons for Being Cyberbullied

2 ....

3 ....

4 ....

PART 4   🔊 MP3 51

Questions 1-4

Complete the summary below.

*Write **NO MORE THAN ONE WORD** for each answer.*

Technology in the workplace has streamlined many business processes, e.g. the sending of **1** ...., but business owners should run the most current version of their software. Data and **2** .... can both be stolen by hackers if a business is running on obsolete software. Another perk of technology is that people can work from anywhere now. However, **3** .... can suffer if employees' attention is diverted from the task at hand by checking email. If business leaders implement rules about the use of technology in the office, the **4** .... employees get from their work will increase along with efficiency.

Answer Key | 答案

Pre-Lesson Skills Practice

Skill 1 Working with summary

Summary 1 (After a few months ... 16 to 20 hour shifts!)
Summary 3 (I thought about it ... the nursing programme faculty.)
Summary 2 (At last, I made up my mind ... free days in the woods.)

Skill 2 Identifying embedded questions

1 How much will the proposed project cost?
2 Who suggested Carl change his major?
3 Where was John on holiday when he first thought of becoming an entrepreneur? //
   When was John on holiday when he first thought of becoming an entrepreneur?
4 What kind of feelings do many people experience when they move abroad?

Skill 3 Understanding graph and chart language

1 ✗	3 D	5 G	7 B
2 E, H	4 H	6 A, F	8 C

Some possible answers include:

9 48% // about a half // just under a half // almost a half // about 50% // just under 50%
10 71% // under three-quarters // less than three-quarters // around three-quarters //
   around 75%
11 18% // less than a fifth // under one fifth // nearly 20% // around 20%
12 30% // less than a third // (just) under one third // around a third

Listening Strategies ⑪ Summary Completion

11.1

❶ One or two words. No, numbers are not possible.
❷ Some possibilities:
   1 Past participle // Adjective // Past participle + Adverb
   2 Adjective // Past participle used as an adjective
   3 Noun // Adjective + Noun
   4 Noun // Adjective + Noun

❸ Some possible paraphrases:

1   <u>lessons can be</u> → course materials can be // lesson plans can be
    <u>adjusted to meet individual ... needs</u> → customised for individuals // tailored for
      individual students' needs

2   <u>instant unlimited sources of ... information</u> → all the information you could ever want,
      at the click of a button // immediate unlimited knowledge

3   <u>the development of</u> → the growth of
    <u>relationships will suffer</u> → it will be hard to make friends / keep friendships // their
      social life will not be healthy

4   <u>placing</u> → putting // setting
    <u>on electronic devices</u> → on gadgets // on cell phones and the like

❹ 1   What can be done to lessons that helps them meet individual students' needs?

2   What kind of information does technology allow instant unlimited sources of?

3   What may technology in schools have a detrimental impact on?

4   What can be placed on electronic devices that is not effective enough to stop
    distraction?

[11.2]

1   customised // customized   3   interpersonal skills

2   current   4   filters

Listening Strategies ⓬ Matching Tasks with Charts or Graphs

[12.1]

❶ Some possible paraphrases:

1   4:10 → just over 4 hours // roughly 4 hours

2   2:22 → just under 2 and a half hours // nearly two and a half hours

3   0:45 → three quarters of an hour

❷ Some possible observations:

• The most popular social media platform (Question 1) is nearly twice as popular as the
  second most popular media platform (Question 2).

• Adults use each of the last three media platforms for less than an hour per week.

• The last two media platforms are used for a similar period of time, with only a 3-minute
  difference between them.

• There's a difference of six minutes between the fourth and fifth most popular media
  platforms.

• There's an hour difference between the fourth most popular media platform (Question 3)
  and the third most popular one.

❸ Some possible observations:

- **A** is equal among all age groups.
- **C** and **E** are almost equal across all ages except for the 65+ group. **E** is only slightly smaller in the 65+ group.
- **F** becomes larger the older the participants become. It's the majority for all age groups except the youngest. It's over half the day of the oldest age group.
- **B** becomes smaller the older the participants become. It appears to be the most popular platform for the youngest age group, only slightly more popular than **F**.

12.2

1 C	**3** A	**5** D
2 E	**4** C	**6** F

Task Practice

PART 3

1 C	**2** D	**3** C	**4** A

PART 4

1 receipts	**2** funds	**3** productivity	**4** satisfaction

LESSON 9

Map or Plan Labelling /
Diagram Labelling

地圖題 / 圖表填空題

Map or Plan Labelling / Diagram Labelling
地圖題 / 圖表填空題

Lesson Overview

本課內容

In this lesson, you will become familiar with ***map or plan labelling*** and ***diagram labelling*** tasks on the IELTS. You will learn how to approach the two tasks and will become aware of common problems that IELTS candidates encounter in these questions.

在這堂課中,我們將會介紹「地圖題」和「圖表填空題」。你會學到這兩種題型的答題技巧,以及一般考生最常遇到的問題。

We will be working with IELTS Listening Part 1 and Part 4 for these two task types.

我們會透過 IELTS 聽力測驗 Part 1 和 Part 4 來練習這兩種題型。

♦ **Listening Part 1**
- Questions 1-10
- A conversation between two speakers
- The topic is non-academic, e.g. job interview, booking accommodations, etc.
- Form completion task is common in Part 1, but any question type is possible

聽力測驗 Part 1
- 第 1～10 題
- 兩人對話
- 非學術的對話主題,如:工作面試、預訂住宿等
- 表單填空題在 Part 1 相當常見,但也可能是其他題型

♦ **Listening Part 4**
- Questions 31-40
- A monologue (a lecture)
- The topic is academic
- Notes completion is the most common task for Part 4, but any completion task is possible
- Generally said to be the most challenging part of

聽力測驗 Part 4
- 第 31～40 題
- 單人獨白(一場講座、演說)
- 學術的主題
- 筆記填空題在 Part 4 最常見,但也可能是任何填空題型
- 一般認為是聽力測驗中最困難

the Listening Test, and for many people, of the
entire IELTS

的部分，對許多人而言，甚至
是 IELTS 測驗中最困難的

Lesson Vocabulary Bank:
Places / Directions / Shapes / Oceans

課程字彙庫：
地點 / 方向 / 圖形 / 海洋

🔊 MP3 52

- abundant 形 充足的；豐富的
  [əˋbʌnd(ə)nt]
- abundance 名 充足；豐富
  [əˋbʌnd(ə)ns]

- adapt 動 使適應；改編
  [əˋdæpt]
- adaptable 形 適應力好的
  [əˋdæptəb(ə)l]
  (↔ unadaptable　無法適應的)
- adaptation 名 適應；改編
  [͵ædæpˋteɪʃ(ə)n]

- ascend 動 上升；攀登
  [əˋsend]
- ascent 名 上升
  [əˋsent]

- branch off into 片 分支，岔出

- capacity 名 容量；能力
  [kəˋpæsəti]

- chemist 名 化學家
  [ˋkemɪst]

- deepen 動 加深
  [ˋdiːp(ə)n]
- deep 形 深的
  [diːp]

- depth 名 深度
  [depθ]

- defective 形 有缺陷的
  [dɪˋfektɪv]
- defect 名 缺陷，缺失
  [ˋdiːfekt]

- descend 動 下降
  [dɪˋsend]
- descent 名 下降
  [dɪˋsent]

- cylindrical 形 圓柱狀的
  [sɪˋlɪndrɪk(ə)l]
- cylinder 名 圓柱體
  [ˋsɪlɪndə(r)]

- flagpole 名 旗桿
  [ˋflægpəʊl]

- foam 名 泡棉；泡沫
  [fəʊm]

- hostel 名 青年旅館
  [ˋhɒst(ə)l]

- intersect 動 相交，交叉
  [͵ɪntəˋsekt]
- intersection 名 十字路口
  [ˋɪntəsekʃ(ə)n]

○ parallel 形 平行的 名 平行
[ˈpærəlel]

○ pastry 名 茶點，點心
[ˈpeɪstri]

○ pave 動 鋪平（道路）
[peɪv]

○ paved 形 已鋪設的
[peɪvd]
（↔ unpaved 未鋪設的）

○ pavement 名 人行道
[ˈpeɪvm(ə)nt]

○ paver 動作者 鋪路機
[ˈpeɪvə(r)]

○ perpendicular 形 垂直的
[ˌpɜːpənˈdɪkjələ(r)]

○ press 動 壓
[pres]

○ pressure 名 壓力
[ˈpreʃə(r)]

○ situate at... 片 位於…

○ spherical 形 球面的
[ˈsferɪk(ə)l]

○ sphere 名 球面；範圍
[sfɪə(r)]

○ submerse 動 使沉入水中；浸沒
[səbˈmɜːs]

○ submersible 形 能沉入水中的
[səbˈmɜːsəb(ə)l]

○ submersion 名 沉沒
[səbˈmɜːʃ(ə)n] [səbˈmɜːʒ(ə)n]

○ toiletries 名 盥洗用品
[ˈtɔɪlətriz]

○ vertical 形 垂直的
[ˈvɜːtɪk(ə)l]

Pre-Lesson Skills Practice | 高分技巧訓練

Skill 1　Understanding basic shapes

技巧 1：認識基本圖形

- Basic shapes as well as slightly more complex shapes may be featured in the types of IELTS tasks you will practise in Lesson 9.

第 9 課介紹的題型中會出現基本的圖形，有時還會有稍微複雜一點的圖形。

- Words or phrases used to describe angles may also be featured.

描述「角度」的字詞有時也會出現在考試中。

*Match the following descriptions of shapes or angles with the images **A-J** below. Each image will be used twice.*

Tip: Try to fill in all blanks first without the use of a dictionary first. Skip over questions you do not know and return to them later.

請看以下敘述，將正確的圖形 A-J 填入空格中。每個圖形會用到 2 次。

小提醒：先不要查字典直接作答，跳過你不知道的題目，之後再回頭寫寫看。

1 .... a circular object

2 .... two straight lines that never touch

3 .... a box

4 .... a wavy line

5 .... a triangular object

6 .... two straight lines that meet at an angle

7 .... a four-sided shape which is wider at the top than the bottom

8 .... a curved line which continuously curls inward toward a central point

9 .... a can-shaped object

10 .... a four-sided object balanced on one point

11 .... a cylinder

12 .... a sphere

13 .... two parallel lines

14 .... a cube

15 .... a diamond-shaped object

16 .... a spiral

17 .... a 90-degree angle

18 .... a gently curving line

19 .... a four-sided object balanced on its narrow end

20 .... a three-sided object with a wide base

A

B

C

D

E

F

G

H

I

J

* Answer Key p. 215

Skill 2　**Understanding map vocabulary**　　技巧 2：認識地圖用詞

- Understanding map vocabulary is important in the types of IELTS tasks you will practise in this lesson.

認識地圖用詞對於這一課要練習的題型很重要。

- Map questions almost always give you 'landmarks' to help you find your way around the map. Landmarks could be entrances, plants, labelled buildings, or rooms, among many others.

地圖題會給你一些標示好的地標，幫助你判斷出正確的方向。地標可能是出入口、植物、已標示出名稱的建築物或房間等。

- The speaker will give directions based on the view of someone inside the map, so practise imagining yourself **in** the map.

說話者會以站在地圖中某處的視角說明方向，所以請練習想像自己身在地圖中。

The phrases listed below are common on IELTS map tasks.

以下是 IELTS 測驗的地圖題常見的字詞。

above	在⋯上面	inside	在⋯裡面
across from...	在⋯對面	intersection / junction	交叉口；十字路口
along	沿著	just past...	剛經過⋯
(run) alongside	沿著；並列地	left-hand side	左手邊
before you get to...	在你到⋯之前	next to...	在⋯旁邊
behind	在⋯後面	north / south / east / west	北／南／東／西
below	在⋯下面	northeast / northwest / southeast / southwest	東北／西北／東南／西南
between	在⋯之間		
beyond	在⋯之後	outside	在⋯外面
corner	轉角；角落	right-hand side	右手邊
dead end	盡頭，死巷	to the right	⋯的右邊
fork in the road	路的岔路	to your right	你的右邊
go straight	直走	turn left	往左
in the centre of... / in the middle of...	在⋯正中間	turn right	往右

Looking at the map below and answer the following questions.
請看以下的地圖並回答問題。

City Shopping Area

1   What landmarks are given to you on the map?

    ....

2   Where is the shopping area's garden?

    ....

3   What is directly on your left after you've entered the shopping area?

    ....

4   If you stand facing the cinema entrance, what is to the left?

    ....

5   What do you see on your left as you come out of the bookshop?

    ....

6   What is located just beside the shopping area's garden?

    ....

7 What store is opposite the cinema?

....

8 Describe the location of **C**.

....

9 Describe the location of **B**.

....

∗ Answer Key p. 215

Select all the phrases that can be used in the blank. Some questions will have more than one answer. Some answers may not be used.

Note: Some phrases may be grammatically correct but not logical or not commonly used. Try to select only the answers that work both logically and grammatically.

請將合理的選項填入空格中,有些題目會有多個答案,有的選項則不會用到。

注意:有些字詞填入空格後,雖然文法沒有錯誤,但不符合邏輯或不是常見用法。請試著選出文法正確又符合邏輯的答案。

A intersection / junction

B north / south / east / west

C below / above

D outside / inside

E right-hand side / left-hand side

F beyond

G before you get to

H just past

I northeast / northwest / southeast / southwest

J next to

K alongside

L to your right

M turn right / left

N go straight

O runs alongside

P dead end

Q	in the centre of / in the middle of	**U**	between
R	along	**V**	to the right of
S	corner	**W**	fork in the road
T	behind		

10 My office is located .... the men's restroom.

11 Stop .... the information desk, and turn right.

12 Go straight for half a kilometre, and then you will reach a(n) ....

13 The hospital is to the .... of the library.

14 .... the river is a walking path.

15 A walking path .... the river.

16 .... when you reach the café, and it will be on the left.

17 You'll find benches to sit on .... the courtyard.

* Answer Key p. 215

Listening Strategies ⑬
Map or Plan Labelling

聽力答題策略 ⑬
地圖題

Look at the example of a plan labelling task below.

請先看以下「地圖題」的例題。

Label the plan below.

*Write the correct letter, **A-J**, next to questions 1-5.*

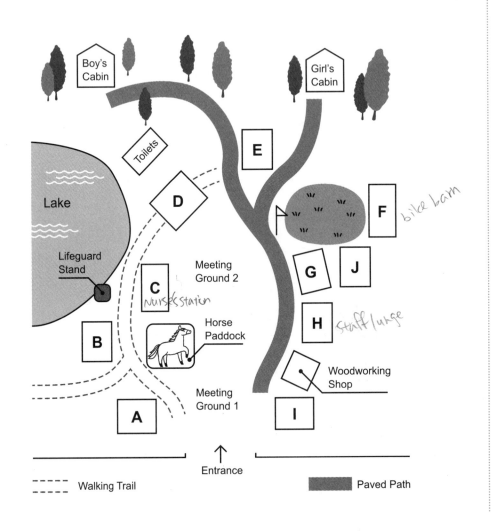

1   Games centre

2   Pottery studio

3   Sports pavilion

4   Lake equipment hut

5   Dining hall

Tips

Map or Plan Labelling Tasks are common in Part 2, although they are possible in any of the parts. Follow all pre-listening advice that we have used in our other lessons (read directions, look where the numbers start and finish, etc.). For maps and plans, look at the labelled things near the question gaps. For instance, what is 'A' next to?

Pay attention to other clues in the maps as well, like compass points (North, South, East, West) if they are provided. Speakers will also often tell you where they are standing when the listening begins. Note this carefully. This will help you follow their directions.

地圖題在 Part 2 相當常見,也可能出現在其他部分。作答前請依照前幾堂課教過的策略進行準備(例如:仔細閱讀題目說明、注意地圖上的題目順序等)。作答地圖題時,請特別注意題目標示附近的東西。例如:A 旁邊有什麼?

此外,也要多注意地圖上的其他線索,例如方位標示(東、西、南、北)。音檔中的說話者往往一開始就會先說明自己站的位置,一定要掌握這個資訊,接下來才能依照音檔所說的方向正確作答。

13.1

Study the plan labelling task above. Answer the following questions.

請觀察上一頁的地圖題,並回答以下問題。

❶ Does the plan have an explanation key for any symbols? If so, what do the symbols represent on the plan?

① 這張地圖有任何圖例嗎?如果有,它們分別代表什麼?

....

❷ What features are already labelled on the plan?

....

❸ Describe the locations of **A-J**.

....

＊Answer Key p. 216

② 有什麼東西是已經標示在地圖
　 上的？

③ 請描述地圖上 A-J 的位置。

13.2　◀)) MP3 53

Now, listen to the recording of the plan labelling task on p. 208. As you listen, write the answers in the gaps.

＊Answer Key p. 216

現在請練習第 208 頁的地圖題，
將答案填入空格中。

Listening Strategies ⑭
Diagram Labelling

聽力答題策略 ⑭
圖表填空題

Look at the example of a diagram labelling task below.

請先看以下「圖表填空題」的例題。

Complete the diagram below.

Write **NO MORE THAN ONE WORD OR A NUMBER** *for each answer.*

Ocean Zones Diagram

0 m Sea Level

Hydrostatic Pressure 101 kPa

Sunlight Zone
200 m

- Sunlight enables abundance of **1** ....
- -30 m **2** .... capacity reduce to 33%

Twilight Zone

- Slow life pace
- Available food low in **3** ....

1000 m

4 .... kPa

Organic nutrients

5 .... **Zone**

- Harsh environment leads to frightening adaptations

4000 m

6 .... kPa

Ocean Floor

Tips

The range of possibilities for diagram labelling tasks is endless, so prepare by exposing yourself to as large a variety of labelled images as you can. This could be anything from IKEA assembly manuals to educational diagrams on the Internet.

圖表填空題的主題沒有任何範圍，所以你只能盡量多看看各式各樣有文字標示的圖片，包含 IKEA 家具的組裝指南，或是網路上的知識性圖表。

In diagrams, as in flow charts, abbreviated English is used for space constraints. Yet speakers use proper grammar, so listen for keywords matching the shortened terms in the diagrams.

圖表中的文字和流程圖中的文字一樣，因空間有限，常會使用簡化過的英文，不過音檔中還是會使用一般的說法，因此請仔細聆聽能夠對應圖表內容的關鍵字。

Read directions carefully, as you will not receive a point if you write too many words.

一定要仔細閱讀題目說明，如果你寫的答案字數太多，就得不到分數。

14.1

Within 30 seconds, preview the task on p. 211. What should an IELTS candidate do before listening to a diagram labelling task?

＊Answer Key p. 216

請用 30 秒先瀏覽一下第 211 頁的題目。IELTS 考生在聆聽圖表填空題前應該做些什麼？

14.2   ◀)) MP3 54

Now, listen to the recording of the diagram labelling task on p. 211. As you listen, write the answers in the gaps.

＊Answer Key p. 216

現在請練習第 211 頁的圖表填空題，將答案填入空格中。

Task Practice   題型練習

PART 1   🔊 MP3 55

Questions 1-4

*Listen and label the map with **NO MORE THAN TWO WORDS**.*

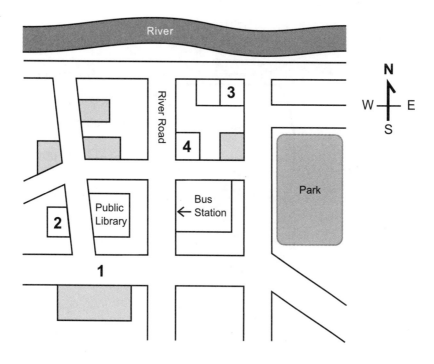

PART 4   🔊 MP3 56

Questions 1-4

Complete the diagram with **NO MORE THAN ONE WORD**.

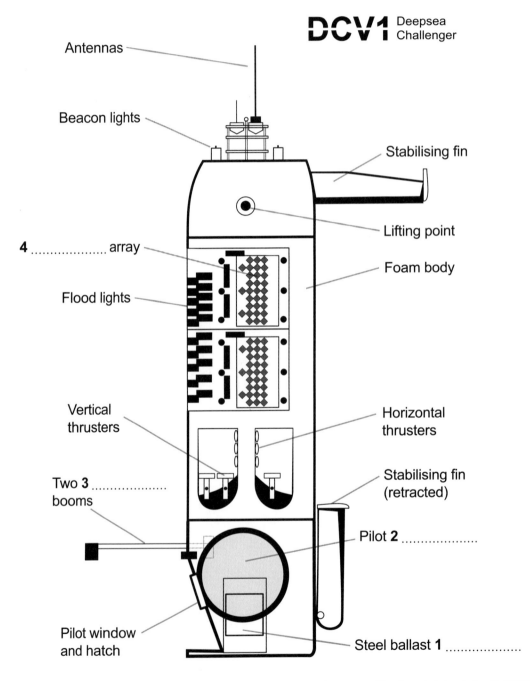

DCV1 Deepsea Challenger

Antennas

Beacon lights

Stabilising fin

Lifting point

4 .... array

Foam body

Flood lights

Vertical thrusters

Horizontal thrusters

Two **3** .... booms

Stabilising fin (retracted)

Pilot **2** ....

Pilot window and hatch

Steel ballast **1** ....

(By Zuckerberg - Own work, CC BY-SA 3.0, https://commons.wikimedia.org/w/index.php?curid=18867589)

Answer Key | 答案

Pre-Lesson Skills Practice

Skill 1 Understanding basic shapes

1 A	**6** I	**11** E	**16** J
2 G	**7** F	**12** A	**17** I
3 D	**8** J	**13** G	**18** H
4 H	**9** E	**14** D	**19** F
5 B	**10** C	**15** C	**20** B

Skill 2 Understanding map vocabulary

1 a bookstore, a department store, a gift shop, etc.

2 It's a short walk from the entrance, located in the middle of the shopping area.

3 department store

4 gift shop

5 A

6 D

7 department store

8 It's located outside the entrance to the shopping area, next to the department store.

9 It's right/just outside the gift shop. // It's to your right as you exit the gift shop.

....

For questions 10-17 below, phrases that are grammatically correct but not commonly used (as they describe very specific or unusual situations) are marked in the brackets.

10 F, H, J, V [C, D]

   C could mean that the office is directly above or below the men's restroom on the floor above or below it. This would not be a common way of describing the office's location, though.

11 G, H, J, V [T]

12 A, P, W [S]

13 B, E, I

14 F, H, J, K, R, V [B, C, Q]

15 O

16 M, N

17 D, F, G, H, J, K, Q, T, V [C]

Listening Strategies ⓭ Map or Plan Labelling

13.1

❶ Yes. They represent two types of walkways. The grey walkway symbolises a paved path, e.g. a sidewalk. The walkway with the dotted border symbolises a walking trail, e.g. a natural path that is not paved.

❷ the entrance, Meeting Ground 1 and Meeting Ground 2, the lifeguard stand, the lake, the horse paddock, woodworking shop, toilets, girls' cabin and boys' cabin. There is also a flag located near the paved path, which may or may not be mentioned in the recording.

❸ Some possible answers:

- **A** is just to the left of the entrance, and **I** is just to the right of the entrance. **A** and **I** are opposite each other.
- **B** is located at the fork in the walking trail.
- **B** and **C** are near each other, on opposite sides of the walking trail.
- The horse paddock is next to **C**.
- **D** is just beyond **C**.
- **E** is the furthest away from the entrance.
- **E** is located at the fork in the paved path.
- **F** is across the grass.
- **F** is near / close to **J**.
- **J** is behind **G**.
- **H** is next to / beside **G** and near / close to **J**.
- The woodworking shop is between **I** and **H**.

13.2

1	E		3	J		5	D
2	G		4	B			

Listening Strategies ⓮ Diagram Labelling

14.1

You should read instructions, quickly identify where each question is, and predict the type of word needed for each gap.

14.2

1	life		3	energy		5	Midnight
2	Lung // Lungs'		4	10,153		6	60,412

Task Practice

PART 1

1 Broad Street   **2** hostel   **3** convenience store   **4** French café

PART 4

1 weights   **2** sphere   **3** utility   **4** Battery

Listening Scripts

音檔逐字稿

Lesson 1

Pre-Lesson Skills Practice

Skill 1 **Writing letters or numbers** ◀)) MP3 02

Example: W-H-I-T-E-H-A-double L

1 T-A-Y-L-O-R
2 30
3 I-M-O-G-E-N
4 A-X-T-O-N
5 674 028 double-4 62

Skill 2 **Predicting** ◀)) MP3 03

Example: How much is a one-way ticket?

1 What's the fee for one-hour parking?
2 What did you do in France last year?
3 How many days did you stay in France?
4 Could you describe your teacher's appearance?
5 What do you do in your English class?
6 When is it coldest in your city?
7 Could I get your age?
8 What is the first thing you do every morning?
9 What university are you going to attend?
10 Nice to meet you. Could I get your name?

Skill 3 **Identifying parts of speech** ◀)) MP3 04

Example: Wash. I wash my hands often. Wash.

1 Remove. Please remove your shoes. Remove.
2 Polite. Your son is very polite. Polite.
3 Red. I prefer red apples. Red.
4 In the kitchen. You cook in the kitchen. In the kitchen.
5 Atmosphere. The house has a peaceful atmosphere. Atmosphere.

Skill 4 **Spelling common words**   🔊 MP3 05

Example: Rose. My name is Rose, just like the flower. Rose.

1   Brown. She has brown hair. Brown.
2   Modern. It's a very modern city. Modern.
3   Ceremony. The wedding ceremony was beautiful. Ceremony.
4   Children. The children are asleep. Children.
5   Furniture. The furniture in the house is old and shabby. Furniture.
6   Wednesday. Today is Wednesday. Wednesday.
7   Public. Public transportation in my city is excellent. Public.
8   February. It's quite cold in my city in February. February.
9   Eastern. Shanghai is on the eastern coast of China. Eastern.
10 Award. She won an award for having perfect attendance in school. Award.

Listening Strategies ❶ Form Completion

1.2   🔊 MP3 06

You will hear a caller asking for information about volunteering at an animal shelter. Listen and answer questions 1 to 7.

Beth:	Second Chance Animal Shelter. This is Beth speaking. How may I help you?
Tim:	Hi, uh, I'm just calling to enquire about volunteering opportunities.
Beth:	Splendid! We can always use more help around here. We're very short on volunteers at the moment.
Tim:	That's what a friend told me. Ur, I'm an exchange student, though, from Australia, and I was just wondering if I'm still allowed to volunteer if I'm from overseas.
Beth:	Oh, definitely! We do have a special form for non-local volunteers. It's not too different from the usual form, but it's not on the website yet. Let me see if I can just find it... Ah yes. Here it is. I can just take down your information now and fill it out for you. It should only take a few minutes.
Tim:	I do appreciate that.
Beth:	Not a problem. Let's see. Could I have your name?

Tim:	It's Tim Beasley. That's B-E-A-S-L-E-Y.	Q1
Beth:	Got it. And a number to reach you at, Tim?	
Tim:	My mobile is 913 6726.	Q2
Beth:	916 27...	
Tim:	No, no. It's 91 *three*... 67... 26.	
Beth:	Sorry. There. Got it. And could I have your address? Ur, your current address here in England?	
Tim:	I live at 40 Tattersall Road.	Q3
Beth:	Could you spell that?	
Tim:	It's T-A-double T-E-R-S-A-double L.	
Beth:	And how old are you, Tim?	
Tim:	I'm 19.	
Beth:	Okay. Tim, have you ever volunteered anywhere before?	
Tim:	Oh, yes. For starts, I work at the local soup kitchen with my parents every Christmas Eve.	Q4
Beth:	That's lovely. And what do you do when you volunteer there?	
Tim:	We help make the Christmas dinner, and then we wash up all the pots and dishes afterwards. We started doing that when I was ten, and it just kind of became a tradition in my family.	
Beth:	A wonderful tradition. Anything else?	
Tim:	I was also part of a clean-up crew as extra credit for an Environmental Science class I was in. That was... last February, I believe. We picked up litter on the beach. There was an awful lot of it. You wouldn't believe how dirty people can be.	Q5 Q6
Beth:	Oh, I'd believe it. Now, Tim. One more question. Are you fine with both dogs and cats?	
Tim:	Well... I'm a little uncomfortable around cats, to be honest. I had a bad experience with one as a child, and uh...	
Beth:	Say no more. We won't make you work with any animals that aren't a good fit for you. I'll put down that you prefer dogs only.	Q7

Listening Strategies ❷ Table Completion

2.2   🔊 MP3 07

You will hear the rest of the conversation about volunteering at an animal shelter. Listen and answer questions 8 to 10.

Beth:	Right. Now Tim, this next part is quite important. Do you have a pen and paper to write this down?
Tim:	Oh, let me see. ... Ah, here we are. Ready.
Beth:	Right. All volunteers, no matter which animals they're working with, must attend a compulsory General Orientation where we will briefly go over the shelter's rules in addition to giving you a guided tour of the establishment.

Q8

Tim:	All right... Got it. What day is that?
Beth:	That will take place at the end of the month, on the 31st and it's from 10 to 10:30 AM.
Tim:	Great. And will I learn my volunteer duties during the orientation?
Beth:	Oh, no, there wouldn't be enough time for that. No, we have separate classes to teach you how to care for each animal. Yes, the Cat Class will be held on July 31. It starts at noon, and it's thirty minutes long.
Tim:	Ur... Do I have to attend that one?
Beth:	What? ... Oh! No, no, of course not! I'm sorry. I forgot you're only working with dogs. No, your class will be on August 8, starting at half-ten and going until 12. It's a bit longer than the Cat Class because there's more information to go over, like walking the dogs, and washing them, and handling the larger breeds.

Q9

Q10

Task Practice

PART 1   🔊 MP3 08

You will hear a conversation between a receptionist at the enquiries desk of a private events hall and a woman who wants to book a room. Before you listen, you have some time to look at questions 1 to 5.
[30 seconds]
Now listen and answer questions 1 to 5.

Listening Scripts

Receptionist:	Hello, Richmond Freemason's Hall. How may I help you?	
Woman:	Oh, hello. I'm calling to enquire about hiring a room for an event on the evening of July 9th.	
Receptionist:	Let me just take a look at our calendar here. ... Ah, you're in luck. All of our venues are fully available on that evening.	
Woman:	Oh, that's a relief.	
Receptionist:	Could I just get your name first?	
Woman:	Yes, it's Mary Swaine. That's S-W-A-I-N-E.	Q1
Receptionist:	Okay. And a phone number?	
Woman:	My cell is 624 875 double 6 37.	Q2
Receptionist:	624...879...	
Woman:	No, not nine. It's 87 *five*.	
Receptionist:	Sorry. You said 875 double 6 37.	
Woman:	That's right.	
Receptionist:	Great. So Ms. Swaine, what kind of event are you hosting? A wedding, a work event...?	
Woman:	Yes, this is for a work event. An award ceremony, to be specific.	Q3
Receptionist:	Ah, well, in that case, I can recommend that you book our Theatre. It's ideal for award ceremonies.	
Woman:	The Theatre. Hmm. I'm just wondering if that's going to be large enough.	
Receptionist:	How many guests are you expecting?	
Woman:	We've already had RSVPs for 120, but the event is still three months away. It's likely we'll have at least... oh, I'd say at least 160 and at most 200 guests.	Q4
Receptionist:	Right... And what kind of refreshment is your company planning to provide?	
Woman:	We're going to do a full dinner, and there will be an open bar as well.	Q5

Before you hear the rest of the conversation, you have some time to look at questions 6 to 10.
[30 seconds]
Now listen and answer questions 6 to 10.

Receptionist:	Right. We actually have several options you could go with. All of them include access to the kitchen, so your staff would be able to prepare dinner for the guests beforehand. It's a spacious kitchen, too, so nobody will be bumping into each other and getting in anyone's way.
Woman:	That's great.
Receptionist:	Let me just go over some of the details with you, and you can decide what's right for you. Let me know anytime if you have a question.
Woman:	Okay.
Receptionist:	All right, I'd say a very suitable venue for you is our Main Dining Room. It's a conference setting with group tables set up in such a way that everyone is able to see the stage.
Woman:	Oh, it actually has a stage?
Receptionist:	Yes, though not one like you would have in the Theatre, which I'll get to next. No, this stage is a medium-sized platform with a lecture podium and a microphone.
Woman:	Ah, right. I see.
Receptionist:	The hall has had this particular stage since 1925, as a matter of fact. That brings me to my second point. The furniture in the Main Dining Room is incredible. It's all antique. The chairs were obtained during the second World War, and the tables date back to 1919.
Woman:	Goodness!
Receptionist:	Yes, it's quite impressive. Anyway, the Main Dining Room can hold up to 250 guests, and the cost for the venue is $500. That doesn't count the deposit, which is a flat rate of $250 for all the venues.
Woman:	And what's the next choice?
Receptionist:	The next choice is my personal favourite, the Theatre. It's quite famous locally because its atmosphere is so unique. It features a balcony, old hand-painted sets, and seating for up to 350. That one runs $600 per night.
Woman:	But the dinner, though... Where would we eat?
Receptionist:	Oh, right. You'd have to set it up on a long table in the outer hall and have guests eat buffet-style.
Woman:	Hmm. That doesn't sound ideal.

Q6

Q7

Q8

Receptionist:	No, I suppose not. There is one more option, and this has been quite popular lately with conferences and ceremonies about the size of yours. You could book our East Wing. That consists of what we call the Noble Room and Maple Hall.	Q9
Woman:	So the East Wing is two rooms, in fact?	
Receptionist:	It is, but the wall separating the two is removable so that it becomes one large space. With tables and chairs brought in, it can accommodate 200, and the $400 cost is quite a fair fee.	Q10
Woman:	Well, this is a lot to think about. I'm really torn between the Dining Room and the East Wing. Let me just talk to my colleague, and I'll call you later to let you know.	

Lesson 2

Pre-Lesson Skills Practice

Skill 2 Recognising general paraphrasing   🔊 MP3 10

Example: I'm thinking about applying to two jobs, but I haven't done it yet.

1   I still have to buy my textbooks.
2   How soon can I enrol?
3   If you're a new student here, you qualify for these benefits.
4   We've already decided where the swimming pool will be built.
5   I can only write the essay after I've done the title page.
6   Our bank has offices only in China and all across Europe.
7   He told me how to get to the station.
8   She's the only professor who won't give assignments for extra credit.
9   Sometimes I go to the library at night to study.
10   Nearly every client can get their fee reduced.

Listening Strategies ❸
Multiple Choice with a Single Answer

3.2   🔊 MP3 11

You will hear a conversation between an enrolment agent at a community college and a man interested in signing up for a class. Listen and answer questions 1 to 5.

Agent:	Hello. How can I help you?
Man:	I'm interested in joining one of your evening classes for adult learners. I've just retired, so I find myself with a lot of free time on my hands and no idea how to use it. I don't want to be idle.
Agent:	Well, you've come to the right place. Just have a seat here, ur...
Man:	John's the name.
Agent:	John... Now. What kind of class are you interested in?
Man:	I'm not sure, to be honest.

Agent:	Let me just show you our programme of night classes. You see our community classes are held on Mondays and Tuesdays.	
Man:	What time do they begin?	
Agent:	It varies. Start times are anywhere from a quarter to seven at the earliest to half eight at the latest, and you'd be done anywhere from 8:15 to 10 o'clock.	Q1
Man:	I see. Well, I don't want to get home too late.	
Agent:	So you'd prefer one of the earlier courses. Right. And do you have any preference for Monday or Tuesday?	
Man:	Either is fine.	
Agent:	That's good. That gives you more options. As you can see here in our programme, both nights provide a variety of classes. We've got language classes, fitness classes, cooking, technology, and a number of arts and crafts.	
Man:	Hmm. I know I should take a language class at some point, maybe brush up on my French. For now, though, I think I want something more hands-on. That isn't to say that learning a language isn't useful—it certainly is—but I want to *make* things.	Q2
Agent:	I see. The cookery class on Mondays is very popular.	
Man:	Hmm. I can already cook, though.	
Agent:	How about web design? The instructor for that is very popular. She designed our college website, in fact.	
Man:	Web design... It's not quite what I'm looking for, myself, but I have a friend who might be interested in it. I have no doubt the instructor is good. I visited your website before and found it to be quite user-friendly. That's saying a lot for a technophobe like myself. I'm a person who usually spends at least fifteen minutes trying to understand what all the links and buttons are for.	Q3
Agent:	You should certainly tell your friend about the course. As for you... let's see... Ah. Yes. I think this is something you might enjoy. 'Woodworking for Beginners.' It's taught by a highly skilled artist who's been working with wood for over thirty years and teaching for around, ur, fifteen, I believe. He's only been at our college for the last three years, but his classes are so effective that they fill up very quickly every semester.	Q4

Man:	Hmm. That does sound like what I'm looking for. What are the details?
Agent:	It's on Mondays at 7 to 9 PM. Ur, wait, no. That was last semester's time slot. The instructor had to change the start time to accommodate his schedule. Let me see... it's 7:30 to 9:30 PM now. Is that all right? **Q5**
Man:	It should be fine.

3.4   ◀)) MP3 12

You will hear a man giving a talk to a group of parents at a school. Listen and answer questions 1 to 4.

Good afternoon, everyone. Some of you may know me already, but for those of you who are new here, I am Sam Reese, president of the Parent-Teacher Association here at Carford Academy. We've called this meeting to inform you all about the changes that will be made to our campus over the coming summer.

So, as you are already aware, here at Carford we pride ourselves on our cutting-edge curriculum that prepares pupils for the modern world beyond the classroom. But in contrast with our state-of-the-art educational philosophy and goals, a number of our   **Q1** school facilities, although clean and well-kept, have simply fallen behind the times and are not suited to the demands of today. This is especially true concerning the library and classrooms, though the upgrades are not going to be limited to these areas.

You see, while academic quality has always been the mainstay of our school, we cannot ignore health, fitness, and the teamwork skills and confidence that come from doing sport. It is for this reason that the gymnasium—and that includes the tennis   **Q2** courts, swimming pool, and changing rooms—are being fully renovated. In fact, the progress that we have made on the gymnasium so far is able to be seen from the main road outside the school's front gates. You no doubt noticed the construction as you arrived this morning. We do hope that you will please excuse our dust.

There are bigger changes to come, though, for a reason that we are all particularly pleased with. Our excellent reputation precedes us, it would appear, and our student numbers have grown by 5% since we first opened our doors. This affects student housing, as you may imagine. Most dormitory rooms currently accommodate three or four students, but even with everybody following the rules—keeping noise levels down, picking up after themselves, following curfews, and so on—four per room can be a bit uncomfortable. We want half that number of students in each room if possible, with three only at the upper limit, and that, of course, means that more housing is needed. You can expect to see a new student hall behind the English Building by next spring.

Q3

Another area of campus that will see developments is the garden behind Johnson Hall. Many of you already know the garden. It's a focal point when family and the public visit, and we want it to look its best for everyone. You may recall that last spring saw a considerable improvement in the garden's seating options, as we added more variety of comfortable surfaces for all ages and physical conditions. We've decided to further beautify the garden, specifically the area just beyond the oak trees, by commissioning a local artist to install a sculpture there.

Q4

Now, as to the new... (fade out)

Task Practice

PART 1　🔊 MP3 13

You will hear a caller asking for information about an Arts Education Conference. Before you listen, you have some time to look at questions 1 to 6.
[30 seconds]
Now listen and answer questions 1 to 6.

Gary:	Good morning. This is the Civic Conference Hall office. Gary speaking.
Sue:	Oh, hello. I'm in town for a few days and heard that there's an Arts Education Conference being held in your hall this week.
Gary:	That's right. It runs from Friday evening to late afternoon on Sunday. There's a registration fee to get in, and that includes access to all the lectures and discussion panels.
Sue:	Great. Well, Friday evening and Saturday morning I'm handling family business, but I'd like to see what's on at the conference for the rest of Saturday. I'm unfortunately leaving on Sunday afternoon and probably will be too busy to stop by the conference that morning.
Gary:	OK. Ur, are you a teacher yourself?

Q1

Sue:	Yes. I teach art to 12- and 13-year-olds.
Gary:	Right. My first recommendation is an evening lecture by a well-known sculptor and art teacher. It's about 3D painted art using unwanted objects.
Sue:	You mean... using junk?
Gary:	Yes.
Sue:	That sounds interesting. What time does it start?
Gary:	That one begins after the 30-minute break that goes from 2:45 to 3:15 PM. Let me just see... Yes. The lecture runs from 3:30 to 4:30. **Q2** There's a short question and answer session afterwards, but the convention hall closes at 5.
Sue:	I see.
Gary:	There are also a number of published scholars presenting their academic papers on art education. There's a huge range of topics. **Q3** Let's see. On Saturday, there are one or two in the morning, a couple around noon, and the majority are in the afternoon.
Sue:	That sounds perfect.
Gary:	You'll also be able to see a few exhibitions of exceptional artwork made by professional local artists. They have paintings on display in the Red Room and ceramics in the Green Room. There's also **Q4** a student art exhibition in the Yellow Room, with all mediums on display.
Sue:	I'll have to check those out.
Gary:	Something else you might be interested in is a performance by the local school's youth orchestra. They came first in the regional contest **Q5** in May this year—it was the very first time that a youth orchestra from our city has won. It's a great honour. Next year they'll be representing the region in the national competition.
Sue:	That's fantastic. I really would like to hear them.
Gary:	You're in luck, because they're only playing at the convention on Saturday. Now let me see. They're doing three performances. The one at 10 AM is in the atrium. At noon they're playing on the lawn, **Q6** and a couple of hours after that is the final concert, which is in the theatre.
Sue:	That will be perfect. Well, you've been such a help... (fade out)

PART 2　🔊) MP3 14

You will hear a woman talking to a group of new library volunteers. Before you listen, you have some time to look at questions 1 to 6.
[30 seconds]
Now listen and answer questions 1 to 6.

Good afternoon. My name is Shelly Wilson, and I will be giving you a short but hopefully informative introduction about volunteering here.

First off, though, thank you for choosing to spend your free time helping us out. As a library volunteer, you will be providing invaluable support for professionally trained librarians and staff throughout the system—a system that cannot function without people like you. In return, the benefits you gain from volunteering are immense. You will learn new skills, gain work experience, and even make important networking contacts. These are all important, aren't they? To me, though, seeing so many new faces every day is what makes volunteering most worthwhile, especially in this digital age when many of us are so isolated from others.

Q1

I'll start with some guidelines about how to interact with library users... ur... since they are the ones we are all here for. So... first of all, what should you do if a library user approaches you with a question, request, or even a complaint? Well, unless it's something as simple as 'Where's the restroom,' we ask that you direct all users to a paid library staff member without exception. If a library member receives false information or is unhappy with some aspect of our service, we'd want the responsible party to be a paid employee rather than a volunteer. It dramatically simplifies the handling of issues and makes your volunteer experience more enjoyable.

Q2

Now, what do you do whenever you arrive for your assigned shift? The first order of business is to sign in. Please don't forget to do this, as keeping tabs on volunteer hours is important for the library statistics. If you realise half-way into your shift that you forgot to sign in, just drop what you're doing and do it right away. You can then come find me in my office on the second floor, and I will initial it for you. Hopefully, forgetting to sign in won't be too much of an issue, as the sign-in sheet can be found at the reception desk just opposite the main entrance.

Q3

Immediately after signing in, you will make your way to the back of the library. There, you will find the locker room, where you will store any personal possessions—mobile phone, keys, and so forth, in your own locker. Each of you will report to a designated staff person today who will issue you a locker and a volunteer badge for identification. After this little meeting is complete, you can find your name and your designated staff person on the list next to the entrance to the Children's Section. Your designated staff person will train you for all tasks you will perform, and they will also be the person who handles any enquiries you might have during your volunteer shift. Keep in mind that *they* are prepared to help you, whereas someone else, ur... the circulation supervisor, for instance—may have no idea what you're supposed to be doing.

Q4

I've one more thing to talk about, and that is parking. Be aware that the staff parking lot is only available to paid staff. Parking for volunteers is in the public parking lot. You are, however, invited to enjoy your breaks together with staff in the lounge at the back of the reference centre. You may store your own cup in the cupboard if you wish. Just make sure that you clean up after yourself. Ur, that advice goes for everyone, of course, volunteer or paid staff member.

Q5

Lesson 3

Pre-Lesson Skills Practice

Skill 1 Spelling academic words   ◀)) MP3 16

1   References. It's important to make a list of all your references when writing a research paper. References.
2   Attendance. I had perfect attendance in all my classes until I got the flu. Attendance.
3   Knowledge. To further your knowledge of the first World War, I suggest reading the class notes. Knowledge.
4   Statistics. Statistics indicate that childhood obesity is more common among certain populations. Statistics.
5   Architecture. Architecture majors study both art and science subjects. Architecture.
6   Experimental. Experimental physics involves unique scientific and technological challenges. Experimental.
7   Assessment. The final presentation is part of my assessment for the course, so I have to do a good job. Assessment.
8   Management. Time management is important when you are involved in a group project. Management.
9   Psychology. Psychology is the study of the mind and behaviour. Psychology.
10 Faculty. Dr. Evans has been a member of this university's faculty for twenty years. Faculty.

Skill 2 Recognising academic paraphrasing   ◀)) MP3 17

Example: When you've finished writing an essay, the most important thing to do afterward is to look over your work, checking it for mistakes.

1   I expected the lecture to be dull, but I was proven wrong.
2   A: What did Professor Higgins say about collecting data for our research project?
    B: She said that we could include a questionnaire in addition to reviewing the literature.
3   After finding a high concentration of chemical toxins in the river, we deduced that the fish died because of water pollution.
4   This study is very clear and thorough in its explanation of each component of the research, and the researchers especially excel at clarifying the sample and data collection.
5   The course on Italian cinema will continue next term, but the one on Scandinavian literature that's currently available will be replaced by more specialised courses.

Listening Strategies ❹ Classifying

4.2　　🔊 MP3 18

You will hear a conversation between a professor and two students about textbooks. Listen and answer questions 1 to 5.

Professor:	Ah, Greg and Lisa, come in and have a seat. I just want to discuss the feedback about the textbooks we used in class. I assume you've got the results ready from the student survey you carried out?
Lisa:	We do, professor.
Professor:	Great.
Greg:	Shall we give you a copy of the data, sir, or...?
Professor:	No, no. For now you can just tell me the main points, though I would like to see the raw data later. I suppose my biggest concern for now is whether there was a major issue with any of the books. I know from experience that other texts by Millican have sparked some controversy in class. Students can find him quite tedious.
Greg:	Not this time, sir. As a matter of fact, the survey shows that our class's edition of the Millican book is far less dry than many other legal texts. It provides a lot of case studies to keep you engaged and learning.
Lisa:	Exactly. We all thought we'd be quite bored reading it—it *is* a law text, after all—but the author provides many exercises to chat about in class, and several students even wrote on their feedback that it actually makes for an interesting read.
Professor:	Hmm. I would have expected them to say that about the Conway text.
Greg:	Well, Conway's book was also certainly enjoyable, but that was no surprise. After reading a few chapters, I immediately started coming up with different ideas for start-up businesses. The author is really good at inspiring creativity, and a good many other students said so in their surveys as well.
Lisa:	Yeah, Conway is a great, easy read without a doubt. The class really liked how the information is presented in a casual tone instead of the traditional, uptight and formal feel you usually get in a text. I suppose that's necessary when you're writing about a topic people normally consider dry.

Q1

Professor:	It's not necessary, I'm afraid, but it's certainly helpful.	
Lisa:	I noticed that Travers and Polski also write with a sense of humor to try to maintain your attention on what could easily be a very dry subject. It's not easy to inspire your readers to get a laugh out of Business Statistics.	Q2
Professor:	Yes, Travers and Polski are quite famed for their use of wit.	
Greg:	You know, the only problem I have with Conway is that there are tons of inserts in the chapters. 'How to be green.' 'How this person achieved their dreams.' 'This company is awesome,' and so forth. It's a bit too much, and it tends to be pretty distracting when every other page has the chapter interrupted by another 'pop-up' type message.	Q3
Lisa:	I agree. It really does stand out as a disadvantage when you compare it to Travers and Polski's format. Theirs is clear and does a really good job dividing the information into different sections and categories, for instance, colour-coded notations for the different concepts: red for vocab or green for headers or subheaders. It makes it easier to comprehend the material and to section it off.	Q4
Professor:	Yes, Conway certainly has something to learn from Travers and Polski about formatting, though I suppose that's more an issue to take up with the publishers than the writers. Were there any comments about the structure of the Millican book?	
Greg:	Not really. It's pretty standard as far as Business Law texts go.	
Lisa:	It is a bit long, though, isn't it? I mean, at almost a thousand pages, it's one of the densest textbooks I've ever had. But I suppose the length is reasonable, considering the seriousness of Millican's subject. I mean, I don't feel like it could have been shorter.	
Greg:	I know what you mean. With Travers and Polski, on the other hand, we all tended to get a bit tired of the long exercises at the end of each chapter. Some of the questions seemed like repeats of others and could probably have been cut.	Q5
Professor:	Well, you two, this has been quite helpful. I do appreciate the feedback. I'll let you go now, as... (fade out)	

Listening Strategies ❺ Sentence Completion

5.2   ◀)) MP3 19

You will hear a conversation between a tutor and a student about a research project. Listen and answer questions 1 to 5.

Tutor:	Ah, come in, Jack.
Jack:	Thank you.
Tutor:	Now, you wanted to discuss your research topic with me, is that correct?
Jack:	That's right.
Tutor:	And what topic have you decided on?
Jack:	Well, I'm really interested in doing something about the effects of technology on peoples' minds.
Tutor:	That's quite relevant in today's world.
Jack:	I thought so, too. It's just... well...
Tutor:	Let me guess your problem: There are *too many* useful resources.
Jack:	Exactly! Yesterday I found myself in the library staring at a full section of books and journals that all seem suitable as references for my topic. There's *so* much information out there. It's overwhelming! I don't even know where to start.
Tutor:	Well, you've encountered a very common problem, Jack—your topic is too broad. Lucky for you, though, you discovered this before you got too deep into the research and wasted a lot of time. Once you narrow the scope of your topic, the breadth of resources will become much more manageable.
Jack:	That's good. But how do I narrow down my topic?
Tutor:	Well, there are a few methods. They're all basically designed to help you take something general and make it more specific. I think the best way is to apply question words to what you've already got.
Jack:	Question words. You mean...
Tutor:	Who, what, where, when, why, and so on.
Jack:	Ah, I see. Could you give me an example of how that would work?

Q1

Q2

Tutor:	Right, you've got 'effect of technology.' Well, what kind of technology? There's an infinite number of possibilities, isn't there?	
Jack:	Oh, I see. Like, 'the effect of computers' or 'the effect of mobile phones.'	
Tutor:	That's it.	
Jack:	Yeah, there were loads of resources about mobile phones. I actually started taking notes from some of the articles I found because they seemed like really good leads. Like, several studies have proven that teens who spend too much time with their cell phones are more prone to stress and fatigue.	Q3
Tutor:	Now that sounds like a start. There's a good 'who' for your research question. Teens.	
Jack:	I see. Oh! Alternatively, I could look into the way all these electronic gadgets are affecting young children! When I was looking through the journals, I saw a statistic that really struck me as surprising. Children under 8 spend close to 4 hours per day using electronics for entertainment. That's 28 hours out of their whole week! Can you believe that?	Q4
Tutor:	There you go. 'The effect of electronics on the minds of children under 8.' But you still have 'effect on the mind.' The mind is vast. What aspect of the mind will you focus on if you go with the topic of children?	
Jack:	Hmm. Well, there were several articles saying that kids seem to be losing their ability to focus on one task or topic for an extended period of time. The thing is, it's always been normal for children to get bored more quickly than older students, but teachers are reporting that the attention span of their pupils has actually shrunk compared to the days when smartphones weren't so commonplace.	Q5
Tutor:	That would be quite a worthwhile research topic. Well, Jack, I think you've got it. You just have to pick one topic and stick with it. Now, if you've no other questions...?	
Jack:	Or I could do 'the effect of video games on the self-esteem of boys aged 8 to 14!' That would be really interesting because... (fade out)	

Task Practice

PART 3   🔊 MP3 20

You will hear two students discussing a research project on learning a second language. Before you listen, you have some time to look at questions 1 to 5.
[30 seconds]
Now listen and answer questions 1 to 5.

John:	Hey Elsa, have you got a minute? I was hoping to talk to you about the research presentation for Professor Bates' class.
Elsa:	Sure. How are you coming along on that, by the way? I'm still working through the literature review. It's interesting, but there's *so* much to look at. I've got loads of sources saved on my computer. I mean, I'm not complaining. It would be simply terrible to not be able to find anything.
John:	My feelings exactly. Anyhow, Professor Bates told me your topic is a bit similar to mine and that we ought to compare notes. You know, just to make sure we don't have too much overlap in our content.
Elsa:	Good idea. It would be awful to make the class watch two presentations that just repeat each other. *Some* repetition would be acceptable, but I can understand that Professor Bates wants most of our content to be different. So, what's your topic? **Q1**
John:	I'm doing mine on the best way to use subtitles when learning a new language.
Elsa:	Brilliant! Subtitles saved my life when I was studying French! It took me the longest time to be able to comprehend a complex sentence without being able to read it.
John:	And your topic is...?
Elsa:	'The use of electronic media in language learning.' Subtitles are mentioned a lot in the research, which makes sense considering how important visual information is to humans. **Q2**
John:	Very true. Well, here are the research articles I've used so far. Take a look.
Elsa:	Hmm. 'Huang and Eskey, 1999.' I've not read that one. What was their study on?

John:	They were trying to see if reading English-language subtitles during a TV programme affected how much new vocabulary students were able to learn from the show. That, and how much of the programme students were able to understand. They had two different groups of mid-level English learners watch a TV programme. One group watched with English subtitles and the other with no subtitles—just as regular TV, in other words.	
Elsa:	Oooh, I bet I can guess what the results were! The group who watched with the subtitles *did* understand more and learned more vocabulary. Right?	
John:	Right. Oh, and something very interesting they noted from their study was that how long students had been learning English and the age at which they began learning seemed to have no impact on their listening comprehension test.	
Elsa:	Wait. So, people who had been learning English for, say, ten years, did just about as well on the listening test as people who had been learning for only five?	
John:	Pretty much.	
Elsa:	That's surprising!	
John:	Isn't it? Huang and Eskey did mention, though, that the results might only be due to the small size of their experimental group. If they'd had a lot more participants in the study, the results could have been different. ... What about you? Have you found any particularly interesting sources?	Q3
Elsa:	There's one by... Wang, Chou, and Wang...	
John:	Oh, I have that one on my reading list but I haven't read it yet! What's it about?	
Elsa:	Well, you know there are different types of subtitles, right?	
John:	You mean different languages available, sure—	
Elsa:	No, not just different languages. With regular subtitles, you've got the option of just one language on the screen while you watch a programme, but there are also 'bimodal subtitles,' which are where you've got two languages subtitled on the screen, for instance, Chinese and English at the same time...	Q4
John:	Oh right! I've seen those before. Bimodal subtitles. I get it.	

Elsa:	Right. But there are also educational subtitles added to films by companies that produce foreign language learning DVDs. They're called 'real-time difficult word subtitles.' So whenever a foreign word perceived as 'difficult' is spoken on the programme, it will show up on the bottom of the screen under the other subtitles, with a definition of the difficult word in the first language. **Q5**
John:	So, the Wang study used these real-time difficult word subtitles?
Elsa:	Right, they had two groups of private high school students watch a Disney film. The two groups watched the movie with both Chinese and English subtitles, but the experimental group also got real-time difficult word subtitles. This group performed significantly better on the listening comprehension test.
John:	That's not surprising. Every study I've read so far had similar results.
Elsa:	You know, John, it's really too bad we can't team up for this presentation.
John:	I know. But Professor Bates said our next research project can be done with a group.
Elsa:	Great. Next time, then.

You will hear three students, John, Elsa, and Katya, discussing the distribution of work for their research project. Before you hear the conversation, you have some time to look at questions 6 to 10.
[20 seconds]
Now listen and answer questions 6 to 10.

John:	Well, now that the three of us are all here, I suppose the first order of business is figuring out who's going to do what.
Elsa:	Agreed. The sooner we do that, the sooner we can start.
Katya:	Would it be helpful if I type up notes for this meeting and email them to you guys later? I mean, I've got my computer open right now, so it's no trouble.
John:	Thanks, Katya! Very helpful.
Katya:	Sure. First, let me just write down the title of our study... 'Students' Response to Common Second Language Learning Activities.' Is that what we decided?
Elsa:	That sounds good.

Katya:	Great. Now. First things first. John, you volunteered to write the survey that asks students how they feel about different activities they do in their language classes. How are you coming with that?
John:	I've got it right here. I finished it this morning.
Elsa:	Oh, well done, John!
John:	Thanks, Elsa. I've emailed it to you both as well, so you can just look it over and make edits to the file itself.
Katya:	What about afterward, when the survey is ready to go out? We need to make sure we get enough responses for the results to be significant.
Elsa:	Oh, I do part-time work in the Language Centre. I could put a big stack of surveys on the study table with a box of lollipops, and offer one candy to anybody who completes a survey there and returns it to me directly. Sugar is a good motivator. **Q6**
John:	And my Spanish professor is always very helpful. I could email the survey to her, and she could send it to all the students in her classes.
Katya:	It sounds like we'll get plenty of feedback that way. Hold on. Let me just finish noting that down. 'John ... administer survey ... via ... email.'... Now, what about the research paper?
Elsa:	I think we should all write bits of it.
John:	Agreed.
Elsa:	I wouldn't mind writing the introduction with the background of the study and the limitations of the research and all that.
Katya:	Great. And I volunteer to type up the list of sources that we all use for the bibliography at the end. And since John created the survey and you two are going to administer it, I think it's only fair that I write the methods section as well. **Q7**
John:	I have no objections to that.
Katya:	Great. Now, when it comes to looking at the results of the surveys—
Elsa:	I think we should all do that together. All that counting can be tiring.
Katya:	Okay.
John:	Do you think we should also outline the discussion section together, too? You know, since we have to interpret the meaning of what we learned?

Elsa:	I do.
John:	And I could actually write the discussion section, if you two don't mind.
Katya:	Okay... 'John ... write discussion'. Ah, and I can write up the results section once we've all finished looking at the survey answers. ... Oh, no. **Q8**
Elsa:	What is it?
Katya:	Well, to present the results in the clearest way possible, some of the information needs to be given in charts and graphs.
Elsa:	So?
Katya:	I'm terrible at doing graphs! It takes me forever, and they never look nice at all. My word processing software is so outdated.
John:	You should really get your software updated, Katya. It's quite easy to do pictures and things if you've got the right tools.
Katya:	I know. I'm just a bit of a technophobe.
Elsa:	Well, *I'm* not. So don't worry, Katya, I've got the graphs covered. Just send me the information once you've completed writing it. **Q9**
Katya:	Thank you! ... One more thing, though. The review of the literature, which goes after the introduction.
John:	We can all contribute to that, can't we? We've done so many literature reviews on this topic in class so far.
Elsa:	I think she's talking about collecting the relevant articles and putting them all together, John.
John:	Ah.
Elsa:	I'd be glad to do that, but I don't know if time will allow, what with me doing the graphs and all that.
John:	Since I can only write my portion of the paper when the results are done, it wouldn't be too much trouble for me to do the literature review. **Q10**
Katya:	Brilliant. So, that's done! Of course, if any of this needs to be changed, we can just shoot each other an email. In the meantime... (fade out)

Lesson 4

Pre-Lesson Skills Practice

Skill 1 **Focused listening with paraphrasing**   ◀)) MP3 22

Example A: Another possible benefit of online social networking is that it may have a positive impact on self-esteem.

Example B: In 1975, the school board voted to expand the campus and add a number of new sports facilities, such as basketball courts, to the eastern side of the grounds.

1   Business schools typically try to differentiate themselves from their competition by specialising in a specific sector.
2   In the 17th century, the wool industry in England—a crucial part of their economy—was centred in the east and south of the country.
3   In the 19th and early part of the 20th century, there was a large demand for egret plumes as European and American milliners—commonly known as 'hat makers'—responded to the fashion demands of their customers.
4   Kenya's tourism industry faces several challenges, one of which is that a great number of its main tourist attractions are located in spots with unpaved roads, and this particularly limits access during the country's rainy season.

Skill 2 **Listening and reading at the same time**

◀)) MP3 23

Example: Another possible benefit of online social networking is that it may have a positive impact on self-esteem.

1   Business schools typically try to differentiate themselves from their competition by specialising in a specific sector.
2   Kenya's tourism industry faces several challenges, one of which is that a great number of its main tourist attractions are located in spots with unpaved roads, and this particularly limits access during the country's rainy season.

◀)) MP3 24

3   In the 17th century, the wool industry in England—a crucial part of their economy—was centred in the east and south of the country.

4   In the 19th and early part of the 20th century, there was a large demand for egret plumes as European and American milliners—commonly known as 'hat makers'—responded to the fashion demands of their customers.

Listening Strategies ➏ Notes Completion

6.2   🔊 MP3 25

You will hear a university lecturer giving a task about the history of shoes to a class of students. Now listen and answer questions 1 to 10.

It is my pleasure today to talk to you about one of the most long-lasting inventions that humankind has ever known—the shoe.

Far from the comfortable, often synthetic materials of today's footwear, a look back into early human history shows us that shoes normally consisted of natural resources that were largely unprocessed, or raw. For instance, the earliest known shoes are   **Q1** sandals dating back to approximately 7000 or 8000 B.C., these sandals were made from the bark of the sagebrush plant. In addition to this, pictures have been discovered in ancient Egyptian murals dating back to 4000 B.C., showing citizens wearing papyrus thong sandals, the ancestor of the modern-day flip-flop sandal. Ötzi the Iceman's shoes, dating to 3300 B.C., probably had insides made of grass. Outside, they featured bases made of bearskin, deerskin side panels, and a bark-string net that pulled tight   **Q2** around the foot. If you think they sound uncomfortable, you're not alone. However, these shoes were recently recreated by an historian and worn on a hiking trip in the Alps, where he discovered that they were especially effective at keeping the wearer's foot safe when walking through frozen water.

The Middle Ages and Early Modern period saw a significant increase in the complexity of shoe design as footwear evolved to look more similar to what we wear today. An excellent example was the espadrille, a common casual shoe in the Pyrenees during the Middle Ages. Many of you ladies in the class today probably own a pair of espadrilles yourselves! This is a sandal with soles made of jute, a rough, braided plant fiber. The shoe's upper portion is made of fabric, and the design often includes fabric laces that tie around the ankle, giving the shoe its unique appearance. But when   **Q3** it came to making more traditional-looking shoes in the medieval era, the turnshoe method of construction was usually used by shoemakers. This means that the shoe

was put together inside-out, and then was turned right-side-out once it was finished.   Q4
Although the turnshoe method had mostly disappeared by the 1500s, it is still used
today for some dance and specialty shoes.

In the 15th century, shoe complexity further increased along with height. In this era,
a shoe called a pattens became popular for both men and women in Europe. These
are commonly seen as the ancestor of the modern high-heeled shoe. Also during the
15th century, chopines were created in Turkey, and these were usually 7-8 inches high.
That's about 17 to 20 centimetres! These shoes, popular in Venice and throughout
Europe, revealed the wearer's wealth and social standing, making them a highly
notable status symbol. During the 16th century, members of royalty started wearing   Q5
high-heeled shoes to appear taller or larger than life, famous examples being Catherine
de Medici or Mary I of England. By 1580, even men wore high heeled shoes, and a
person with authority or wealth was often referred to as 'well-heeled.'   Q6

Besides the high heel, another feature of today's shoes that we take for granted has
been with us since at least the 1600s. I'm talking about the sole of the shoe, the bottom
section of your footwear. Everyone, take a look at the sole of your shoe. If you happen
to be wearing finer-quality dress shoes today, your sole is probably sewn on, which
is standard for this type of footwear now. Since the 17th century, most leather shoes   Q7
have used a sewn-on sole, and some of them also have a welt, a strip of leather which
runs along the perimeter of a shoe and attaches the upper to the outsole. Interestingly,
until around 1800, welted rand shoes were commonly made without any differentiation
between the left and right foot, so you could put your foot into either shoe and go on
your way. Breaking in a new pair of shoes like this was not easy, especially when there
were only two possible widths per size. If you needed a shoe that was wider than the   Q8
widest option in your size, you were out of luck. Only gradually did the modern foot-
specific shoe become standard.

Up until 1850, all shoes were made with practically the same hand tools that were used
in Egypt as early as the 14th century B.C. In the 33 centuries between the Ancient
Egyptians and the mid-19th century, shoemakers added only a few simple pieces of
equipment to the chisel-like knife and the scraper. Attempts had been made to develop
machinery for shoe production, but they had all been unsuccessful for various reasons.
Finally, in 1845 the first machine to find a permanent place in the shoe industry came
into use. Gilmore's rolling machine, used for hardening sole leather, could do in under
two minutes what formerly took a worker half an hour of pounding on lap-stone with a
hammer. This cut down on labour drastically. Then, on the 10th September 1846, Elias   Q9

Howe Jr. invented the lock-stitch sewing machine and took out his master patent number 4750 in the USA. Howe's invention was originally intended for domestic **Q10** use, but innovative shoemakers soon realised the machine could also make a huge difference to work done outside the home, and almost immediately applied the sewing machine to their own leather. The success of this major invention seems to have set up a chain reaction of research and development that has gone on ever since. Today, nearly all of the major operations in shoemaking are done by machine rather than by hand.

Task Practice

PART 4 🔊 MP3 26

You will hear a student giving a presentation about the use of feathers in human cultures. Before you listen, you have some time to look at questions 1 to 10.
[60 seconds]
Now listen and answer questions 1 to 10.

Today, I am going to talk about the ways that birds' feathers have been used by human societies worldwide.

Let's briefly consider the two main types of feathers: contour and down. Contour feathers are found on the outside of the bird, including on its wings and tail. These feathers provide the bird's colour and shape, and thus have been coveted by humans for centuries due to their perceived beauty. Down feathers are located at the base of the contour feathers. These feathers provide the insulation birds need to keep warm. While contour feathers are flat and sharp-tipped, down is fluffy. Down is also significantly softer than the contour feathers. **Q1**

Although nature gave feathers to the birds, humans have found numerous ways to put feathers to good use in our own lives for thousands of years. Pillows have been filled with feathers and down since around 400 C.E. And prior to the invention of steel pens in the mid-nineteenth century, the finest writing instruments, quills, were made from the **Q2** contour feathers of the goose. Feathers have also been used as toys for cats, props for magic, and even in cleaning equipment. But perhaps the most widespread use of feathers across time and culture has been for items considered sacred and for personal **Q3** decoration.

What do feathers symbolise to different societies? I could talk for hours about that, so I will simply say that feathers are often associated with spirituality in a number of cultures. In ancient Egypt, the ostrich feather was a symbol of truth. It was often seen in depictions of Ma'at, the goddess of truth and justice, who judged the souls of the dead. Indigenous peoples of the Amazon have been recorded as using feathers in religious ceremonies and ritual dances. During the dry season, certain members of the Tapirapé society wear feathered masks in ceremonies as they circle their village and sing songs. Yanomamö men of the Amazon wear feathered armbands high on their upper arms. This gives them the appearance of having wings, thus bringing them closer to bird spirits. As a final example, the Native American war bonnet was an impressive headdress made of feathers from a golden eagle's tail. This headdress symbolised honour, accomplishment, and bravery.

Q4

By the late nineteenth century, feathers had become a universal fashion necessity in Western culture, and the demand for them was endless. To supply feathers for such fashion items at this time, an estimated 5 million birds were killed each year. In 1886, Frank Chapman, a bird expert at the American Museum of Natural History, observed feathers—or sometimes even whole birds—on 542 out of 700 hats worn by ladies in New York City. For the next few decades, bird species were overhunted drastically in the United States, Burma, Malaya, Indonesia, China, Australia, New Zealand, and throughout Europe. As a result, some species were greatly threatened, with several even dying out completely. Perhaps the most famous examples of this phenomenon were the Great Egret and the Snowy Egret, which nearly suffered extinction due to a large demand for egret plumes as European and American milliners—commonly known as 'hat makers'—responded to the fashion demands of their female customers.

Q5

Q6

Bird protection laws were enacted in the early twentieth century when environmental concern emerged about the world's plummeting bird populations. Queen Alexandra of England showed support for the effort by disposing of all of her own hats with feathers on them in 1906. In 1918, the United States and Canada signed the *Federal Migratory Bird Treaty Act*, which limited a sportsman to shooting migratory birds no more than three and a half months a year. In 1937 a similar treaty was established between the United States and Mexico, and the *Endangered Species Act of 1973* contains important provisions for the protection of migratory birds as well. The next few decades marked the start of an era of environmental awareness, and many more efforts were made to replenish birds' dwindling numbers. By the early 2000s, most wild birds were protected. In the United States, for instance, it is now illegal to use feathers from songbirds (such as chickadees), marsh birds (such as egrets), and birds of prey (such as eagles) for

Q7

clothing and accessories.   Q8

While these laws undoubtedly aided in the reduction of the number of birds being killed for use in fashion, perhaps the biggest factor that helped save birds on the endangered species list was a change in fashion. In the eras when women wore large, feather-topped hats, their hair played an important role in anchoring these heavy accessories to their heads. However, young women in the 1920s cut their hair so short that it could not properly support such large hats. Feathers did reappear on hats in the 1930s, 1940s, and 1950s, but this headwear was generally much smaller than that of the previous decades, and the feathers were usually just an interesting accent of shape or colour instead of the foundation for the hat. By the late 1960s, very few women wore   Q9
hats on a regular basis, and the bare-headed trend has continued up to this day. That doesn't mean feathers are out of style, though. They are still popular decorations for clothing and accessories, but the birds they come from are not endangered species. Also, technology has allowed fake feathers and fur to look very realistic. That way,   Q10
we can have the uniqueness that feathers bring to a look, without harming any of our feathered friends.

Lesson 5

Pre-Lesson Skills Practice

Skill 1 **Focused listening for verb tenses**　🔊 MP3 28

Example : I used to buy a pastry for breakfast every morning.

1　It's been raining all day.
2　I went to the library this morning.
3　I've lived in this city since 1997.
4　I've been to Thailand.
5　I've been in Taipei for three years.
6　I'll clean my room.
7　There used to be a lovely garden behind the building.
8　He's just finished mopping the floor.
9　I would have met you at the bus station.
10　There haven't been so many visitors to the park in years.

Skill 2 **Spelling non-academic words**　🔊 MP3 29

1　February. I went to Thailand in February. February.
2　Manager. She is the manager of the restaurant. Manager.
3　Snake. Did you see that yellow snake in the garden? Snake.
4　Fund. The fund was established to help the poor. Fund.
5　Housekeeping. The housekeeping staff keeps the hotel neat and clean. Housekeeping.
6　Snack. Fruit is a healthy snack to eat between meals. Snack.
7　Accounting. The accounting department handles the money. Accounting.
8　August. I'm going to England next August. August.

Listening Strategies ❼ Short Answer

7.2　🔊 MP3 30

You will hear two people discussing a sports centre. Listen and answer questions 1 to 4.

Greg:	Hello?
Sara:	Hi, Greg. It's Sara. How are you doing? Are you enjoying your new job? You're working at the public sports centre, right?
Greg:	Yes. I started there when it re-opened back in August. I'm really enjoying it. I'm even looking to get my trainer certification starting in April, when the courses open.
Sara:	That's great. Good for you! David and I have actually been meaning to join the sports centre for a while. We've been so sedentary recently. We're both working from home, you know.
Greg:	Oh, you should join. The fee is quite reasonable, and it has so many more facilities than it used to. It's even got a café now, where you can get any kind of snack or meal—sandwiches, salads, smoothies, coffee. It's really comfortable, too. The café manager added a bookshelf with a variety of books and magazines on health-related topics. Some people come and work out at the gym and then spend their whole afternoon in the café reading lounge.
Sara:	Mmm. I wish I had that much free time to spend!
Greg:	Yes, you're probably busy lately with the children, right?
Sara:	Yes. Their summer holidays just started. We're considering taking them to France, to the beach, but they haven't learnt to swim yet, so we're not sure.
Greg:	Well, the sports centre has got swimming classes for young learners. They are taught by a very experienced athlete. It would be perfect for your kids.
Sara:	Mmm, that sounds good. I'll have to look into that. What about you? Do you still swim often?
Greg:	Once a week or so. I've recently been playing basketball a lot. I do that two or three times a week.
Sara:	Oh, that reminds me, Greg! David was wondering if there's a racquetball court at the new sports centre. He's only played three times at most since we started working from home. It's really sad. He used to play twice a week before work got so busy.
Greg:	Yes, we've got a few courts for racquetball. There are even two tennis courts outside.
Sara:	Well, it sounds lovely, Greg. We'll look into it.

Q1

Q2

Q3

Q4

Listening Scripts

Listening Strategies ❽ Matching from a List

8.2 🔊 MP3 31

You will hear a woman describing exhibits at a museum. Listen and answer questions 1 to 5.

Good morning, everyone, and welcome to the museum. We've got some great new exhibits and events running, and I'd just like to tell you a bit about them before you wander off to explore.

'Oh Captain, My Captain!' is an exhibition of objects taken from the living quarters of a 19th century sea captain. You'll be seeing these antiques in their natural setting, as experts have recreated the captain's cabin as accurately as possible in our new Starboard Hall. Just go out the front door here, walk along the marina, and you'll see the signs pointing the way.   Q1

Moving on, most of you have heard of Molly Gray, who is something of a local hero. In our '180 Days Alone' exhibit, you'll get a chance to explore the 11.2 metre yacht Molly sailed alone around the world for nearly six months in 1987. This exhibit has been wildly popular, and I'm sure you've seen it on TV or read about it in the papers.   Q2

Then there is 'Happy Ocean, Happy Earth,' which you'll find in the Media Wing of this building. This is a film project featuring interviews with top environmentalists, scientists and academics working to help protect our oceans' future. This one is recommended for anyone 12 and over, as younger museum-goers may find themselves a bit restless.   Q3

Something really popular for all ages, though, is 'Monsters of Yesteryears,' where you will see what sea creatures of the past looked like. There are some huge replicas in this exhibit, and really exciting multimedia games. How fast can your team put together a dinosaur using only its fossils?   Q4

Finally, it's my pleasure to introduce you to 'A Tradition Unbroken.' This national touring exhibition honours the long-standing art of shell necklace making among the Indigenous Peoples of Australia. On display, we have stunning shell necklaces created in the 1800s alongside necklaces from celebrated makers of today, plus necklaces from a new group of stringers who learnt the tradition at cultural workshops. You mustn't miss it!   Q5

Task Practice

PART 1   🔊 MP3 32

You will hear two colleagues, Tom and Jean, at a hotel discussing a party. Before you listen, you have some time to look at questions 1 to 5.

[20 seconds]

Now listen and answer questions 1 to 5.

Jean:	Hi Tom, thanks for coming. You know we've been asked to organise something for Mary's goodbye party?
Tom:	I do, yes. I was just thinking myself that it's time we started working out the details.
Jean:	Absolutely. We don't want to leave it too late and give ourselves double the work.
Tom:	Agreed. So, shall I take notes?
Jean:	That'd be great, thanks.
Tom:	Right, first thing is, when should we hold it?
Jean:	Well, she's leaving on the fifteenth of February. **Q1**
Tom:	Hmm. What about the thirteenth, then?
Jean:	That sounds about right. It's close enough to the day. And what about the venue? Here at the hotel, I suppose?
Tom:	That'd be best, I think. That's easiest for everyone. What room, though?
Jean:	Mary has always liked the Rose Room.
Tom:	The Rose Room is already booked for the thirteenth. I took the reservation just this morning.
Jean:	That's too bad. What about the Dining Hall? **Q2**
Tom:	I think it's available that night. Let me just check... Yes. The Dining Hall is free.
Jean:	Let's do it there, then.
Tom:	And then we ought to be thinking about the invitations. Mary's touched everyone's lives here. Who mustn't we forget about?
Jean:	The regional manager and her husband, for one.
Tom:	Right.

Jean:	The housekeeping staff.	Q3
Tom:	Right. And the Front Desk team. The kitchen staff as well.	Q4
Jean:	Yes. What about the gardener? He's quite new, isn't he, and doesn't know Mary particularly?	
Tom:	I'm sure he'd like to be included.	
Jean:	Yeah, you're right.	
Tom:	When should we get the invitations out by?	
Jean:	Not too early, but enough time.	
Tom:	How about the sixth of February?	Q5
Jean:	Mmm, make it the fourth. Give them a few extra days.	
Tom:	Right. February... 4th.	

Before you hear the rest of the conversation, you have some time to look at questions 6 to 10. [20 seconds]

Now listen and answer questions 6 to 10.

Jean:	Now, we just have to get her a present.	
Tom:	Would you mind collecting the money for that?	
Jean:	Not at all. We usually pass around an envelope in the break room, don't we?	Q6
Tom:	Yeah. That's the best place for it. Everyone's got their money ready.	
Jean:	Should we suggest an amount, or is that a bit pushy?	
Tom:	No, I think people appreciate it. We suggested five dollars last time for Mark.	
Jean:	There are a lot more people coming to this party, though.	
Tom:	True. Would two dollars be a good suggestion?	Q7
Jean:	I think that's more like it.	
Tom:	Have you thought about what we ought to get her?	
Jean:	A few of us have been talking about it. Something for her kitchen is the most popular idea. You know Mary adores anything related to cooking.	
Tom:	She mentioned to me recently that her ice cream maker broke last summer.	

Jean:	Did she? That would be perfect. I'll check the price on them.	
Tom:	As for decoration in the party room, let's not have anything that would take too long to clean up.	
Jean:	Right. No confetti.	
Tom:	Balloons?	
Jean:	A few would be nice. Not too many.	
Tom:	How about a big, colourful banner on the wall?	
Jean:	We could do that. What would it say?	
Tom:	Something like, 'Thank You for 25 Years.'	Q8
Jean:	Has Mary been here that long? Impressive.	
Tom:	I know. She was one of the first employees ever hired... Uh... Now we need to think a little more about the money. We talk to Accounting for the party fund, right?	Q9
Jean:	Yes. But how much does the party fund cover?	
Tom:	It covers a certain amount of food.	
Jean:	And drinks?	
Tom:	Yes.	
Jean:	Will it be enough for a group this large, though?	
Tom:	In the past, we've asked guests to bring some snacks. Let's do that as well this time. They don't need to bring drinks, though, because the party fund ought to cover that.	Q10
Jean:	What about music?	
Tom:	We can use the sound system in the Dining Hall.	
Jean:	Lovely! So, is that all for now?	
Tom:	I think so.	
Jean:	Great. Thanks ever so much, Tom. I'll see about... (fade out)	

PART 2   ◄)) MP3 33

You will hear a man talking to a group of new employees at a summer youth camp. Before you listen, you have some time to look at questions 1 to 5.

[20 seconds]

Now listen and answer questions 1 to 5.

Good morning, everyone. Before we begin our tour of the camp, I just have a few things to say to everybody.

First off, I would like to introduce everyone to Bruce, here. Bruce has been our full-time camp groundskeeper for thirteen years. He's the reason our grass is always mown and our hiking trails are clear. He's also the person who keeps our equipment in good repair. Group A—that's our custodial crew—you will be working under Bruce and will help him keep the campgrounds clean and tidy. Any questions or issues you have, take them to him.

Q1

Next, our lifeguards are also key players on our team. Because of them, everyone can feel safe when they're out having a dip in the lake. Group B, that's you, lifeguards, please bring your CPR and First-Aid certificates to the Nurse's Station when this meeting is over so we can have them on file.

Q2

Group C are our esteemed camp counselors. They are with our campers from morning to night, throughout every activity and game that we offer. Out of all of us, they spend the most time with the kids, so be sure to thank them for their efforts.

Q3

Another work group that deserves appreciation is the kitchen crew—Group D. They keep us all fed and make sure the dining hall is clean. It takes a big crew to do all this, and there was a shortage this year of kitchen crew, so I want to thank those of you from other work groups who have volunteered to cover a few kitchen shifts.

Q4

Last but not least, Work Group E, our nurses, see to the health and wellbeing of everyone at camp. The Nurse's Station can be found in the centre of our campgrounds, but you can easily identify the nurses from the distinctive white vests they wear over their T-shirts.

Q5

Now, let's all go over... (fade out)

Lesson 6

Pre-Lesson Skills Practice

Skill 1 Following a list 🔊 MP3 35

Table	Between	Specialist	Atmosphere
Published	Sacred	Wallet	Impactful
Sedentary	Interactive	Elephant	Standard

🔊 MP3 36

Since graduating, my three best friends in college and I have met each other every year for a holiday as a way of maintaining our friendship. Usually we go somewhere relatively close to where we all live, but [1] last year was unusual in that I met up with them in Bangkok, Thailand. We'd decided we should travel in Asia while we're still young, and we'd seen some gorgeous pictures of the beaches in the southern part of Thailand. [2] They looked like paradise, these pictures, so that's where we headed.

We spent only [3] a few days in Bangkok, which was a fascinating cultural experience itself, but we were [4] ready to hit the beaches by the third day. So we got on a cramped bus and rode for twelve hours until we arrived at last on the southern coast of the country. We were so exhausted from having hardly slept that I can't really recall the boat ride over to the island. I do remember [5] arriving at the port, though, and getting on a truck with a lot of other tourists. There was such a thrill of excitement, a sense of adventure, as we rode in the open air along a dusty road lined with palm trees.

Skill 2 Recognising paraphrasing in a list 🔊 MP3 37

I'm a bit of a foodie. What I mean is, [1] I tend to seek out the best meal possible wherever I am. So when I went to Beijing for a business trip last March, I absolutely *had* to find the best Beijing roasted duck and try it for myself. [2] I told my colleagues what I wanted, and they booked us a table at a restaurant famous for its duck. I recall there was quite a crowd already waiting outside the door as we came in, which is always a good sign at a restaurant, you know. [3] But we were able to breeze right by them and be taken immediately to our seats. The duck was indescribable. It had a rich, fatty flavour. [4] It was served with paper-thin pancakes on the side. One of the biggest surprises was the skin. It was crispy and rich, and our waitress showed us how to dip it in sugar. [5] This was a new idea to me. We don't dip our meat in sugar back home. In fact, a lot of people don't even eat the skin of fish or chicken. Anyway, the two flavours, sweet and fatty, complemented each other so well! I tried it with chicken skin when I went back home. To be honest, sugar did *not* taste the same as it had with duck skin. [6]It was *not* nice. My wife thought I was crazy for trying it. I suppose this might be because of the higher fat content of the duck.

Listening Strategies ❾
Multiple Choice with More Than One Answer

9.2　🔊 MP3 38

You will hear a woman answering questions for a farmer's market survey. Listen and answer questions 1 to 5.

Man:	Hello, there.
Alina:	Oh, hi.
Man:	I hope I'm not intruding, but I'm conducting research for the farmer's market association. Do you happen to have a few minutes to take part in a survey? We do appreciate any feedback we get about peoples' experience here.
Alina:	Sure, I don't see why not. My husband has just taken the kids off to grab a snack.
Man:	Wonderful. Let me just tick here... you are female. Here with... family. Right. Oh, and could I get your name?
Alina:	Alina. A-L-I-N-A.
Man:	Thank you. So to start, Alina, is this your family's first visit to the farmer's market?
Alina:	Oh, no. We come here every week.
Man:	That's great to hear. And what would you say is your main motivation for visiting us?
Alina:	Well, honestly, it's only a few minutes' drive from our house, so the convenience is a big draw, but... is that our main motivation? I mean, we *do* have a conventional supermarket almost equal distance from our house in the other direction...
Man:	Is it cheaper to buy your produce here?

Alina:	Hmm. Some things, yes, but not everything, honestly. No, I'd say we come *here* instead of *there* mostly because of the environment.
Man:	The environment?
Alina:	Yeah. What I mean is, if we take our kids to the regular supermarket, they just get bored and start whining to go home, but if we bring them here, it's stimulating for them to see all the colours and the different booths. Another big incentive—if I can say two things...?
Man:	Of course!
Alina:	As I was saying, another incentive for my husband and I is that the kids can meet the real farmers who grew the produce. It's very important, we feel, for people to develop a sense of gratitude for the resources we consume. And if we tell the kids, 'This carrot was grown by this man or woman right here,' it's suddenly much more personal to them.
Man:	I see. That's great. And here's a question about what you buy. Which items do you specifically seek to purchase here?
Alina:	You mean what we come here for particularly instead of other shops. Hmm. Well, I know you've got really fantastic steaks and sausages...
Man:	Oh yes, indeed.
Alina:	But my brother-in-law runs a butcher shop downtown, and we'd just feel too guilty getting our meat anywhere else.
Man:	That makes sense.
Alina:	Although...
Man:	Yes?
Alina:	My brother-in-law—the one who's a butcher—the chicken he sells isn't antibiotic-free. That worries me, frankly. We don't eat chicken all that often, but when we do, we definitely buy it here.
Man:	Ah good. Yes, our farmers are passionate about that.
Alina:	There's also this rub for steaks that's sold by one of the vendors here. I've never found it anywhere else. She makes it herself. It's got salt and pepper and all the usual spices that go on a meat rub, but there's a few other spices in it I can't remember... Well, anyway, I come here for that in particular when I've run out.
Man:	What about baked goods? Breads, pies, and so on.

Q1-2

Q1-2

Q3-5

Q3-5

Listening Scripts

Alina:	We don't do sweets as a rule. And I bake my own bread.	
Man:	Ah.	
Alina:	Though if we come here and we do happen to see fresh baked pies, we might pick one up as a special treat.	
Man:	As you should. They're marvelous.	
Alina:	Also, our family is fond of peaches, and one of your farmers here grows very juicy ones. When we have a craving, we always come here for those. Carrots, too, and corn.	Q3-5
Man:	I see. And what about dairy items, milk and so on?	
Alina:	My son's allergic, so we stick with soy and almond milks, which I've looked for here but haven't found.	
Man:	Ah, that's too bad. Well, that's all the questions I've got. Thank you for your time.	

9.4　🔊 MP3 39

You will hear an excerpt from a university lecture about the fishing industry. Listen and answer questions 1 to 2.

I'm here to talk to you today about food—not just any type of food but a form that has been and always will be important for people on this planet: aquatic food, food that comes from the water. There are two main sources of aquatic food that I'd like to talk about today: the products that come from fishing and those that come from aquaculture. Before we go into the differences between the past and the future of these two industries, let's first define what they are.

Simply defined, fishing occurs when people catch or harvest aquatic plants and animals. When fishing for commercial purposes, people typically fish in special areas called fisheries. These can be in saltwater or freshwater. Fisheries are established where fish or other aquatic life are naturally growing or living. In other words, we didn't put the fish there; we found them. On the other hand, aquaculture involves people farming or cultivating fish or other aquatic life deliberately. So in some ways, you can think of fisheries as involving 'hunting' for fish while aquaculture involves 'farming' fish. As with other types of fisheries, there is aquaculture in the oceans and aquaculture in inland waters such as lakes.

Fisheries, including aquaculture, have been and continue to be an important source of food, employment and income in many countries and communities. But in the middle of the 20th century is where we started to see major shifts in how much food people were able to obtain from fisheries. The 1950s and 1960s saw a remarkable increase in the capture of fish in both marine and inland waters, but world fisheries production has   Q1-2
levelled off since the 1970s. Why? Overfishing is the main cause. Vital fishing areas seem to have reached their maximum potential for production. In other words, we are using up the majority of fishing stocks so that there is no room left for growth. Thus, it is   Q1-2
very unlikely that we will see this trend reverse in the future.

In contrast, marine and freshwater aquaculture production has followed the opposite path. It started with an insignificant total production and grew by roughly 5% each year in the 1950s and '60s. Then it saw an 8% annual increase in the '70s and '80s. In the 1990s, we were looking at a 10% yearly increase in production. This dramatic growth rate offers a counterbalance to the reduction in the ocean catch of fish. This is good news, especially for inhabitants of Asian countries, where most aquaculture is now located. Freshwater aquaculture is a vital source of food security in these areas, especially in places far from oceans.

Task Practice

PART 1   🔊 MP3 40

You will hear a woman talking on the phone to a manager about a wedding reception. Before you listen, you have some time to look at questions 1 to 3.
[20 seconds]
Now listen and answer questions 1 to 3.

Woman:	Hello?
Man:	Good afternoon, Miss Easton, this is Peter, the manager at Rizzo's Italian Restaurant.
Woman:	Oh, lovely! How are you, Peter?
Man:	Quite well, thank you. I just wanted to confirm the details of the booking for your wedding reception and go over a few other matters.
Woman:	Okay.
Man:	Now, your reception is booked under the name Queen, is that right? Q1

Woman:	That's right, Peter. My great-aunt is paying for the reception and that's her surname—Queen.
Man:	Oh, good. And... the date of the event is July 13th.
Woman:	That's right.
Man:	And it's to be a party of 40, is that correct?
Woman:	It's looking more like... ur... 45 to 49 now. My old high school pal and her husband can make it after all. And one family who originally thought they'd be away have just let us know they can come, too. Oh, and I also have one couple who haven't gotten back to me yet, but I'd be surprised if they didn't come. Is that all right?
Man:	Certainly. I'll just say 49 here on the form. We'd rather be prepared with too much than get caught with not enough. **Q2**
Woman:	Very wise.
Man:	Now, you mentioned there's an extra family coming. Are there any children in that group?
Woman:	They have two children, yes. Three, actually, with the baby. Or wait. I wonder if they'll bring the baby...
Man:	Shall I make a special note to have a high chair handy in case they do?
Woman:	Yes, I think that would be a good idea.
Man:	Now, there were originally 35 adults in the party and five children, so now that brings us up to... 42 adults.
Woman:	Wouldn't it be 41? The original 35, plus my high school friend and her spouse, the two parents in the family, and the pair who haven't responded.
Man:	Ah, right you are. 41. And the new number of children...
Woman:	Eight. **Q3**
Man:	That's counting the baby, though. We won't include the little tyke unless they'll be having our food.
Woman:	Oh, I see. Yes, one less than that, then.

Before you hear the rest of the conversation, you have some time to look at questions 4 to 10.
[30 seconds]
Now listen and answer questions 4 to 10.

Man:	Now that's settled, I need to run through some of the finer points about the food. I'm just going to go through the general menu options with you. Let me know if there's any item you want removed or changed.
Woman:	Okay. I'm ready.
Man:	Right. Now, for banquets you have a choice of whether to have a pasta course before an entrée course, or to skip the pasta course and go straight to entrées.
Woman:	We have a saying in my family: 'you can never have too much pasta.' I think my guests would go mad if there weren't any.
Man:	Pasta it is, then. And now for the entrées. These are my recommendations: chicken with mushrooms, pork with clams, beef with red wine sauce, a lovely spicy veal, and a vegetarian dish with aubergine.
Woman:	Hmm. About the veal...
Man:	Yes?
Woman:	I know some of my family would object to that, so maybe we could put in something else instead, if it's not too much trouble.
Man:	Certainly. Any issues with spicy food, though?
Woman:	No, not at all.
Man:	I'll note that down.
Woman:	The chicken and the beef will be fine. The aubergine, too. Ur, the pork with clams, though... I've got an aunt and a cousin who are both seriously allergic to shellfish. I know your kitchen would keep the different foods separate, but I don't think I'd be able to relax knowing there were clams even on the table.
Man:	I understand perfectly. Let's forego the clams. Pork is all right, though?
Woman:	Oh yes.
Man:	Then we'll replace that with pork loin.
Woman:	That would be great.
Man:	Now, Miss Easton, I would just like to remind you of the restaurant facilities available to you and your party. We do this with all our guests to ensure you're aware of what is and isn't part of the banquet cost.

Q4-5

Q4-5

Woman:	Okay.
Man:	Firstly, if you decide you want a specialty product, a cake or other dessert, for instance, that our restaurant does not provide, you can work with an outside vendor. There would be no extra fee from us. We can give you a list of preferred vendors that we are partnered with.
Woman:	Oh, that's very nice!
Man:	Yes. Just, make sure it's from our preferred vendors, otherwise there would be a charge.
Woman:	I see.
Man:	I do need to clarify, though, that specialty items from our preferred vendors do *not* count toward your party room's sales minimum. Now, don't worry. It's easy to meet the minimum if 90% of your adult guests show up and eat. Spending less than the sales minimum, however, would result in a room rental charge added to the final bill.
Woman:	That's fair, I suppose.
Man:	We believe it is. Now, in addition to the option of using preferred vendors, we do have a nice selection of audio-visual equipment available for rent at your party—things like microphones or a TV.
Woman:	If we rent the microphone, where does the sound come out? Does the room have a loudspeaker?
Man:	Ah. Rental of the microphone includes a sound system. Uh, but do be aware that we cannot allow music to be played through the speakers. The larger banquet hall is the only one soundproofed for music.
Woman:	That's all right.
Man:	Lovely. Now, Miss Easton, be sure to turn in your guaranteed number of guests within three business days before the dinner. Having *more* guests than stated on the guaranteed guest count list would result in extra charges.
Woman:	Can I email it?
Man:	Certainly. Now, one last thing I have to tell you, as I tell all banquet hosts. Cancellation within one week of the event would incur an additional fee. So if you *do* have to cancel, for whatever unexpected reason, please make sure to do it at least eight days before the dinner.

Q6-7

Q6-7

Woman:	Hmmm.
Man:	Yes?
Woman:	It's just... well, obviously I have no plans to cancel, but... I remember my boss held a dinner party here before and he mentioned there was *no* cancellation fee.
Man:	Ah. Your boss must be a member of our Planner Benefits programme. There are three member types: Standard, Select, and Premium. Your boss must be a Premium member, since only they get the cancellation fee waived.
Woman:	Hmm. What do the Standard members get?
Man:	Standard membership gets you event consultation at no charge, plus more freedom to personalise your event's food options—choose anything you want, basically. Select members get the same benefits as Standard, except audio-visual equipment comes free.
Woman:	Wow, that's quite a perk.
Man:	Of course, Premium members get all the benefits of the other two groups, plus regular gift cards to online shops as well, and no deposit for their events.
Woman:	Sounds nice, Peter, but I don't think I plan events often enough to need a membership.
Man:	I understand. Now, if you have any questions... (fade out)

Q8-10

PART 4   ◀)) MP3 41

You will hear a professor giving a lecture about salt and healthy diets. Before you listen, you have some time to look at questions 1 to 10.
[60 seconds]
Now listen and answer questions 1 to 10.

Hello, everyone. I am going to talk today about one of the most ubiquitous substances on the planet and within our own bodies—salt. First, I want to talk a bit about how much salt people should be eating compared to how much they *are* eating. Then I'll move into how we can choose foods with healthier salt content when we're out shopping. Finally, I'll touch on the topic of iodine, a necessary element in our diets and with which table salt is commonly fortified.

The first question I often hear from the public is, 'Is salt the same as sodium?' In fact, though the phrases 'salt' and 'sodium' are often used interchangeably, they are not exactly the same thing. Sodium is a mineral that can be found naturally in foods, added during the manufacturing process, or both. Sodium occurs naturally in foods like celery, beets and milk, but the amount of sodium found in these sources is minimal when compared to the amount in packaged and prepared foods. In European and North American countries, 75% of sodium intake comes from processed foods. In Asian as well as in many African countries, salt added during cooking and present in sauces and seasonings represents the major source of dietary sodium.

Q1-2

Q1-2

Now let's turn to table salt, which is a combination of sodium and chloride. Roughly 90% of the sodium we consume is in the form of sodium chloride, which by weight is approximately 40% sodium and 60% chloride. The remaining 10% of our sodium intake comes from other forms of sodium that show up in our food like sodium bicarbonate, commonly known as baking soda. These sodium-containing ingredients are used to preserve food, enhance its colour or even give it a firmer texture.

Q3

Now, salt is indeed vital for life. We need about 1 gram per day, about a pinch, for our bodies to function. Bear in mind, though, that this is the minimum. The current government recommendation is to eat no more than 5 grams of salt per day—about a teaspoon. However, most people are consuming too much sodium through salt— on average, about 9-12 grams per day. This is because many are unaware of dietary guidelines regarding salt.

Q4

One question I hear often from people is how to determine whether a food is a wise choice in terms of sodium content when they're out shopping. If you take a look at this visual, you find that foods low in salt contain less than 0.3 grams of salt per 100 grams of food, or 0.1 gram of sodium. Foods with a medium salt content have 0.3 grams to 1.5 grams of salt or 0.2 to 0.4 grams of sodium per 100 grams of food. And on the higher end of salt content, we're looking at over one and a half grams of salt or half a gram of sodium per 100 grams of food. If you want to know approximately how much sodium is in a given amount of table salt, you can consult the reference below. A quarter teaspoon of salt contains 575 milligrams of sodium, while half a teaspoon of salt has 1,150 milligrams. Moving into higher salt content foods, you will find 1,725 milligrams of sodium in three-fourths a teaspoon of salt, and 2,300 milligrams of sodium in a teaspoon of salt.

Q5

Q6

Q7

In terms of overall health, less salt is good news. It must be remembered, however, that table salt is the most common food vehicle for iodine fortification worldwide. Iodine is crucial in our diets, and iodine deficiency can have devastating consequences in pregnant women, women nursing infants, and young children. However, fortifying salt with iodine may no longer be the best method of getting this element to consumers. This is because different populations consume different amounts of salt. Moreover, many people are now lowering salt intake as health knowledge increases.

Bread has been suggested as a vehicle for iodine via iodised baker's salt, but it would be difficult to monitor and control the fortification process, and different populations consume varying quantities of bread. Milk is another possibility, but again, the problem is that different populations consume different amounts of milk. That leaves water, which is consumed daily on a predictable scale unlike bread and milk. There are just a few problems with iodising water—pretty significant problems. For one, although it is effective for the most part, the financial cost and the systems needed to monitor the   Q8-10 process present many more difficulties than when iodising salt. One reason for this is that there are so many sources of water, which would make it difficult to ensure that the iodisation process is carried out correctly and systematically. Furthermore, iodine is   Q8-10 stable in water for no longer than 24 hours, a fact that would require repeated doses of iodine in the water supply.

Countries which have had success... (fade out)

Lesson 7

Listening Strategies ⑩ Flow Chart Completion

10.2　🔊 MP3 43

You will hear a speaker talking about how to organise a community clean-up. Listen and answer questions 1 to 7.

So, you want to help out your neighbourhood by organising a community clean-up. Here's what you need to do to make this worthy goal a success. First of all, you need to select the area that you want to clean up. This may be your entire community or a small area within a community such as a neighbourhood. This will be the area where you distribute information, collect bags of debris, and clean up public places. If you're going to publicise your event through newspapers or flyers, it will be helpful to choose an area with boundaries people can readily identify—a park, for instance, to avoid **Q1** confusion. Something else you can do in addition to identifying public areas that will be cleaned up is to choose to encourage residents to clean up the curbs and driveways in front of their houses.

Once you've chosen your clean-up zone, the next thing to do is to get in touch with your community or city maintenance office. They can help you with maps and the hours for compost sites. Also, if they sweep streets, they will provide you the scheduled dates for this. *You* give *them* an informational fact sheet or brochure about the clean-up you are **Q2** putting together. Let them know that this is a pollution prevention project that supports the hard work its employees do to keep the streets clean and you would appreciate any help they can offer.

After you've communicated your intentions to the city office, it's time to choose a time and a date for your event. Weekends are popular days for community clean-ups since more people of all ages are free to take part. It is best to select a date at least one month in advance to allow time for thorough preparation. As for which season to **Q3** choose, clean-ups can be scheduled in the autumn or in the spring of the year. Keep climate in mind, though, as snow storms, fallen leaves, and rainstorms must be planned around. One other thing to consider. Before choosing a day, check with your city to determine if and when street sweeping is conducted. Schedule your clean-up prior to this time to keep a majority of the debris out of lakes, rivers and streams. However, scheduling it after street sweeping will clean up all remaining materials.

When your day and time have been decided, it's time to recruit volunteers. Consider enlisting the help of friends, family and neighbours to recruit sufficient volunteers to help with publicising the clean-up. Depending on the size of the clean-up area, you will need between 6 to 30 volunteers. Be sure to remind volunteers to bring gloves, rakes, shovels, brooms, and safety vests if possible, and to dress suitably for the weather conditions. You will also want volunteers with support vehicles such as pickup trucks or trailers to transport the bags to the compost site. Finally, depending on your resources, volunteers can also be asked to bring a box of yard waste bags.

Q4

Q5

So. The next step is to publicise your clean-up. Approximately three weeks before is the ideal time to let community members know about the programme through an article in the local newspaper. If you decide to distribute a door hanger or flyer by hand rather than through the paper, place the flyer or door hanger in each resident's newspaper box or on the front door knob in the area covered by the community clean-up. Identify as many ways as possible to get the message out about your clean-up to benefit the entire community.

Q6

Before you know it, it will be clean-up day. Whichever site you've determined for your volunteers to meet—a local park, community centre or school—place a check-in station near the parking area to register all volunteers. Be sure to go over all clean-up instructions and thank special guests, sponsors and volunteers. Everyone has given their free time to lend a helping hand to the community.

Q7

10.4   🔊 MP3 44

You will hear a lecturer giving a talk about the processes used for removing caffeine from coffee beans. Listen and answer questions 1 to 6.

Most coffee drinkers have at least some idea about how coffee is made. Beans are grown, harvested, roasted, and so on. But what about decaffeinated coffee, coffee that has had its caffeine removed? How is decaffeinated coffee made? No, it does not grow from special caffeine-free coffee beans. Coffee beans destined for decaf drinkers must undergo a process to have their caffeine removed, starting when they are still what we call green coffee beans—beans that have not yet been roasted.

Have a look at this chart, which describes the coffee decaffeination process—or processes, I should say. As you can see, there are actually two common processes used to take coffee beans from caffeinated to decaffeinated. One method involves the use of chemical solvents, which are chemicals that can dissolve other substances. The other method, developed in Switzerland in 1933, utilises water as a main component of its method. Today, I'd like to compare the steps in these processes side by side to give you some idea of their differences and occasional similarities.   **Q1**

Looking at the chemical solvent process, we can see there are in fact two possible methods of chemical solvent decaffeination. With the direct method, the coffee beans come into contact with the chemical solvent. With the indirect method, they do not. The direct method of the chemical solvent process begins with the coffee beans being steamed. This opens their pores, preparing their surfaces to receive the chemical solvent. Compare this to the indirect method, where the initial step is to soak the coffee beans for a number of hours in near-boiling water. Soaking the beans pulls out the caffeine and the solid components into the water. The Swiss Water Process begins similarly to this, by immersing the beans in a water solution for just up to 8 hours, extracting both their caffeine and their flavourful components.   **Q2**

The next step in the direct chemical solvent process involves rinsing the steamed coffee beans in the chemical solvent. This is performed repeatedly, and during these rinses 99.99% of the caffeine is eventually flushed out of the beans. With this step, this particular process is complete. With the indirect method, the beans are separated from the water. What happens to the beans? They will be used later.   **Q3**

With the Swiss Water Process, after the soaking phase, things start to get interesting. At this point, things have progressed quite similarly to the indirect chemical solvent method. This water solution now contains caffeine and flavourful components extracted from the beans during the soaking phase. As with the indirect chemical process, the beans are removed from the water. What happens next, however, is very different. The coffee beans are in fact discarded! Once they are discarded, all the focus now goes to the caffeine-laden, flavourful water, which is referred to as green coffee extract.   **Q4**

For the next step in the indirect chemical solvent process, the solvent is introduced into this now caffeinated water where the beans have been soaking, removing the caffeine from the water. Compare this to what happens in the Swiss Water Process: The green coffee extract, which still contains caffeine, don't forget, is passed through a carbon filter. This filter is a fascinating part of the process, designed to catch only the caffeine molecules but to allow the flavourful components of the green coffee extract, and the liquid, of course, to flow through.

In what is essentially the final step in both processes, the step in which the final product—decaffeinated coffee—is produced, two very different things occur. With the Swiss Water Process, the green coffee extract is used to wash and filter the next batch of coffee beans, removing the caffeine from the beans while preserving as much flavour as possible. Notice that no chemical agents have been introduced to either beans or water in the process. In the indirect method, on the other hand, the process culminates in the bean-flavoured solution being reintroduced to the original beans, which allows many of the oils and flavours to be reabsorbed.

Q5

Q6

As for the chemical solvents in both direct and indirect method chemical processes, those are either rinsed or evaporated from the beans. The coffee roasting process, as well, further helps ensure they are mostly gone by the time the coffee reaches consumers. The trace amounts at which they remain are harmless.

So there you have it: the methods for decaffeinating coffee. So what do... (fade out)

Task Practice

PART 3   ◀)) MP3 45

You will hear two students, Arial and Tim, discussing how to revise a term paper. Before you listen, you have some time to look at questions 1 to 5.
[30 seconds]
Now listen and answer questions 1 to 5.

Arial:	How are you doing, Tim?
Tim:	Oh, hey, Arial. I'm fine. Well, that is... I'm worried about my paper for Professor Jenkins' class. I didn't do so well on my last one, so I really need an A on this one.
Arial:	Have you started revising yet?
Tim:	That's the problem. I've checked it over for errors—typos, spelling, and things like that—but I did that for my first paper, too, the one I got a lousy grade on.

Arial:	Well, checking for typos and spelling errors isn't revising. That's just proofreading. You've got to take a closer look at your content after you've finished the paper and make changes. I usually revise my paper twice, first a few hours after I've finished, and then, several days or even a week later, I revise one more time.	
Tim:	Oh... I always thought revision takes just a few minutes. What do you do when you reread?	
Arial:	Well, the first thing I do is reread everything to make sure I've stayed on track—you know, that I haven't veered away from what my paper's focusing on.	
Tim:	Hmm. So you check the focus of the paper first.	Q1
Arial:	Exactly. And once I'm sure that's all good, I take a closer look at my thesis statement.	
Tim:	For what?	
Arial:	Well, occasionally I've found that I don't even still agree with my thesis after doing the paper.	
Tim:	Oh, dear.	
Arial:	But that's rare. No, the main thing there is to make sure I've taken a specific position and not generalised too much. Like in the paper I'm working on now for Professor Jenkins, on ocean conservation, my original thesis was the idea that schoolchildren should be educated about pollution's impacts on ocean life. But I narrowed that down to using one particular case study to educate kids on plastic pollution in oceans.	Q2
Tim:	Ah, I see. That's really good.	
Arial:	I thought so, too.	
Tim:	So... you said you revise twice.	
Arial:	Right. In the second revision stage, you want to start by making sure the paper's in proportion, like you didn't spend too much time on one point and neglected another one. Or sometimes you might find you gave lots of details in the beginning but became more general at the end. What you're essentially doing is checking your paper's balance.	Q3
Tim:	I see.	
Arial:	Once you've seen to the balance, you make sure your information is organised properly, that it follows a logical pattern and you move the	

reader smoothly from one point to the next.

Tim:	Oh, right. Transitions. I've never been good with transitions. Conclusions are my personal strength.	Q4
Arial:	It just takes practice. Anyway, before you check your conclusion, you have to go over the information in the paper. Make sure you've cited all your sources properly and that the statements are accurate.	Q5
Tim:	I see. Well, thanks, Arial. This has really been helpful. It turns out I have some revising to do.	

PART 4   ◀)) MP3 46

You will hear a tutor giving a presentation on the manufacturing process for ketchup. Before you listen, you have some time to look at questions 1 to 6.
[20 seconds]
Now listen and answer questions 1 to 6.

Welcome to our exploration of the intriguing ketchup manufacturing process. It's a fascinating journey that transforms fresh tomatoes into the condiment we know and love all around the world.

Our journey begins when ripe tomatoes are harvested, cleaned, and sorted to remove any defective specimens. These selected tomatoes then undergo a pulping process, where they are crushed in order to extract their juice. Once this juice has been extracted, it is separated from the seeds and skins, creating the foundation of our ketchup.   **Q1 Q2**

Moving forward, the tomato juice is heated to evaporate excess water, resulting in tomato paste. This concentrated paste serves as the core ingredient of ketchup. To enhance its flavour and preservation, vinegar, usually made from acetic acid, is added. The vinegar's acidity not only imparts a tangy taste but also acts as a natural preservative.   **Q3**

Ketchup's signature taste emerges from the harmonious blend of spices, salt, onions, and garlic, carefully formulated to create that distinct flavour profile. The perfect balance of sweetness is achieved through the addition of sugar. These ingredients are added to the mixture, followed by another round of heating, allowing the flavours to blend, melding together perfectly.   **Q4**

To ensure safety and product stability, this mixture must be pasteurised. To achieve
this, it is subjected to a final heating, which eliminates any remaining microorganisms.
After this final heating, the ketchup is rapidly cooled to set its consistency.

Q5

As our journey nears its end, the ketchup is meticulously packaged into bottles, jars, or
other containers, and the containers are sealed to maintain freshness. Finally, labels
are affixed, and the products are ready for distribution.

Q6

The ketchup manufacturing process exemplifies the art and science of food production,
resulting in a condiment enjoyed worldwide. It's a testament to the careful balance of
ingredients and the adherence to rigorous quality and safety standards that ensure its
consistent and delectable taste.

Lesson 8

Listening Strategies ⑪ Summary Completion

11.2   ◄)) MP3 48

You will hear part of a lecture about the use of technology in the classroom. Listen and answer questions 1 to 4.

Whether we like it or not, technology has entered our homes, workplaces and classrooms and is here to stay. Is this a positive or negative phenomenon? Well, it depends who you ask. Some believe that technology is invaluable in all areas of our day to day existence, while others see its presence as a threat. Still others, myself included, take the middle ground.

Let's first consider the role technology plays in the classroom. If used well, it motivates students and raises their self-esteem. This can be largely attributed to the fact that it allows for more customised teaching. Every student learns differently, and using technology enables teachers to adapt their lesson plans to suit each individual student's needs. Gone are the days when every learner was taught in exactly the same way, because today's market offers countless computer programs and apps that can track the progress of each student and determine how he or she learns best.

Q1

Another benefit of using technology in education is that it provides access to an infinite amount of knowledge. Before computers and the Internet found their way into schools, the sole sources of information were teachers, students, and textbooks. Human minds have obvious limitations, however, and as for books, the world changes more quickly than publishers can update editions. As a result, textbooks are likely to contain some outdated information. But with technology in the hands of teachers and students, knowledge in today's classroom is unlimited, current, and immediate.

Q2

Technology is not without its faults, though. Opponents fear that students will lose their ability to communicate in social situations because of their constant use of technology. They claim that interpersonal skills are not developed when students are given technological devices in school as less time is spent interacting with peers, thereby condoning antisocial behavior. This will have negative impacts on students' future relationships with friends, family, workmates, and romantic partners.

Q3

There is also the potential issue of distraction. Ignoring the outside world can be easy when you're immersed in your device. Naturally, effective teachers set rules for the use of gadgets in their classrooms and even place filters on electronic devices to prevent students from accessing non-educational materials. But there's a problem with this which is unique in human history: today's youngsters are often more tech-savvy than their elders. If a student would rather play a game or text with a friend than research historical facts, he or she probably knows a way to disable the filter or can ask a classmate for help.

Q4

Listening Strategies ⑫
Matching Tasks with Charts or Graphs

| 12.2 | 🔊 MP3 49

You will hear two students presenting the results of a survey they conducted about social media use. Listen and answer questions 1 to 6.

Tutor:	Our next presentation is from Polly and Dan.
Dan:	Thank you, Professor Howard. So ur, Polly and I thought it would be fascinating to know something about how media usage differs among age demographics. We used a survey to collect the data, and we administered it, fittingly, through email and over social media. We asked people to log the number of minutes they spent on different media platforms for one week. We ended up with a sample size of just over 300 people.
Tutor:	Impressive!
Polly:	Yes, and we found the results to be really interesting. Some of our expectations were met but other details came as a bit of a surprise.
Tutor:	Hmm, what surprised you?
Polly:	Well, Dan and I expected watching TV to be much less popular, I suppose because we ourselves spend an average of just around 40 minutes a day watching it. But if you take a look at this chart here, you'll see that the adults we surveyed spend an average of over four and a half hours per day watching television. When you break that down into the two types of TV, the majority by far is spent viewing live TV, and this 36 minutes down here at the other end of the chart

Q1

represents, like, DVR viewing, time-shifted TV.

Tutor: Ah, I see. What was your expectation, if I may ask?

Dan: Before we looked at the data, I was convinced that people spend no more than a quarter of an hour per day using apps or the web on their smartphone, but that activity actually amounted to almost two and a half hours a day. **Q2**

Tutor: As a teacher observing students with their smartphones, I'm not surprised.

Dan: I just thought most people were too busy for that!

Polly: Something else I didn't expect was the fact that people generally spend only six more minutes surfing the web on tablets than they do on computers. **Q3**

Tutor: Wait, say that again?

Polly: People spend only six more minutes per day on tablets than on their computers—though both activities account for less than an hour. I just expected people to use their tablets a lot more than they use computers, since tablets are so convenient.

Tutor: Hmm, I see. Now, what happened when you broke it up into different age demographics?

Polly: Well, you can see in the next chart that all four age groups spend an average of exactly 7% of their day using a tablet. This was very similar to the amount of time they spend using the Internet on a computer—except for the over 65s. They spend only about 4% of their day on the computer. Another similarity across all groups is that everyone spends an average of between 14 to 16% of their day listening to radio. **Q4**

Dan: Yeah, I personally found that surprising as well, but I suppose if you take into account driving to work and school and so forth, it makes sense.

Polly: Now, here is where things start to get really interesting. Look here at the figures for TV-connected devices and also for app and web on a smartphone. You'll notice that the amount of time people spend on devices like this is inversely proportional to age. That is, the percentage gets smaller the older the subjects get. The younger group spend 14% of their day using devices connected to the TV and 29% of their day using their smartphones. In contrast, the over **Q5**

65s spend an average of merely 2% of their day on TV-connected devices, and 13% of their day on their smart phone.

Tutor:	Was that a surprise?
Polly:	No, not really. Something else that wasn't a surprise were the figures for all forms of television viewing, which accounts for over half of the day for the oldest age group and just over a quarter of the day for the youngest.

Q6

Tutor:	Very interesting. So what conclusions did you... (fade out)

Task Practice

PART 3   🔊 MP3 50

You will hear two students, Martin and Tessa, discussing a project about the Internet. Before you listen, you have some time to look at questions 1 to 4.
[30 seconds]
Now listen and answer questions 1 to 4.

Tessa:	Hi, Martin.
Martin:	Oh, hi Tessa. Right, so let's get these charts made, and then I think that's everything done for our project.
Tessa:	Whoo, I can't believe we're almost at the end. Okay, so let me just pull up the results of our survey. Here we are. So I'll read out everything for you and you can do the chart?
Martin:	That works. Let me just get the title... 'Prevalence of Online Harm Among Adult Internet Users.'
Tessa:	Okay, so the most common negative experiences among our respondents were getting junk mail, being victims of scams, fraud, and identify theft, and accidentally downloading viruses or malicious software. The most common problem was junk mail, which one fifth of our respondents complained about.

Q1

Martin:	That's a problem I can certainly identify with. I'm so thankful for whoever invented the delete button.
Tessa:	You and I know to delete it—when the spam box doesn't catch it, that is—but a fairly high proportion of people are vulnerable to it. On a similar note, here's our next figure: just over 10% of our subjects

Q1

	have experienced scams, fraud, or identity theft.	
Martin:	Did they give any details?	
Tessa:	Yeah, ... ur... 40% of that number is attributed to credit card fraud from online shopping.	
Martin:	Hmm.	
Tessa:	And this is interesting. An equal proportion of people have ended up with viruses or malware on their computer.	Q1
Martin:	You mean equal to...	
Tessa:	... the percentage who've experienced scams, fraud, and identity theft.	
Martin:	Ah... okay, that's *that* one done. Now for the second chart. This one's on 'Teenagers' Reported Reasons for Being Cyberbullied.' Is that right?	
Tessa:	Yes. So just over 60% of teens in our study reported being bullied online because of the way they look.	Q2
Martin:	How awful!	
Tessa:	I know, and a quarter of them say that being perceived as intelligent or making good grades brought about online verbal abuse.	
Martin:	I just can't understand why.	
Tessa:	Other kids are jealous, most likely. And uh, 17% of the teens report having been cyberbullied due to racial discrimination.	Q3
Martin:	Mmm.	
Tessa:	Religious beliefs was the next most prevalent reason for being bullied—wait no, that's not right. The next one was due to how much money the kids' families had. Religious beliefs was just over ten percent. The remaining 20% were bullied for other reasons.	Q4
Martin:	I really do hope the Internet is a safer place for kids in the future—or for everyone, actually.	
Tessa:	So do I. Well, that's why people do studies like this one—in the hopes of learning the facts so that we can find the best way to take action.	

PART 4　🔊 MP3 51

You will hear a lecture about the use of technology in the workplace. Before you listen, you have some time to look at questions 1 to 4.

[30 seconds]

Now listen and answer questions 1 to 4.

Technology has undoubtedly revolutionised the 21st century workplace. Software, hardware, and online capabilities provide countless benefits to business owners and employees. Businesses become more efficient and effective by employing faster and simpler working methods. For instance, receipts in the past had to be posted by hand   Q1
to clients, but they can now be sent automatically through online systems. However, this use of technology comes with some degree of risk, particularly to small business owners who tend to use outdated software and not update often enough. In this case, hackers find it all too easy to steal data or even divert funds into their own accounts.   Q2

Another benefit of technology in the workplace is that it allows for a more mobile workforce than ever before in history. Workers can access company programmes from virtually anywhere—their homes, the subway, or even on an airplane. Non-mobile workers benefit from this technology, too, in that corresponding with clients can be done with the click of a button via email. Even customers' signatures can be obtained on documents sent online. This all saves time for everyone and globalises many business operations.

The danger with all this convenient technology is, of course, the possibility of distraction. With our mobile phone sitting on our desk, it can be difficult to stay focused on the job. Time-wasting habits also become formed with Internet access on work computers. Even an employee trying to do work-related research on the web can veer off track on an unnecessary trail and find that they have wasted hours of time. Employees can also get distracted by checking email too frequently while waiting for a response from a client. This takes their attention away from what they're working on, if even momentarily, which reduces productivity. So what does this all mean? Well,   Q3
business leaders need to set policies to prevent employees from taking advantage of technology at work. This will help employees develop good technology work habits, which maximises productivity and job satisfaction. In the end, everyone will be able to   Q4
benefit.

Lesson 9

Listening Strategies ⑬ Map or Plan Labelling

13.2   ◀)) MP3 53

You will hear a woman talking to a group of new employees at a summer youth camp. Listen and answer questions 1 to 5.

Right, here's a plan of our campgrounds, so you can all get an idea of where everything is. As you can see, we're here at Meeting Ground 1. There's the Admin Office to our right, with the horse barn and horse paddock both to our left. Camp counselors, when it's time to take your group of campers to their cabins, you'll want to follow the paved path here up to the flagpole. Boys' counselors, you lot will then branch off to the left, and girls' counselors, you'll go to the right. We've strict rules about this—no girls on the boys' side, no boys on the girls' side—but the games centre is for everyone. You'll see that situated between the two forks in the path.   **Q1**

Now, when you aren't on duty you'll be able to spend your free time in the staff lounge. It's got a small kitchen and a fridge, and computers with Internet access. You will find the staff lounge just up ahead along the paved path. It's the building between the woodworking shop and the pottery studio. You're also welcome to go cycling in your free time. There are communal bikes in the bike barn, and of course those of you who've brought your own bike can store it there. You can't see the bike barn from where we're standing as it's situated a bit off the path, but you won't be able to miss it once you've made your way to the flagpole. To reach the bike barn, you'll just step off the path once you reach the flagpole and cut to the right through the grass. You'll see the bike barn right up ahead of you. From the grass, you could also veer off to the right instead of straight to the bike barn and go to the sports pavilion if you prefer. You'll find it situated behind the pottery studio.   **Q2**   **Q3**

Now, dining hall staff, you'll be spending most of your time in the stretch of camp nearer the lake. To get to the dining hall, you'll follow the walking trail behind the horse paddock. The trail branches off in two directions just as you reach the Lake Equipment hut. Take the right turn and keep following it along the lake past the lifeguard stand, which sits in front of the Nurse's Station. Keep walking, and you'll soon come out onto the clearing with the dining hall, which you can actually see off in the distance ahead if you look just past Meeting Ground 2.   **Q4**   **Q5**

Listening Strategies ⑭ Diagram Labelling

14.2   🔊 MP3 54

You will hear a tutor giving a talk about the parts of the ocean. Listen and answer questions 1 to 6.

Good morning. Today, I will be talking about the layers of the ocean, specifically how they are distinct from one another in terms of the presence of life and the hydrostatic pressure at different depths of water.

The Sunlight Zone, the part of the ocean we land-dwellers are most familiar with, extends from the surface of the sea down to a depth of about 200 metres. From bony fishes of all shapes and sizes to warm-blooded oxygen-breathing mammals, life is   Q1
abundant at this level thanks to the presence of sunlight.

Now, at sea level, the air around us presses down on our bodies at 14 and a half pounds per square inch. We don't feel this because the fluids in our own bodies push outward with the same force. Scientists measure pressure in kilopascals, abbreviated as kPa. So as you can see here on the chart, this standard atmospheric pressure we feel right now is defined as 101 kilopascals. As divers in the sunlight zone descend, they start to feel the pressure against every square inch of their bodies. The feeling is especially noticeable in their lungs. At a depth of around 30 metres, the size and   Q2
volume of these organs is reduced to one third of their capacity at sea level.

The next zone of the ocean is noted for very low levels of sunlight and virtual darkness for human eyes. From 200 to 1,000 metres below sea level lies the Twilight Zone. Life in this zone is remarkable for its slow, sleepy pace, as the type of foods available to these creatures tend to be energy-poor. Pressure in the Twilight Zone grows ever   Q3
higher, and at 1,000 metres below sea level, where light can no longer reach, the hydrostatic pressure is at 10,153 kilopascals. Specialised suits and diving vehicles are   Q4
necessary for humans to explore in this zone and below.

Finally, from about 1,000 metres down to 4,000 metres is a place of unending darkness, and so is appropriately referred to as the Midnight Zone. Despite the   Q5
perpetual blackness of this place, life that exists here depends indirectly on the benefits of sunlight. When creatures in the sunny upper layers of the sea die, a steady flow of organic nutrients rains down to feed the life forms living at or near the bottom. Deeper still, below 4,000 metres down to the ocean floor, lies the ocean's most profound and

darkest region. Many of the creatures living in the deep sea have developed unique, frightening-looking adaptations to survive in this harsh environment where hydrostatic pressure can be up to 60,412 kilopascals.   **Q6**

Then, of course, we have the trench zone... (fade out)

Task Practice

PART 1   ◀)) MP3 55

You will hear a woman asking for directions at a tourism information counter in the bus station.
Before you listen, you have some time to look at questions 1 to 4.
[20 seconds]
Now listen and answer questions 1 to 4.

Tina:	Hi, excuse me....
Clerk:	Yes, how can I help you?
Tina:	I just have a few questions about how to get around the area. I've just arrived, and my cell phone is out of batteries.
Clerk:	Oh. You know, we've got a phone charging station here at the back of the bus station, but of course I'm happy to help out.
Tina:	Oh, thank you! Well, the first thing I need is just to get to my hostel. They told me it was close to the bus station, but I'm not sure...
Clerk:	Let me just see the name... Ah, yes. I know that hostel. Very popular.
Tina:	Is it close enough to walk?
Clerk:	Certainly. Let me just show you a map here. See, River Road runs north and south outside the bus station...
Tina:	I see...
Clerk:	And you've got these two streets running parallel to each other on either side of our block. The one nearer the river is Station Lane, and the one further away, to our left, is Broad Street.

Q1 (appears beside the highlighted text "The one nearer the river is Station Lane, and the one further away, to our left, is Broad Street.")

Tina:	Okay.
Clerk:	Now, you could take either Station Lane or Broad Street. If you take Station Lane, you'll walk west just along this block on the map. You'll come to an intersection with the public library on your left, and a

	department store on your right. Turn left at that street—that's Carter Street—and you'll see your hostel on the right-hand side of the road in no time.	**Q2**

Tina: Oh, that's great. Very close, like you said.

Clerk: Mmm-hmm. Anything else I can help you with?

Tina: Well, actually yes. I realised on the bus that I forgot my toiletries bag back home. Is there a place near my hostel where I could buy just a few personal items?

Clerk: Coming from your hostel, you say. Hmm. Yes. I'll tell you the simplest way. So, from your hostel, you'll go out and take a left back onto Carter Street. Turn right when you reach the river and walk along that block until you pass River Road on the right. On that block facing the **Q3** river you'll find a chemist shop on your right and a convenience store a few steps further down, just beside it. I bet you'll find everything you need between those two.

Tina: Great. And do you happen to know if there are any restaurants near there? I'll want to grab lunch after I go shopping.

Clerk: Oh, yes. Well, you ought to know there's a fantastic salad bar across the road from your hostel, opposite the department store I mentioned earlier. But there's also a Greek restaurant and a French café just across the street from the bus station on the other side of Station Lane.

Tina: Oh, they both sound good right about now.

Clerk: There's a lovely view of the park from the Greek restaurant. But **Q4** the French café has delicious sandwiches and pastries, so you win either way.

Tina: Thanks so much. You've been such a help!

Clerk: You're welcome. Enjoy your time in the city!

PART 4   🔊 MP3 56

You will hear a lecturer describing a deep-sea vehicle. Before you listen, you have some time to look at questions 1 to 4.
[30 seconds]
Now listen and answer questions 1 to 4.

Today, I will be describing the Deepsea Challenger, a submersible vehicle that can withstand massive hydrostatic pressure and freezing temperatures. With this vehicle, scientific explorers can travel to the furthest reaches of the deep sea.

The Challenger spins like a bullet as it travels with the help of two stabilising fins, one above the central foam body, and one below. Despite this striking difference in design from other submersible vehicles, the way the Challenger sinks to the bottom of the ocean is similar to that of previous submarines. If you look at the diagram here, you will notice that down at the base of the vehicle are 1,100 pounds of steel weights as ballast. **Q1** When it's time for the Challenger to ascend back to the surface, the ballast is released at the ocean floor and the vehicle floats back up.

Just above the steel ballast weights is where the pilot sits. This small area is shaped like a sphere because a sphere is the strongest shape for resisting pressure. At just **Q2** 43 inches wide (or 109 centimetres), the interior of the pilot sphere is so small that the pilot must keep his knees bent and can barely move. Yet from this small space, he can control the submarine's various instruments, such as its four external HD cameras. Two of these cameras are mounted side by side on one of the two utility booms, which **Q3** you can see positioned just above the pilot's window and door hatch. Together, these two cameras can create 3D images with lighting provided by two sources: the spotlight on the other utility boom, and the flood lights. You can see the flood lights here on the diagram, located inside the central foam body above the vertical thrusters and beside the battery array. All of the submarine's tools, thrusters, lights, and cameras get power **Q4** from this battery array. It is highly dependable, but just in case of emergencies, the pilot sphere contains independent batteries under the seat which can run the life support system if the main battery array fails.

Now, lets' talk about... (fade out)

國家圖書館出版品預行編目 (CIP) 資料

IELTS 雅思聽力最後 9 堂課／Robyn Blocker 作 .
-- 初版 . -- 臺北市：眾文圖書股份有限公司, 2023.12 面；公分
ISBN 978-957-532-638-8（平裝） 1. CST：國際英語語文測試系統 2. CST：考試指南
805.189   112013225

IE012

IELTS 雅思聽力最後 9 堂課

定價 600 元
2023 年 12 月 初版一刷

作者	Robyn Blocker
責任編輯	黃婉瑩
譯者	眾文編輯部

總編輯	陳瑠琍
主編	黃炯睿
資深編輯	顏秀竹
編輯	黃婉瑩・蔡若楹・范榮約
美術設計	嚴國綸
行銷企劃	李皖萍・楊詩韻
發行人	陳淑敏
發行所	眾文圖書股份有限公司
	台北市 10088 羅斯福路三段 100 號 12 樓之 2
網路書店	www.jwbooks.com.tw
電話	02-2311-8168
傳真	02-2311-9683
郵政劃撥	01048805

ISBN 978-957-532-638-8
Printed in Taiwan